Mastered

OVER THE LINE

THE 10TH ANNIVERSARY EDITION

SIERRA CARTWRIGHT

Over the Line
ISBN # 978-1-80250-585-6
©Copyright Sierra Cartwright 2023
Cover Art by Kelly Martin ©Copyright November 2023
Interior text design by Claire Siemaszkiewicz
Totally Bound Publishing

OVER THE LINE

Dedication

For Theresa Martin with thanks! For Darlene
Good with appreciation.
To the Pineapple Gang—Scarlett, Goldi, Lexy,
Mel.
And for some fun, new fabu friends—Jean, Leslie,
Carolyn, Shelley, Laurie, Leaundra, and Susan—
you help keep me sane. Either that, or you're such
good friends, you join me on my journey!
Don—always and all ways…

Chapter One

Michael Dayton caught a whiff of spiced vanilla on the night air, and he turned his head to find the source.

The view of the woman passing by walloped him. He only managed a brief look at her face, not enough to make out her eye color, but on a primal level he noted the softness of her mouth and the sexy pout of her beautiful lips.

She kept moving in the direction of the Den's firepit. Fascinated by her beauty, as well as her confidence, he didn't look away. How could he? She was tiny, compact, with blonde hair tumbling over her shoulders, the strands an untamed, riotous mass. She walked with determination, her hips swaying seductively as she navigated the uneven flagstone patio. Her grace was even more remarkable given the unyielding leather dress and her crazy-high heeled sandals. Even though the shoes added extra height, he doubted she'd reach his chin.

A need to protect flared in him. The sensation was as unexpected as it was unwelcome.

Several times a year, he attended BDSM play parties here at the Den, a mountain retreat owned by his friend Master Damien. On occasion, Michael scened, and he'd been sexually attracted to many of the subs he'd played with.

But he'd only had this kind of visceral reaction one other time in his three decades. Recklessly, he'd ignored his intuition and the warnings of others and had ended up married within three months.

A few years later, he and his bride had been in court, and he'd spent most of his inheritance to hold on to the Eagle's Bend Ranch. The two thousand acres had been in his family for over eighty years. If he'd lost it to some scheming bitch, his father would have haunted him from the grave. The lessons Michael had learned while rebuilding his life and fortune had made him harder, smarter, and significantly more cautious.

He adjusted his cowboy hat and continued to look at the blonde. She had joined a group of people near the fire. Her figure-hugging dress did as much — and maybe more — to arouse him as her nudity would have.

Until this moment, he hadn't missed having a woman in his bedroom, tied to his rustic four-poster bed, arms and legs spread wide as she lay there for him, willing and waiting. Last night he'd gone to bed alone after masturbating to ease the day's tension. Tonight, he hoped things would be different. He was glad he hadn't simply tossed away the invitation to the Den's late-summer party.

As if sensing his scrutiny, she glanced over her shoulder. They made eye contact for less than five seconds, but it was enough, more than enough for him.

Nearby, a male voice flatly stated, "She's trouble."

Michael blinked and reluctantly turned toward the newcomer, Gregorio, the Den's caretaker.

"Don't go there," Gregorio advised, coming to a stop in front of him.

But Michael was already thinking about her, despite the fact she didn't resemble the women who generally caught his eye. He preferred a more rounded, feminine form — a woman who could withstand the rigors of ranch life as well as his Dominant demands.

"Her name's Sydney," Gregorio said.

Michael was aware of Gregorio's voice, but his focus was elsewhere. *Sydney. Unusual name.* He let it roll around in his mind. *How will it sound when I say it aloud as I command her to her knees?*

"She used to dance nude in a cabaret in Vegas and has a boa constrictor as a pet. It killed her last Dom and dragged him out to the backyard. She's on the run from the law. We heard she's wanted in ten states and two Canadian provinces." Gregorio snapped his fingers near Michael's face, jarring him from his reverie. "You listening to me, Mike?"

"What?" He shook his head and looked at Gregorio.

"I figured you weren't listening, otherwise you'd have decked me for calling you Mike." Gregorio chuckled. "If you want to play, there are a number of subs here tonight — they're wearing the house's purple wristband. That means they're available for a scene, they know the rules, and they follow them. Any one of them would be much better for you than Sydney."

Gregorio, as Damien Lowell's right-hand man, knew things. Gregorio understood human nature and, since he tracked all the membership applications, he had insider knowledge of everyone at the Den. He served as a house monitor and sometimes participated in scenes. Because he was so well respected, Doms and subs alike listened to him. Those who didn't often regretted their decision.

For the first time, Michael wanted to ignore Gregorio's unsolicited advice. "I didn't see a collar around her neck." He took in the people she was standing with. "And she doesn't seem to be here with anyone."

"She doesn't have a Dom."

"I'll bite. What's wrong with Sydney?"

"Other than the snake and the problems with the law?"

"What the hell are you talking about?" Michael asked, taking a sip of his energy drink and looking back at her. A waiter approached with a tray full of sparkling water, and she snagged a flute. Her back was to him, and he couldn't drag his gaze away from her shapely derriere. "Is she a Domme?" He'd bet money she wasn't.

"She's a sub," Gregorio said, giving the answer Michael wanted. "But one with no real interest in a relationship with a man."

He blinked. "She's gay?" Please God, no, not now that he was imagining her legs wrapped around his waist as he drove into her slick pussy.

"She likes men just fine. What I mean is, she'll start playing, if a guy interests her. If he bores her, she bails."

"Meaning she'll leave in the middle of a scene?"

"It's happened a handful of times." Gregorio folded his arms across his chest. "She's earned the name 'the Brat' around here."

Something he could handle. "Challenging."

Gregorio laughed. The sound was both ominous and sympathetic. "A few other Doms have felt the same way," Gregorio said. "Sydney has a history of battering hearts and egos. Protects herself emotionally — with good reason. And she never plays with the same person twice."

Water in hand, she walked around to the far side of the firepit and stood there alone. He responded to the unspoken cue. After finishing his beverage, he crumpled the can and passed it off to Gregorio. "Wish me luck."

Gregorio shook his head. "You'll need more than luck, my friend."

Michael moved toward her.

Perhaps hearing his approach, she looked up and watched as he closed the distance.

"Evening, ma'am," he said, as he stopped near her and tipped his hat.

"I was hoping you would be brave enough to come and talk to me," she admitted with a smile that could roll his socks down. "I saw you talking with Gregorio. No doubt he tried to frighten you away with tales of how terrible I am."

"And are you?"

"I suppose there could be some truth to it." She shrugged easily. "But a good story is always entertaining, isn't it?"

This close, she smelled potently dangerous—spiced vanilla blended with unadulterated pheromones. The combination created a cocktail he couldn't get enough of. "Either way, not much scares me."

"A man among men."

"Michael Dayton. Master Michael." Although the sun hadn't completely vanished behind the distant mountain peaks, torches were being lit, adding to the ambience and catching streaks of red in her hair. He wanted to touch those strands, to curl them around his fist as he held her down and made her scream out his name.

"Sydney Wallace," she said, returning the formality.

"May I call you Sydney?"

She rolled her glass between her palms. With a tease in her voice, she said, "I'm hoping you can be considerably more creative than that."

He tipped back the brim of his hat to get a better look at her. She intrigued him. "So name calling is not on your limits list."

A server, this one a woman in a French maid's outfit that left nothing to the imagination, walked nearby. Though she was curvy with luscious bare breasts, he only had eyes for the woman he was with.

Sydney placed her glass on the tray. He appreciated the fact that she didn't need something to toy with.

When they were alone again, she said, "I understand you're divorced, Mr. Dayton. No kids. You have a ranch you'd like to protect from gold diggers. You scene every once in a while, and you're not looking for a serious commitment."

"Do you know my blood type?"

"No." Her quick grin was engaging. "I only asked about the important stuff."

"You found out a lot in a short amount of time."

"I like being prepared. If I'm going to spend an hour with a man, I want to make sure the time is worth it. I don't think it's fair to either of us if there are false expectations."

"You're mistaken, Sydney."

"About which part?"

"We'll be spending more than an hour together. I can't get you properly warmed up in under sixty minutes, and I intend to keep you on the edge, writhing for an orgasm for much, much longer than that."

Her eyes widened, and for the first time he noticed how blue they were, a shade of ice, a shocking contradiction to the heat she radiated.

"That's a bold statement, Michael."

He captured her chin gently. "Find out for yourself. Let's have an experiment here at the Den to see if we have chemistry. After that, we can head out to my ranch. It's about forty-five minutes from here. Or if you'd prefer, we can go to your place. Wherever you feel most comfortable."

Michael allowed his gaze to wander down her body, taking in her shapely, bare legs. Until now, he'd been a stockings man. "Are you wearing underwear?"

"I…"

With his index finger, he stroked her cheekbone. "I asked you a question."

"Yes."

"What kind?"

She hesitated for a moment, and he wondered if she was going to answer or whether she was going to run. He held her lightly enough that her movements weren't restricted.

"Boy shorts," she said.

"Please remove them for me."

"Now?" She blinked. "Here?"

"Maybe you're the one who should be afraid," he said quietly, "rather than me. Gregorio says you often bail out of scenes. I wondered at first if it was because Doms asked too much from you. But I'm thinking they probably didn't ask enough. I've known you less than five minutes, but I've figured out you're assertive. You know what you want, but I'm guessing you're not always good at asking for it. Furthermore"—he leaned in closer—"I'm willing to bet you're bored with anyone who isn't as aggressive as you are. Am I wrong about that?"

She shivered. Since the Colorado evening was mild and they were standing near the fire, she couldn't be cold. Clearly, he'd hit a nerve.

Surprising him, she met his gaze. "You're right about the fact I get bored easily." She curled her hand around his wrist. "And you're wrong if you think I'm afraid of anything."

"Fair enough. In that case, I told you to take off your panties." He released his grip on her chin, and she let go of him. He remained where he was, physically and figuratively refusing to give her space.

He offered his arm, and she held on to it while precariously balancing on her high heels.

Finally, she straightened and looked at him as she dangled the pretty pink material from her index finger. Too late he realized he'd made a mistake by not asking to see them on her first. The material had probably stretched across her derriere, highlighting her butt cheeks perfectly.

He accepted the proffered underwear and stuffed the silk and lace confection into his pocket. Who would have suspected that she wore something so tantalizing beneath black leather? "What are your limits?"

"I haven't found any," she said.

"Then you've been playing with the wrong Doms."

She shrugged. "That's possible. But maybe I'm tougher than you think."

"Perhaps." He met her answer with a great deal of skepticism. Jane, his ex-wife, had let him believe she wanted things raw, but the moment his wedding band had been placed on her finger, the figurative collar had come off her throat. "Humiliation?"

"I don't have a lot of experience with that."

"No one has made you stand in a corner with your nose pressed to the wall and your panties around your ankles when you misbehaved?"

She stiffened.

Have I hit another nerve?

Her lips parted for a moment, just long enough for him to wonder how she tasted. He loved anticipation, enjoyed getting a woman so turned on she lost her inhibitions, but now, with Sydney, unfamiliar impatience nipped at him.

With an impish grin, she returned his volley. "I don't misbehave."

"Of course you do. Enough to be called the Brat."

"Oh." As if bored, she yawned. "That."

"Scares some people away, no doubt."

"But not you?"

"No. I understand that you're looking for something you haven't found."

She heaved a soft sigh. "I'm not open to being psychoanalyzed. Since it's unlikely we'll see each other again, can we skip the bullshit and get to the good stuff?"

Before it formed, Michael quashed his smile. "I don't rush. That's the first thing you need to know, darlin'."

"Really? You like wasting time?"

"You can be certain"—he leaned in a little closer, only to be electrified by the sexual vibes she radiated—"I'll give you what you need, not just what you want."

"That's as unlikely as it is arrogant."

"Find out for yourself," he challenged.

She scooped up a handful of hair and eased it back from her forehead, revealing her annoyance. "I was hoping that since you're a divorced man who doesn't want to go through that nonsense again, you'd be fine with taking what I offered."

"Ouch."

"Do you want an apology for your tender male ego?"

"With me, you don't have to watch your words. I prefer honesty."

"Do you, indeed?"

"I'll return the favor. I'm not against having a relationship. I'm not, in theory, against marriage." Passing the land to his heirs would be nice. He had one sister, who had two girls, but neither of them had shown any interest in running the ranch on a long-term basis.

"Are you looking for something permanent now?" Trepidation wound through her tone.

"No."

"Then if you'd like to play, I would, too." Seductively, sexily, she placed her palm over his crotch.

Heat seared through the denim. Except for lovers he'd been with a long time, no woman had been so bold. He wanted to cave to his baser instincts and take her here, now. Instead, he captured her hand and moved it away.

She pulled back, breaking his grip. *Feeling rejected?* What man in his right mind would have stopped her?

"Don't take it personally," he said. "In the future, you may be welcome to do that. It's not that I don't want you. On the contrary, I want to be buried balls-deep in your hot pussy as you cry out my name."

Her eyes opened wide. She seemed more intrigued than shocked. "What are we waiting for?"

"We need to clear up a few things."

"Right. I have no STDs and no physical limitations. Oh, yes, and I have condoms in my purse—large." She shot a quick, sassy grin. "And medium, just in case you need them."

Do you eat men's egos for breakfast, darlin'? Rather than replying, he changed the subject. "Why do you scene?"

"More attempts to psychoanalyze me?"

"If you'd like to play with me, you'll answer my questions. You've thought about it, surely?"

"Regular sex is boring."

"Hmm."

"And I like to transcend my limits."

When he nodded, she went on. "I thrive on physical challenges. I guide white water river rafting excursions. Completed a triathlon last week, and I'm competing in an upcoming mud race. You know, running up a mountain then doing obstacle courses, under barbed wire, over a wooden wall. My team is doing it for charity."

He looked at her with a newfound respect. When he'd first seen her, he'd had an urge to protect and care for her. Even though he now knew she could hold her own, those instincts hadn't vanished. "What's your safe word?"

"Everest."

Of course it is.

"You don't need to know why."

He figured he already knew, but he looked forward to her telling him about it at a later date. "How about a code for slowing down?"

"I don't believe in that."

"In that case, we'll use the word caution."

She sighed. "If I have to have one, how about we use the word turtle?"

He thumbed his hat. "You trying to insult me, brat?"

"Not at all." Innocently, she made an invisible halo above her head. "That would be rude. I'm just saying that turtles are slow."

Not only was she attractive, but quick-witted and intelligent. It had been a long time since a woman had appealed to him on multiple levels. "How do you feel about public play?"

She hesitated for a second. "I've never tried it."

"Are you willing to?"

17

"I suppose."

"I prefer a yes or no answer," he told her. "Unless you'd rather talk about it?"

"No. I mean yes."

Swiftly, he rebuked her. "Yes, *Sir*."

"Yes, *Sir*," she dutifully repeated.

"Good girl."

Though she gritted her teeth, she said nothing. Seemed his demand that she conform to courtesies had hit a nerve. "What kind of impact play do you prefer?"

Before he could ask further questions, she said, "I find an open-handed spanking to be really pleasurable. I also like belts." She glanced at his waist.

Oh, yeah. He'd happily lay the leather across her sweet, sexy rear.

For a moment, she was quiet. A bit discombobulated, perhaps?

In that moment, an air of vulnerability ghosted through her eyes. But then she blinked and smiled. If he hadn't been paying attention, he would have missed it.

"I'm also fine with a shoe or a ruler." She rushed the words together, filling the sudden silence. "Anything, really. Feel free to be creative. I'm okay with a flogger, open to trying a bullwhip or cane. There isn't a position I'm averse to, over the knee, or a table, or a bed. Standing, lying on top of a spanking bench. Did I miss anything?"

"The 'Sir' at the end of your sentence."

"Of course. Sir." She gave him another of her sunny smiles.

She seemed so guileless, he'd bet it would be difficult for some Doms to hold her accountable. "Clamps?"

She nodded. "Potentially." Would the erotic pain help her get off?

"Anal plugs?"

She fidgeted then replied, "If you insisted, I'd try it."

"No one has claimed your ass?" he asked, stunned.

"No."

That he would be the first to place something up there made his erection press even harder against his jeans. He wanted to readjust his cock, but he reminded himself to focus on her. There were a few other things he needed to know before they got started. "Handcuffs?"

"Any kind of bondage," she said.

"I haven't lassoed a woman... Yet."

Her eyes widened. "Sounds interesting."

Michael was glad he'd ignored Gregorio's advice. The thought of dragging a helpless Sydney toward him was a thrill. If she were barefoot and naked, it would be all the better. "I'm gathering you're open to sex."

"Like I said, I have protection with me. In assorted sizes. In addition to having nothing communicable, I'm on birth control. Anything else you need to know?"

"That will cover it," he responded wryly. "Likewise, I have a clean bill of health, but I also believe in exercising caution. We'll use condoms."

When he said nothing else, she flipped her hair and turned away, heading toward the house.

"Where do you think you're going, Sydney?"

She stopped and looked over her shoulder. With a puzzled frown, she said, "Inside." After dampening her lips, she added, "I thought that was what you wanted."

"Did I say so?"

"No." She returned to stand in front of him. "I apologize."

"I'm going to spank you over there." He nodded toward a short metal fence in the distance.

It bordered the grassy area beyond the horseshoe pits, far enough away that they'd have some privacy. Still, since it was lit by numerous solar lights and torches, anyone who wanted to watch could.

She glanced around, and he waited patiently.

A small group had gathered on one side of the firepit. Some stood around high tables. Elsewhere, a woman sat on a porch swing while her male sub licked her boot.

Another evening at the Den.

"I think you need reminding that I prefer to be called Master Michael or Sir. When we play together, Sydney, I make the rules. I will be sure you understand them and agree with them, but once that happens, they will be enforced. Do you understand?"

"Yes, Sir," she whispered.

"Do you agree to address me respectfully?"

"I do, Sir."

"Good." Satisfied, he nodded. "Please pull your dress up to your waist."

She couldn't have taken more time, but he didn't complain. Watching her obey his wishes was its own reward. Sydney was softness and sensuality wrapped in a beautiful package.

"Ah," he said when she was exposed to him. "Such a pretty little pussy. I like that it's shaved." He looked at her expectantly.

"Thank you, Sir."

Interesting—since he'd drawn harsher boundaries, she seemed softer, more compliant. "Please put your hands behind your neck and bring your chest forward."

Once she had, she asked, "Would you like me to take the dress off entirely, Sir?"

"I'd like you to do as you're told. Nothing more. Are you able to comfortably spread your legs a little farther apart?"

After she was more open to him, he slid a hand between her legs. Her response delighted him. "You're damp, Sydney."

He kept his hand still, but she moved her hips a bit, sliding herself against him. "I generally won't mind if you come without permission. In fact, the more you orgasm, the more I get into the scene." He lowered his voice to an inviting purr. "But not tonight. Tonight, I want you more aroused than you've ever been." After she released a tiny moan, he pulled his hand away. Without giving her a chance to react, he spanked her there.

Crying out, she pitched forward slightly. He caught her and held her against him, liking the way they fit together.

For a moment, she stayed there before drawing in a deep breath and moving away. "*That* was unexpected."

"Turtle?"

"Hell no." She shook her head. "More like that, please."

"Stay where you are. I'll be right back."

He went inside. Brandy, a sub who regularly helped with house functions and parties, fetched him a blanket and two separate cuffs.

"Thank you."

"My pleasure, Sir." She lowered her head.

When he returned, Sydney was still in the same place. She was shifting from side to side a bit nervously, but she'd yet to bail out of the scene. "Are you doing okay?"

"Feeling a little exposed," she admitted. "Sir."

"Seeing you when I came back outside pleased me."

She exhaled. "Did it?" Her words were breathless.

"Indeed." Was he affecting her as powerfully as she was impacting him? "Would you like to continue?"

"You don't think that scared me off, do you? Sir?" The words were sassy and confident, but her voice wobbled, maybe betraying some nerves.

Interesting. "When you're ready, walk over to the fence." Then he scowled. "Are you okay in those shoes?"

"I could hike in them."

We'll see about that. "I'll stay a step or two behind you so I can watch your bare buttocks move."

The view was all he'd hoped for. Her every step was graceful, filled with sultry elegance. Despite her bravado, when she reached the edge of the paved patio, he took her elbow. After helping her over the uneven terrain, he draped the blanket over the top rail.

Without being told, she kicked off her shoes and leaned over the top rail, even remembering to spread her legs wide. Sydney Wallace definitely knew what she wanted. And, whether or not she recognized it, by having her beautifully curved ass upturned and waiting for his attention, she was also meeting his carnal needs.

"Use your safe word if it's too much, your slow word if you're uncomfortable or get a muscle cramp. We can get you readjusted."

"Yes, Sir. I understand."

"Your choice—I can secure your legs in place, or I can cuff your wrists."

She answered unhesitatingly. "I'd prefer you fasten my ankles so I can't get away, Sir."

Which meant that sometimes she attempted to do just that. "I'll expect you to keep your hands in place."

"Anything you say, Sir."

He crouched to attach the cuffs, and he inhaled the heady scent of her muskiness. Keeping her turned on without letting her come was going to be exquisitely rewarding.

To test the bonds, he trailed his fingers up the insides of her thighs. She squirmed and pulled and yet she helplessly remained where he wanted her. Sometime in the future, he'd stick a plug up her ass too, to intensify her sensations. "I'm going to warm you up with a few spanks." He fed the words into her ear. "Then I'll make you beg for more."

"You sound sure of yourself, Sir," she said, her voice muffled.

"I am, Sydney."

"You know, Sir, I have never begged for anything in my entire life."

"Tonight, brat, you will." *You've never been spanked by me.* "I promise you."

"We'll see about that…" Then, after her challenge, she added a saucy, "Sir."

Chapter Two

At Master Michael's confident, arrogant-sounding statement, a thrill that had nothing to do with the evening air arced down Sydney's spine. She had begged before, but not because she had meant it, only because it had been something that made her Top happy.

But if this gorgeous cowboy could truly drive her that far out of her mind…

She'd fantasized about playing with a Dom who was in tune with her, able to read what she wanted and needed and not just what she asked for.

Her visits to the Den were getting further apart, more from restlessness than because of her schedule. When she traveled, she sometimes checked out the scene in whatever city she was visiting. She'd tried new Doms, from renowned Tops to enthusiastic newbies. And she hadn't bared herself to the same man twice.

Like her parents before her, she was a thrill-seeker. Her first encounter with BDSM at a college party had immediately captured her interest. After that, going back to normal sex hadn't been possible. Still, every new high had left her wondering if there was anything else, anything better.

She'd been with some extreme players, and several years ago, she'd knelt to accept a collar. But true affection had been missing between her and Lewis. Finally, things had deteriorated to the point where Gregorio had found someone to cut the silver band off her neck. She'd left the pieces in the middle of the bed and never looked back.

On the other hand, Doms who were overly solicitous, as Master Michael had surmised, bored her.

So far, he seemed different from other men. She'd thought that would be a good thing, but now, being ignored, still half dressed, uncomfortably bent over a rail and hair spilling everywhere with her bottom exposed to anyone who was outside, she wasn't as sure.

When she'd first spotted the gorgeous rancher, she'd been intrigued. She'd only been at the party a few minutes when she'd wandered to the window. From her vantage, she'd watched him accept an energy drink. He'd nodded politely to the pretty submissive who'd fetched it for him.

Some guests, Doms and Dommes alike, ignored servers, but this cowboy seemed to have old-world manners.

Sydney had intentionally timed her walk across the patio. As she'd exaggeratedly moved her hips, hoping to catch his attention, she'd prayed she wouldn't fall off her ridiculously high heels.

When she'd noticed Gregorio moving toward Master Michael, she'd gritted her teeth. But obviously, he hadn't been deterred, and it had been all she could do not to pump her fist in joy.

Now, she was wondering if her enthusiasm had been misplaced. Perhaps she should have asked Gregorio about Master Michael before agreeing to play. "Can we get on with it, Sir?"

"When I'm ready."

Damn you. Earlier, when he'd slapped her pussy, she'd nearly orgasmed. Then he'd restrained her ankles and stroked the insides of her thighs. She had been certain he'd start the action quickly. But since then, he had barely touched her, just enough to intrigue her. And now impatience was curling in her stomach.

She released her grip to stretch her fingers.

"Stay still, please."

"Yes, Sir," she said, not because she meant it, but because it was expected. She understood his rules and she'd play by them to get some skin-on-skin satisfaction.

Startling her, he grabbed both of her ass cheeks. Then he squeezed unbelievably hard, making her gasp.

"Too much?"

God, no. "It was fine, Sir." Once the shock receded, a warm glow settled in. No one had done that before, and damn, the surprise tantalized. She tingled, wondering what was next.

"So is there a reason you're not holding on as you're supposed to be?"

"Sorry, Sir." She grabbed the bar again.

"Do you do that often?"

She frowned. "Sir?"

"Allow your mind to wander?"

"I…"

"Are you always living in the future, Sydney, rather than enjoying the moment?"

"I thought you weren't going to psychoanalyze me, Sir."

He laughed. The sound unnerved her, as if he knew she were trying to goad him into action.

At least fifteen more seconds dragged past before he lightly spanked her right buttock. This time, there was no heat, making her wonder if he really was worth the effort. After all, the night was young, and there were plenty of other Tops here. She could find someone else, get a few orgasms, and be home in bed before midnight.

"Relax." He tapped a few times on her left buttock. "Enjoy it."

Easier said than done.

He continued the light smacks, hardly varying the intensity but sometimes the location.

She exhaled in a frustrated rush.

"Give me what I want, Sydney, and I'll make sure you get what you want."

"And what is that, exactly?"

He didn't respond. From her upside-down position, she saw him take a step back. "Sir?"

"To move at my speed. I'm watching your reactions, learning your body. You might be impatient, but you *are* getting aroused."

Since the gentle breeze whispered on her exposed parts, cooling her, he might be right.

"I know I'm asking you to step outside your comfort zone, maybe beyond what you've experienced before. Would you be willing to trust me for a little while?"

Suspicion and doubt warred in her. "How long?"

"Give me five minutes. If you're not happy after that time, I'll give you an ass blistering you'll never forget."

Her ass tightened at his words. The first part of his sentence had been kind, the second part clipped. The way he used his voice made her react in a visceral way.

"You'd like that, wouldn't you?"

"As a matter of fact, yes."

He chuckled — the sound as sexy as it was diabolical. "Are your manners always this atrocious?"

His casual comment made her bristle.

"I don't know the extent of your training, and some couples don't follow protocols. But I've corrected you a couple of times already. And you've continued to leave Sir out of your sentences, and you are not addressing me as Master Michael. Perhaps no one's demanded good behavior from you before, or maybe you're intentionally trying to live up to your reputation, I don't know. But if we continue on from here, you will comply with my requirements."

In an underwater competition, she'd gone without breathing for almost three minutes, so surely she could get through this frustratingly long discussion. "Yes, Sir."

He spanked her right buttock *hard*.

Yes. So, so much better.

"Did I get your attention?" he asked, rubbing the tender spot.

Playing his game, giving him what he demanded, she replied, "Yes, Sir. Thank you."

"That's better." He grabbed her ass cheeks like he had earlier and squeezed again.

She surrendered to the exquisite pain, letting her body go limp.

"Now, Sydney, we'll enjoy some mutual satisfaction."

"Of course, Sir." Was that the difference between him and other Doms she'd played with? From the beginning, he hadn't wanted it to be about either of them in particular. Some guys were just into their own kink. Others seemed so intent on making her happy that they failed miserably.

Master Michael held her around the waist and pressed his body against hers, forcing her into the fence railings. Denim scratched her skin, and his cock angled suggestively between her cheeks. He rocked his hips, and she moved with him in a primitive, universal dance.

"You're getting hot for me, Sydney."

Her senses were overwhelmed. "Yes, Sir."

"I like that." He moved back a bit to slide his fingers over her hot folds, teasing and arousing, then pressing a thumb against her anal whorl. The fact that she couldn't close her legs made escape impossible. She wriggled, trying to coax him into giving her more.

Skillfully, he stroked her clit, making her rise onto her toes as much as the restraints allowed. "Oh, Master Michael..."

"That's enough," he said, pulling away entirely.

"But—"

With a sharp smack to her pussy, he cut off her protest.

The pain heightened her arousal. She was lost in a delirium of desire, desperate to come.

"You're a very sexy woman, Sydney." He kept his fingers against the small of her back.

Before she could reply, he spanked her repeatedly, and hard.

Needing this desperately, more than she knew, she moaned.

He fondled her pussy.

"Oh, Sir. I want to come."

"Ask."

"May I?"

"Soon."

"May I please come, Sir?"

"That will more likely get you what you want."

But instead of bringing her off, he spanked her again, rapidly, leaving no part of her buttocks unscathed.

Her fingers were now in a death-grip around the fencing, and she needed to hold on so the world wouldn't spin out of control.

When she was sure she couldn't take any more, he gently squeezed her clit.

She whimpered. "I... Please. I want to come."

Again, maddeningly, he denied her.

Sydney rose as high as she could, thrusting back toward him, wordlessly asking, seeking, but her efforts only earned her a pinch on her right thigh.

"Not quite yet," he told her.

It had been a long time since she'd been this turned on, and he was driving her out of her mind. "Don't make me wait, Sir."

He laughed again softly. "It will be worth it. I promise."

Deep inside her, pressure thumped in persistent demand.

"Ready for more, Sydney?"

"Yes, yes, *yes*."

He slapped her left buttock, then quickly stroked between her legs. The momentary friction drove her mad. Before she could react, he smacked her right cheek then teased her again. On and on he went, relentlessly repeating the pattern, not doing any one thing long enough for her to get off.

What he did instead was set every nerve ending on fire.

As the seconds passed, her resistance receded.

"That's it," he said, his modulated, rich voice sounding as if it came from the farthest mountain peak.

"Your butt is turning the prettiest shade of pink. Beautiful, beautiful, Sydney."

Sydney no longer held the bars as tightly, and she didn't struggle against the ankle cuffs. She didn't even wriggle her body in an attempt to press her pussy against his hand when he paused there. Instead, she surrendered.

The world seemed to spin backward, and she stopped being concerned that they were out in the open. She no longer noticed her earlier discomfort. In fact, her body felt as if it were weighed down by a thousand stinging sensations.

"Even more?"

"Oh…" She was already delirious.

"We can stop now, and I can give you the orgasm you've earned. Or we can continue with my belt."

Sydney shivered. He'd taken her past the limits of how long she thought she could hold off her orgasm, and the curious part of her wanted to know what else was possible. Tonight—Master Michael—was the adventure she craved. "Please," she said. "I want more."

"Please…" he prompted.

Frustrating man. "Please, Sir."

"To be clear, Sydney, are you begging?"

"Yes." How long had it been since she'd been this aroused, aware of every muscle in her legs and the throbbing sensation between her legs? "I'm begging. Tell me you're taking off your belt, Sir," she pleaded.

"Damn straight, I'm taking off my belt."

Hunger crawled through her, for the taste of his leather, and for the sight of his naked body. She'd noticed the breadth of him, the long, lean length of his legs and his tight ass. She'd bet he wasn't a ranch owner who let the hired hands do all the work—the calluses on his fingers proved it. "And your hat?"

"That might happen later," he told her.

Later.

Earlier, he'd mentioned going to his place, but she hadn't been convinced she'd accept an invitation. And when he'd mentioned chemistry, she hadn't argued, even though she believed it was nothing more than a word to make insatiable romantics swoon.

She had planned to live by her personal motto—show up and hook up. She'd mingle, looking for unattached Doms, introduce herself then see if a private room was available.

At this point, however, she wanted to see where the evening might go.

Sydney moaned and writhed when he drew the belt across her shoulders. Now—longing to feel the caressing bite of his leather everywhere—she wished he'd had her remove her dress entirely.

She wiggled around, but he took a step back.

With a sigh, knowing he wouldn't be rushed, she forced herself to settle again.

The impending orgasm loomed distantly, leaving her edgy.

She was more than ready when he landed the first two strokes across her buttocks. Her skin was already warmed from his earlier squeezes and spanks, and these new strokes seared her skin.

Although he was nowhere near her pussy, arousal returned full force.

"Thrust your ass out for me. And keep it there."

Before he was done speaking, she presented her rear end as much as possible. *Tur-tle.*

"That's it." He laid several more strokes across her heated body, turning her inside out.

"I feel as if I'm going to come, Sir," she told him.

"If you can, please feel free to do so."

She tried to squeeze her legs together, needing just a little pressure, but he'd been clever in his restriction.

As he increased the intensity behind his swings, she cried out. *This* was exactly what she'd been seeking.

Despite her best intention of staying in one position, the force of his blows made her sway. But within moments, it was as if they'd found a rhythm that worked for both of them.

"Red is my new favorite color," he told her. "And now to add some to the backs of your thighs."

She'd been certain it couldn't get any better. But it did.

He used infinitely less pressure on her legs, but the lashing was just as exquisite.

Slammed against the railing by his relentlessness, she loosened her grip and allowed herself to move freely.

She wasn't sure how long he continued — all she knew was that she was no longer thinking about anything but the moment. Being halfway upside down combined with the Den's mountainous elevation caused a mild oxygen deprivation, leaving her unable to speak.

For the first time in a scene, she wasn't trying to set the pace or manipulate her Dom. She'd turned over control.

Several moments later, she registered the fact that he'd stopped.

Her heart rate increased, and she blinked, trying to clear her mind.

"You did well," he said.

He cupped her heated pussy and squeezed.

"Sir..." The word was a moan wrapped in a breathless plea.

"Now I'll help you to come," he said, scraping her clit with a fingernail.

As if she were flying apart, she trembled.

Relentlessly, he persisted, inserting a finger inside her, fucking her with his hand while putting pressure on her clit. He kept it up until she was shaking, her hips jerking.

Orgasm after orgasm claimed her. And when she was convinced she had nothing left, he abraded one of the welts on her left buttock.

She arched her back, pushing away from the fencing, allowing him in deeper, and unintentionally increasing the force of his touch against her clitoris.

Reeling, she shattered once more. He'd left her breathless, overwhelmed, more satisfied than she'd been in months, if not years.

Her body was drenched in sweat, and her thoughts were scrambled as she gasped for air.

"You're about warmed up," he said.

Warmed up? Her knees sagged.

She was aware of him unfastening her ankles then rubbing her bare legs. Although the touch wasn't erotic, it sent a warm shiver through her.

"Stay where you are," he instructed.

As if I can move.

Her Dom for the night took control again, tugging her dress back into place before he effortlessly lifted her from the ground, scooping her into his arms.

She prided herself on her strength, and she'd never been a snuggler. But he'd worn her out, left her powerless to do anything other than wrap one arm around his neck and lay her cheek against his chest. She breathed in his power and strength, and the fresh mountain scent of his soap. He felt...comforting.

He snatched up the blanket and strode toward the patio.

"My shoes."

"I'll get them in a minute," he said.

Near the firepit, he placed her in a chair. After wrapping the blanket around her, he promised to come right back.

She watched him return to the fence to pick up her heels and the cuffs. Her strappy sandals dangled from his index finger, and she wondered why she found the sight so sexy.

When he was close, he dropped everything in an untidy pile before signaling for a server.

With a "Thanks," he snagged two waters from the man's tray, then uncapped one and offered it to her. "How are you feeling?"

"I..." Hands curled around the bottle, she hesitated. Instead of taking a drink, she regarded him.

Generally she kept her thoughts and emotions to herself. Other than her friend Vanessa and a couple of college roommates, Sydney wasn't particularly close to anyone.

Nearby, the wood crackled and hissed, the light casting intriguing shadows over him. Finally, she settled for a noncommittal answer. "You were right... You made me beg."

He leaned over her, bracing his hands on the chair arms, and said, "That was only an appetizer, Sydney."

They were so close, they breathed the same air. "Is that a promise?"

"Or a threat." With a grin, he pressed one of his thumbs to her lips. "Take it any way you want."

She shuddered.

For a wild moment she wondered if he was going to kiss her. But that was too personal. Wasn't it?

As she blinked, he lowered his hand, then used a booted foot to drag in another chair so he could sit nearby.

Already, she'd gotten so much more than she'd expected here tonight. She still had on everything except her underwear, and she'd yet to catch a glimpse of his naked body. He was right about one thing — what they'd shared had definitely whetted her appetite. Now she wanted the main course.

Although there were many other couples milling about, he'd positioned her so that she felt cocooned, as if it were just the two of them on the vast acreage.

She sipped her water and noticed Gregorio and the Den's owner, Master Damien, looking in their direction.

Master Damien was as dashing as he was rakish. The cuffs of his long-sleeved white shirt were folded back, exposing his forearms. His hair was longer than it had been the last time she'd seen him, and she wondered how many subs, men and women alike, longed to run their fingers through it. To her knowledge, though, he played with no one. His history was an object of frequent discussion, but the man himself provided no answers.

Gregorio stood next to his boss, shoulder to shoulder. If she wasn't mistaken, Gregorio was smiling.

A woman with incredibly long, dark hair joined them. A much, much larger man, apparently her sub, knelt next to them with his head bowed. Even while she talked with Gregorio, she kept her hand affectionately on top of her sub's head.

The man cocked his head a little, looking up at his Domme. It could be her imagination, but the man looked peaceful in a way Sydney had never experienced.

"Mistress Catrina," Master Michael said as if reading her thoughts. "She's training a new submissive."

"Training? They're not a couple?"

"No. To my knowledge, Catrina doesn't have permanent submissives."

"Was your ex collared?" When he didn't answer, she regarded him more closely. The brim of his damnable hat made his expression unreadable. She wanted to see his eyes.

"Not literally, though I'd considered it."

Hoped to? Except for the fact his abrupt answer had closed the conversation, she'd have asked the question aloud.

Saying nothing more, he steepled his fingers and looked over the top of his hands at the fire.

"How about any other submissive you've been with?" she prodded.

He glanced in her direction. "It hasn't worked out that way."

"You're an expert at evasive answers, Sir."

"If—or when—it's appropriate, Ms. Wallace, I'll have no secrets from you."

"Oh?"

He turned to face her. "And you'll have none from me."

She shivered a little, despite the fire, despite the blanket, despite the leather dress.

"So, little sub, is this good night?" he asked. "Or would you like to come home with me?"

Little sub? No one had called her that before. And truthfully, if they had, she might have run, or as forcefully as possible let them know it wasn't acceptable. She liked a bit of adventure with her sex. But submission? That really wasn't her thing. As an occasional part of the act, it was fine. But she wanted nothing more, and if they continued, she'd have to make sure she set him straight about that.

Still… There was something about the way he said those words — tinged with a roughened, raw huskiness — that made them palatable. They sounded like a term of endearment, and that made a forbidden response uncurl within her. "What do you have in mind?" If he was offering another ride on this extremely emotional and physical roller coaster, she was intrigued.

"I haven't had you on your knees." He swept his gaze down her body. "And I haven't tormented your nipples."

Damn. "I have very sensitive nipples, Sir."

"Do you?" he asked, with no concern in his tone. "Then having me drag you onto your toes by them will no doubt be uncomfortable."

Hunger slammed into her, making her shift in her seat.

"So what will it be, Sydney?" he asked again. "Would you like to continue? Or shall we say good night?"

His cock still strained against his jeans. Suddenly she was ravenous for him, wanting him inside her, filling her again and again. She had to see if the night could get even better. "I'd like to continue."

He raised his eyebrows. "Then address me correctly."

"*Sir.* I'd like to continue, Sir."

"At the ranch? Or would you be more comfortable here?"

Staying at the Den had numerous advantages. Gregorio and Master Damien would both look out for her. But she was curious about Master Michael and how he lived.

"I'm also happy to drive to your place, if that's best for you," he continued.

"In Evergreen?" She shook her head. Not only did it not make sense for him to drive back toward Denver, but she didn't invite men to her condominium. She liked her privacy and she needed the freedom to get in her vehicle and leave when she wanted. "Your house is fine."

After he stood, she accepted the hand he extended. Effortlessly, he drew her up and held on to her for longer than she expected. A protective part of her brain urged her to pull away. But her instinctive, feminine senses recognized his strength, power, and masculinity. She couldn't move.

"I'm happy to drive you," he said. "Your vehicle will be fine here, but I assume you'd prefer to take your own car?"

"Yes, Sir."

He nodded. "Just as well. I'd require you to raise your dress again, and the sight of your beautiful bare pussy would distract me."

The things he said were an erotic thrill.

After releasing her, he folded the blanket and picked up the cuffs while she slid back into her heels.

When she'd smoothed her dress back into place, he nodded to indicate that she should precede him.

"I like watching your hips move and remembering the red marks on your cheeks."

Earlier she'd intentionally tried to capture his interest with her walk, but now that she was aware of his scrutiny, she felt self-conscious.

"Sexy," he said.

Master Damien detached himself from the group he'd been visiting with and met them midway across the patio.

Master Michael placed a hand lightly on her shoulder. Knowing she had no choice, she stopped.

"Thanks for your hospitality," Master Michael said, accepting Master Damien's extended hand.

"Always a pleasure. You're leaving already?"

"We are."

Raising one of his impossibly dark eyebrows, Master Damien looked at her directly. "Is everything all right, Sydney?"

This was one thing she had always appreciated about the Den. Damien and Gregorio enforced the rules and looked after the safety of all their guests. "Yes. Everything is fine, thank you." Master Michael tightened his grip on her shoulder, and she said, "I mean yes, Sir."

"May I have a moment with Sydney?" he asked Master Michael.

"Of course," her temporary Dom replied. "I'll be inside when you're ready, Sydney."

She watched until he had entered the house and handed the cuffs and blanket to a perfectly trained sub.

"You've never left with anyone," Master Damien observed. "And Master Michael is not your usual type."

She waited for him to say something further, but he didn't. She marveled at his patience. Master Damien was correct—she usually scened with Doms whose reputation she knew, men who would be satisfied playing in the dungeon.

The instant attraction to Master Michael when she'd seen him talking with Gregorio had been something more visceral. She liked how tall he was, how broad, how focused and, of course, the fact that he was willing to form his own opinions about her. "He's different," she said finally. "Gentle's not the right word." She met

Master Damien's gaze and sighed. "But I can't think of a better one. Measured, maybe. Calculated."

He nodded. "Don't underestimate him."

A small shiver traced her spine. "Are you saying I shouldn't trust him?"

"Not at all."

"Then..."

"I've known Master Michael for eight years, maybe more. He plays by his own rules."

She'd already ascertained that. During their brief encounter near the fence, he'd moved at his speed, not hers, but there was no doubt he'd given her what she needed. And a lot more than she'd anticipated. "Ah, I get it. You're concerned for him, rather than me," she said with a smile.

"Perhaps I am."

"That stings."

He inclined his head to one side. "If you need anything, feel free to call us here. I take my obligations to our members very seriously. Someone will fetch you, if necessary."

"I appreciate your consideration." She nodded. "Thank you, Sir."

Master Michael was waiting for her inside the patio doors, with her purse in hand. Oddly, it didn't detract from his masculinity.

"I took the liberty of asking for your belongings and having your car brought around."

She accepted the small handbag. "That was considerate."

"Unless you've changed your mind?" He captured her chin with his thumb and forefinger.

"You don't scare me," she said, meeting his gaze. His eyes were a deep, dark green, as unreadable as they were inviting.

"Perhaps I should."

The pseudo-threat sent a jolt of adrenaline through her. While he kept her imprisoned, he swept a fingertip across her jawbone. "I'll follow you," she said, feigning a calm that had suddenly deserted her. As Master Damien had pointed out, she didn't go home with men, and Master Michael was nothing like the other Doms she'd played with. But his complexity intrigued her. She'd known him only a short time, yet she'd already figured out he was as demanding emotionally as he was physically. The physical part excited her. The emotional one…? That she could do without.

"Shall we?" he asked, releasing his hold to rest his palm against the small of her back, guiding her through the house and back outside.

An attendant, nattily dressed as if he were a doorman at a New York City hotel—minus a shirt—wished them a good evening.

That Michael drove a new but dusty, oversize pickup truck didn't surprise her. The jeans, cowboy hat, and worn leather boots were obviously not just for effect.

She followed him out of the secluded area where the Den was nestled, and they turned onto Highway 34, heading north. There were distant peaks, seemingly endless miles of high-mountain prairie, but very few headlights from oncoming cars. It was as if they had the world to themselves.

Rather than getting nervous, the kind of anticipation that came from the unknown raced through her. To focus herself, she set her streaming service to her favorite channel, then cranked up the volume, blasting dance music throughout the passenger compartment of her decade-old small sports utility vehicle.

She kept his taillights in sight and she appreciated that he drove a bit over the speed limit. About half an hour later, they left the tarmac behind. A large pothole in a bumpy dirt road almost jarred the wheel from her hands.

This definitely hadn't been what she'd planned when she had shimmied into the leather dress several hours ago. In fact, out here, her attire and sandals seemed ridiculous.

They bypassed several turn-offs, and she had to drop back in order to not get blasted by the dirt spewing behind his tires.

A few minutes later, he followed a fork to the right. She was starting to wonder if it was a road to nowhere when he braked to a stop in front of a well-lit gate. It was buttressed by massive, rough-hewn wooden poles that soared at least twenty feet in the air. A beam spanned the overhead distance, and a metal sign hung from chains. A large raptor with talons extended was emblazoned on the left side, next to the words *Eagle's Bend Ranch.*

With his hat still firmly in place, the lord and master of the place walked back to her vehicle. She pushed a button to lower the window.

"Welcome to my small slice of heaven." He tipped his hat. "Follow me through the gate, then I'll close it behind us." He placed his hands on the door and leaned in.

Damn, he smelled good—of rugged, open space.

"Scared yet?"

"Not a chance."

With a grin, he tucked a lock of her hair behind her ear. "That's my girl."

The easy familiarity took her by surprise. No one had called her anything like that. Nasty sex words, yes.

Syrupy, sugary, hoping-to-get-you-to-bed words like honey and baby, yes. But something that innocuous? Definitely not. It didn't fit her. So why the hell was she smiling back at him?

Without another word, he turned away. Her gaze was riveted on the way his jeans fit his hot rear, and she didn't glance away until he'd climbed back into the truck then driven through the entrance.

She pulled in behind him, then the gates slid shut.

Now she was nervous. He'd effectively blocked her escape.

He stopped by her vehicle again.

"The code for the lock is M-Y-H-M," he said. "Shorthand for my home, so it's easy to remember."

She exhaled. "How did you know?"

"Darlin', you haven't blinked in thirty seconds. You've already told me that not much scares you."

Slowly, Sydney shook her head.

"But the things that scare you are debilitating."

With determination, she shoved aside his direct hit. "There you go with the psychoanalysis again."

"That's just casual observation. I'll let you know what I see when I really have the chance to study you."

Before she could respond, he moved off. As her window slid closed, she took her foot from the brake and followed him.

As they wound their way down the dirt road, lights came on, obviously all equipped with motion sensors.

Off to the right were a number of buildings, a barn among them.

His home finally came into view, and he lowered his window to point to a place for her to park near a large pine tree.

The moment she shut off the engine, he was there to help her, something she appreciated with her sandals and the uneven dirt parking area. "This outfit isn't exactly the best for ranch wear," she said, closing the vehicle door.

"Are you kidding? It's perfect."

In the distance, she heard an occasional moo and something that sounded like the bleating of a goat. While she also lived in the mountains, it was as if she and Master Michael occupied two entirely different universes.

After cupping her elbow for support, he led her toward the house. A huge yard was also fenced, but with horizontally notched wooden rails interlaced with vertical ones. Though it was likely practical, it was also artistic.

With one hand still on her, he opened yet another gate, taking time to ensure it latched securely behind them.

"To keep Chewie out," he said.

"Chewie?"

"Long story. She's a Nigerian dwarf goat."

"I thought ranches had cows."

"I run cattle, yes," he said. "But Chewie is more of a pet. Actually, she qualifies as a pest. She would eat all the grass and the flowers and the trees if I allowed her near the house. Well, and anything else she could find."

"And the fence stops her?"

"It's supposed to. I'm thinking of putting up a surveillance camera. Somehow the gate gets opened far too often. Last I checked, she had hooves rather than opposable thumbs, but I wonder…"

The sight of columbines and other wildflowers surprised her. "Are you the gardener?"

"No. That's thanks to my sister, Melanie. They were my grandmother's flowerbeds, and my mom continued the tradition. Mel doesn't visit often, but she plants, I don't know…stuff. Annuals. Perennials. Bulbs. Seeds. Bushes. Shrubs. As if I'm supposed to know the difference? The goat is hers, and the girls have a horse here, too. The ranch has a few hands who live on-site in the bunkhouse over there." He pointed toward the distance. "Don't worry. We'll have our privacy. And it won't matter how long or how hard you yell—no one will come running to save you."

She looked up. He wasn't smiling, and there'd been no hint of a tease in his tone, which all sent another illicit thrill rocketing through her.

After opening the front door, he ushered her inside.

The home was rustic, with exposed-beam ceilings, hardwood floors, hand-woven rugs, and oversize leather furniture. A stone fireplace dominated the living room, and wood crisscrossed in the grate, waiting to be lit. Dozens of photographs, some in black and white, crowded the mantel.

Just that detail highlighted the differences in their priorities. She had a single picture of her parents. In the small, framed snapshot, she was about a year old and asleep in the pack on her dad's back. They'd been on a pilgrimage in Spain—if she remembered the story correctly.

Her condominium lacked the homey touches that his home had. Hers was impersonal enough to be a hotel room. Until now, she hadn't really noticed.

"Can I get you something to drink?"

She followed him into the kitchen, aware of the staccato sound of her shoes on the rustic floors. "Water is fine, thank you," she said as she placed her purse on the counter.

He poured her a glass from a pitcher stored in the stainless-steel refrigerator.

With a smile of thanks, she accepted it and slid onto a barstool tucked beneath a poured concrete island. The kitchen looked like a designer's dream, with gleaming pots hanging overhead. She rarely cooked, but she appreciated the gas range, double ovens, and miles of countertops.

"I think, Sydney, we should get a few things straight between us." He moved in closer, standing on the other side of the island.

With her hands wrapped around the glass, she looked at him. He folded his arms across his chest. The brim of his hat, as always, cast him in shadows, making it difficult to read his expression.

"Your feedback, verbally as well as physically, matters to me, so I insist on open and honest communication. I want you to get off, and that's more likely to happen if you're interacting with me. I have no interest in just spanking you until you come."

That sounded all right with her. She took a sip of water and squirmed in her seat. Because he demanded a response, she said, "I agree, Sir."

"When I request something from you, I anticipate you will either let me know it's problematic or you'll do as you're told." He raised an eyebrow.

His firm tone brooked no refusal. She took another drink of water to soothe her suddenly dry throat. After releasing the glass, she said, "Yes, Sir."

"In that case, strip and kneel. Hands behind your neck, head tipped back, chest thrust toward me. I believe I promised to torture your nipples."

Chapter Three

Maybe he should have heeded Gregorio's warning.

Michael didn't consider himself much of a risk-taker. He weighed his decisions carefully and he liked having everything in order. Keeping the family's ranch after his parents had passed had never been in question. Although his sister had voted in favor of selling, he hadn't been swayed. His roots went deep into the land. The acreage was as important to him as his next breath.

Yet he couldn't help his attraction to Sydney's untamed streak.

Since his divorce, he'd mostly scened with subs at the Den who wore the house's purple wristband and had no expectations of a continuing relationship. They were professionals who knew all the protocols and could be counted on to behave perfectly.

Sydney, on the other hand, seemed focused on herself. It was all about her, not him, and definitely not about submission.

But he was honest enough to admit that he'd loved the way she'd behaved when he'd had her draped over the fence. Her responses had been real, with no artifice. When he'd brought her to orgasm for the first time, he'd known he'd rather spend the evening with her than anyone else, no matter how well trained they were.

He shouldn't see her as a challenge, but he did. "Do you need me to repeat my order?"

Slowly, she slid from the barstool.

In the curve-hugging dress, she looked so sexy that it was almost a shame to have her remove the garment. *Almost.*

Michael stayed where he was while she revealed her skin a slow, beautiful inch at a time.

As she shimmied, pulling the material over her head, he drank in the whole of her. She had an athletic build, not overly thin, and she had definite curves, along with a waist made for his hands. Her breasts were perfect, not too big, and her nipples were already hard.

After laying the dress over the back of the stool, she removed her lacy bra and dropped it on the seat before bending to remove her shoes.

"Leave them on," he said.

"Of course, Sir."

For a moment, she stood there, and he simply looked at her. Right now, this evening, she was his.

Finally, she lowered herself to the floor and placed her hands behind her back as he'd requested.

Her chest rose and fell quickly, and he appreciated the betrayal of nerves. She projected an aura of confidence that appealed to him, but that he had some effect on her made him hungry. His cock swelled, but he'd had a hard-on for the better part of two hours. He could wait a little longer.

He walked around her, knowing she was aware of the sound of his boots against the wood. To her credit, she didn't turn to look at him. "Good," he said. "That will help you earn an orgasm."

"Earn, Sir?"

"Behave yourself," he reminded her, "and you'll enjoy our time together more."

"That's a tall order, Sir. I'm not sure I've ever been that satisfied."

"Is that another challenge, little sub?"

"No, Sir. That would be wrong. I'm just making a comment."

He grinned. *Yeah.* He would have been smart to have heeded Gregorio's warning. "Cup your breasts, Sydney, and offer them to me."

She did as instructed, drawing them together and lifting them. He crouched in front of her. "Look at me."

Their gazes met.

Earlier, he'd noticed that her eyes were ice blue. But he'd seen her outside—the sun had been fading, and the flickering firelight and torches had hidden the richness of the color. He wondered if she had any idea how expressive their depths were. Now he saw anticipation there, along with a hint of trepidation. "You said your nipples are sensitive."

"Yes, Sir. They are."

He brushed the pads of his thumbs across the tips, making her tremble. *Yeah.* If that gentle a touch caused that reaction, then nipple play would bring them both endless delights. "I want you to stay as you are, even if you're tempted to move. Understand?"

She nodded.

"And your slow word?"

"*Tur-tle*," she said, breaking the word into two distinct syllables. "Sir."

"That will get you an orgasm denial."

"Not a punishment?" She scowled.

"That is punishment for you. I think you'd like another spanking, and you'll get one. But I'm betting that keeping you on the edge and making you practice patience would really be torment."

She opened her mouth as if to say something, but then snapped it closed again.

"Wise choice," he said, approvingly. Still looking at her, he dragged his thumbnails across the tips of her nipples.

His reluctant little submissive sucked in a breath.

He pinched her nipples lightly then let go right away. Even though she swayed toward him a little, she kept her eyes open, her gaze focused on his face. "Good girl," he said.

This time, he took her nipples and used more pressure, squeezing for longer.

"Ahh..."

"They're like small pebbles," he said.

"Yes, Sir. It...hurts."

"Do you want to stop?"

"No."

He released her, giving her a short break, letting her process the sensations, making her wonder what was next.

"Keep holding your breasts for me." After she nodded, he repeated the process twice more. She closed her eyes before quickly opening them. "Ready for more?"

"Yes, Sir."

As he continued, he increased his tempo, pinching her harder, longer. He'd been giving her a handful of seconds to recover and prepare for the next assault, but now he shortened the time between the breaks.

All the while, he held her gaze, watching her for signs of real distress. "Is your pussy getting wet?"

"I'm not sure, Sir."

"You're not sure?" He raised an eyebrow.

Her words were breathless. "I'm a bit overwhelmed."

"In that case, I think you should check."

"Sir?"

"You heard me. With your right hand, touch your pussy."

She blinked, as if confused for a moment, but she let go of her breast and followed his instructions.

"Well?" he asked.

"Yes, I'm a bit wet, Sir."

"Show me your fingers."

Unbelievably, twin streaks of pink stained cheeks. *Are you embarrassed, little sub?* Especially after Gregorio's warning, seeing this side of her surprised him.

She held up her hand, and dampness glistened on her fingertips.

"That's perfect," he said, capturing her wrist and lowering his head to taste her juices. "Delicious. I like how sensitive your nipples are and how you respond to my touch. Please continue to play with your pussy. But this time, use both hands."

"Yes, Sir." She lowered her head and dropped her gaze to the floor.

"No, no. Keep looking at me."

After blinking, she refocused her gaze.

"Better," he said. "Much, much better. I always want to see your expression to ensure you're enjoying yourself." That was especially important if he couldn't always trust that she'd use her safe words. "And I want to be certain you don't come."

"But—"

"Do it *now*."

She slowly moved both hands between her legs.

"That's it. Spread your labia with your left hand. Use your right to slide across your clit and to finger-fuck yourself." As he gave his instructions, he tugged on her nipples.

"Oh, Sir…"

"Do you like that?"

"It's… Sir… Yes. I do." Gyrating her hips, she did as he said.

Damn, she was hot. "Beautiful," he murmured. "Pleasure yourself. Enjoy. Surrender." He continued to torment her while praising her. "Such a good girl."

"Yes, Sir," she whispered.

The deeper she slid into their scene, the easier it seemed for her to call him Sir.

At the Den, even when he'd moved her toward the fence, her back had been straight. It was as if she affected a certain posture to keep others at a distance. But here, now, with his attention solely on her, with no one else around, her shoulders were more relaxed.

As he continued to rapidly pinch, pull, and release, she added a second finger to her pussy.

The tantalizing scent of her arousal made him even more delirious with desire. He wanted to claim her, mark her as his. "Fuck yourself with your fingers," he encouraged.

As her head fell back, she whimpered.

"*Stop!*"

Ignoring him, she continued to work her hand against her pussy.

He moved quickly, releasing his grip on her breasts to grab her hands.

"What?" she demanded.

He yanked her hands above her head and secured her wrists.

She exhaled a shaky breath. "I... Damn you. I almost came," she protested, her mouth slightly parted.

"And I told you orgasm denial was part of your punishment. You haven't earned an orgasm." He leaned in a bit. "The fact you just forgot your manners can be overlooked for now, but if you have any hope of being allowed to come again for the rest of the evening, you need to focus on me."

She drew her eyebrows together and pursed her lips. *Is she going to tell me to go to hell as she hits the door?*

Fascinated, he watched her internal emotional battle play out on her face. She clenched her teeth and set her chin. He said nothing, giving her time to process what was happening. He knew they were on a precipice, and damn, he wished he knew the right way to pull them back.

She was definitely headstrong and unaccustomed to giving up control. From the beginning, he'd known she liked BDSM for the intensity, but he'd bet she hadn't reckoned on this.

Over the course of the next thirty seconds, she remained rigid, glaring at him. Then she took a couple of deep, shuddering breaths, and the tension seemed to drain from her body.

He exhaled slowly. "No doubt I'm different from anyone you've played with," he said quietly. "Demanding things you're not expecting." And she was unlike anyone he'd ever known.

Sydney tried to extricate herself, but since she hadn't used her safe word, he kept hold of her.

"I…"

He waited for her to sort through her thoughts.

"I've been with Doms who practiced orgasm denial before, but not like this."

"Tell me what you mean."

"They've always just changed tactics, so I didn't come as fast. But then, when I did, it was an amazing experience. I've never had it as punishment." She blinked. "I'm not sure I like it."

"You're not meant to. I figured you would happily take a red ass or a flogging. You could feel good that you were being punished for your bad behavior, but you would really just be getting what you wanted because I'd allowed you to manipulate me." He traced a finger over one of her eyebrows.

Her nipples were still hard, and she had some goose bumps on her arms. She'd obviously sweated a little, and now her skin was cooling. Or maybe he'd just unnerved her. "I need you to know one thing—I won't be goaded. And you can stop anytime."

"I don't admit defeat."

"That's what I want you to accept." Michael shook his head. "It's about being honest."

"In that case, I want to come."

"I can have you back there again in minutes."

"You may not be done punishing me," she said, "but I'm so over being punished. Can we move on to something more fun?"

"I'm afraid you don't get to decide that."

She sighed.

"Tell me what you think your orgasm will be like."

"Will it happen in this century?" she countered. "I mean, will it happen this century, *Sir*?"

You really are a brat. With a chuckle, he released her wrists. "Put your hands behind your back. Spread your knees farther apart."

With a scowl, she did as he requested.

He removed his hat, then flicked his wrist to send it onto the nearby stool before running his hand through his short hair.

"It's darker than I expected, Sir. I want to get my fingers in the strands."

"You can hold it when you're on top of me."

"Promise, Sir?"

She definitely should have come with a warning label.

He lay on the floor and shifted so that his face was between her legs. "Your clit is still swollen." He took hold of her waist and pulled her down, forcing her legs farther apart and bringing her lower so that her pussy was mere inches from his face. "Keep your hands where they are. Now move your hips."

"Dear God."

He grasped her labia and tugged. "This skin was made for clamps."

His threat made her jerk.

"That's a girl. Keep moving. Just like that."

"This is embarrassing, Sir."

"Get your clit on my tongue or it will be a cold day in hell before you have that orgasm."

She moved, and he took the opportunity to pinch her clit. Yelping, she jerked, and the movement threw her off balance, bringing her into contact with his mouth. Exactly what he'd hoped would happen.

He licked her from back to front.

"I…"

"Fuck my face, little sub. I won't tell you twice."

The position was obviously awkward for her, but she did so. He tongued her, sucked her clit, captured her around the legs, and held her prisoner as he ate her, showing his appreciation. With a moan, she writhed helplessly. Then, when he brought her to the edge, he stopped.

"Damnable man, Sir."

He grinned and went back to work. This time, he stuck his tongue inside her, savoring her feminine taste.

She lifted up onto her knees, off his face, even though he tried to hold her in place.

"That's... It's too much, Sir."

"Not nearly enough," he countered. "Get back into place."

Her muscles were tight as she complied.

He used his tongue to make her wet and to lap up her intoxicating juices. The moment she made soft mewling sounds, he once again ceased what he was doing.

"*Argh!*"

"Nice try. But your body gave you away. You'll not be sneaking in any orgasms, I'm afraid." He let her go and smacked her right ass cheek. "Kneel up properly." When she did, he moved out from beneath her.

He rose to stand in front of her, and she tilted her head back to look at him. Her lips were parted, and her eyes were wide. The earlier hostility was gone. Her hands were still linked behind her back as he'd requested. Despite her apparent frustration, she seemed softer. "In answer to your question, no. It appears your orgasm will not be happening this century."

"Master Michael, you are a beast."

"Indeed," he agreed. "I'm open to you convincing me otherwise."

"How, Sir?"

"That's a good start." He reached down to grasp her nipples again. Since he believed in keeping his promises, he said, "Stand."

He pulled on the tips, lengthening her nipples and stretching her breasts.

She grabbed his arms for support and hissed through clenched teeth. He continued until she was standing. "Let go of me," he instructed. "Hands behind your back again. Surrender."

Eyes wide with total trust, she did.

He kept up the pressure until she was on her toes. "Beautiful," he told her. "How does it feel?"

"Oh, damn, Sir... It hurts."

"Too much?"

"Yes. And not enough."

He understood and he delighted in her.

Abruptly, he released his terrible grip, only to gather her in his arms and pull her close. "You can relax."

With her chest heaving, she snuggled against him, and he smoothed her hair before cradling her head.

Then he placed his other hand on her back. "You're a brave little sub. In fact, you've almost earned that orgasm."

She looked up. "Sir?"

"My bedroom is on the second story. I'd like you to crawl up the stairs." He was asking a lot from her. She wanted to let go, push the outer edges of a pain-induced adrenaline rush. But this... Being submissive...? "Your choice," he reminded her. "But I want to watch your ass move."

"I'm beginning to think that's one of your kinks."

"It wasn't. Until I saw you walk across the patio at the Den. Now all I can think of is your ass. And I'm wondering if it's red enough."

"I created a monster, Sir."

"You did, indeed. Now get up the stairs. If it's easier, I can fetch a leash."

Her wide-eyed innocent look vanished as she blinked several times in rapid succession. "I can manage on my own, Sir," she assured him, pulling away.

With athletic grace, she lowered herself to her knees.

"Wait a moment," he said. "We'll go upstairs soon."

She remained in position but looked at him with a frown.

He crossed to a kitchen drawer filled with all sorts of random items and dug through it until he found two small clips. They weren't as serviceable as proper nipple clamps, but since his toys were upstairs, these would work for now.

After testing their grip on his pinkie, he returned to her.

Her breasts hung freely, and he'd never seen anything more enticing. "Since your nipples are already sore, these will intensify the sensation." He bent to fondle her left breast, smacking it back and forth until she gasped. Then he brutally squeezed it. "I haven't even touched your nipple and already it's getting harder."

"Yes, Sir."

"Do you want me to clamp it?"

She turned her head to look at him. "Do it. Please."

"My pleasure." He twisted her nipple then released the clip onto it, not right at the edge as that would cause her too much pain, but a little farther back so that she could tolerate the tension.

He tugged on the makeshift clamp, making sure it was secure. "It should stay on," he said. "It would probably hurt if it came off accidentally." Then, just because he could, he flicked it a couple of times.

Arching her back in response, she didn't complain.

"That's a good sub." Her response sounded suspiciously like a growl. "Shall I place the other or leave you lopsided?"

"I don't suppose we could remove this one so that they'd match, Sir?"

Michael kept the smile from his face, but not his voice. "After all the trouble I've gone to?"

"Of course not. What was I thinking, Sir?"

"Hope springs eternal, doesn't it?" He moved around her, admiring her from multiple angles.

Her long blonde hair hung in wild abandon, and he was tempted to grab a fistful as he slammed into her from behind.

It took all his self-control to think only about her, about increasing the pleasure of her upcoming orgasm. He could wait. *Surely.*

He leaned down to play with her right breast, plumping it, releasing it. She moaned and moved away from him, so he toyed with the clamp he'd already placed.

"Sir!"

"Sub?"

That she didn't turn and slay him with a single glance told him she was sinking into the scene.

Michael hoped nothing else matched the high of being with him — a Dom intent on giving her a unique, all-consuming experience.

He gently swatted her right breast and teased the nipple into an erect state. She dropped her head, and he took advantage of her distraction to place the clamp.

"Oww."

"You'll be all right." He caressed her flesh. "Your swollen flesh looks hot." He captured her chin and turned her head so that he could read her expression. Her eyes were wide, and they had a glazed look to them, making the blue even more startling. "How's your pussy? Are you getting as turned on as I am?"

"I…" She licked her lower lip.

The act was a sledgehammer to his solar plexus. The things he could imagine that pink tongue doing…

"Why don't you see for yourself?" she teased in husky invitation.

"I believe I will." He needed to be careful with her — she was as clever as she was sassy. "Present your ass to me."

"Sir?"

"Lower your breasts to the floor."

"That's…"

"Not what you were expecting? Do it."

She moved slowly, as if hoping to minimize the sway of her breasts. Every motion should bring her a wave of pain. But all that would be nothing compared with the agony she'd feel when she complied with his order.

Once she was where he wanted her, he said, "Reach back and spread your buttocks."

He waited while she readjusted herself several times, obviously to find a more comfortable position. Before she was situated, he toyed with her pussy. "You're definitely wet," he told her as he slid his hand back and forth. "I'd like your permission to put a finger inside you."

"Yes." She wrapped the word in a hiss. "Yes, Sir."

He entered her slowly and maneuvered until he felt the difference in the texture of her internal flesh and touched her G-spot.

"Oh! *My God*." She bucked and forced herself back, seeking more.

He indulged her for a few seconds, placing the pad of one thumb lightly against her anal whorl and feathering the lightest of touches over her clit.

"So close," she whispered. "Please, please, please, Sir!"

"Not yet." His cock getting harder and harder, he continued his torture. She was so much more responsive than he'd imagined, and seeing proof of her arousal turned him on.

She continued her sensual, nonstop pleas.

When he was certain she couldn't take any more without orgasming, he pulled his hands away. "That's a taste of what's to come."

She whimpered, her forehead pressed to the wood, her hands still on her buttocks.

With little sympathy and a lot of triumph, he stood and moved to the sink to rinse his hands while she regained her composure.

"*Master Michael!*"

At the sound of confusion and upset in her tone, he turned off the tap and looked over at her. "Sydney?"

When she didn't respond, he devoured the distance in a few brisk strides. "I'm right here." Sitting on the floor, he gathered her into his arms. Who would have suspected that the toughness she projected was mostly a mirage? "Talk to me, Sydney," he urged softly. "Do you need me to remove the clamps?"

"No." She pushed him. "There's nothing wrong. I promise."

"Did it bother you that I left you?" He brushed hair back from her face. "Do you hurt?"

"Everything is okay." She sighed, sounding exasperated. "I think the whole orgasm denial is just driving me crazy. Everything tingles, and there's a gnawing inside me. I haven't felt this way before. Please, don't overreact. I didn't mean to alarm you."

He frowned. At best, that was a half-truth. But he suspected he'd get nothing more from her. Still, he liked having her in his arms, inhaling the citrusy scent of her shampoo and touching her bare skin.

"You worry too much, Sir. I'm okay. I always was. I promise."

He debated what to do. Part of him wanted to talk, but maybe she was right. Maybe he'd heard something in her voice that really hadn't been there.

"Can we continue, Sir?"

An urgent part of him wanted to put each of them out of their misery.

"I am so ready for an orgasm."

"Little sub, you're going to get more than one."

She shot him a sly grin. "The night is not getting any younger, Sir. And neither am I."

Her momentary weakness was gone—if it had ever really been there.

"In that case..." He loosened his grip. "When you're ready, take off your shoes, then head up the stairs."

She moved, but then winced and bit back a groan. When she tried again, her motions were much slower so as not to disturb the clamps.

Once her shoes were off, he pushed them out of the way and watched her climb up onto the first step.

The upward trek couldn't have been easy. The steps had no carpet, and since the house was old, the pitch was steep. The view of her ass, though, gratified him. If he had his way, he'd keep her here, like this, naked and needy. "Second door on the left."

When they reached his room, he instructed, "Kneel up." He assumed she'd been around the lifestyle long enough to know what he meant, and clearly she did, kneeling with her legs slightly parted and her hands on her thighs.

He removed all the pillows from the top of the bed and piled them beneath a window. He left the blinds open, and a smattering of stars were visible against the inky sky.

After turning down the comforter, he said, "Please get on the bed and lie on your back." As she climbed onto the massive four-poster that his father had constructed from local trees, their gazes met.

Michael wasn't a mind reader, but he was convinced he saw trust in the way her eyes were open so wide. If there was anything headier, he had no idea what it was. "I'm going to remove these clamps."

"They're fine, Sir."

"I should have said *replace them.* I want clovers that will stay on, even if I pull on them."

"Ah... I've grown quite fond of these, Sir."

"As I've mentioned, that's not a decision you get to make." He sat next to her and gently plumped her right breast. "This may hurt, but I'll try to mitigate it."

"I'm ready. Maybe..."

He continued to hold the flesh as he released the clamp. With a moan of pain, she gasped. Immediately he replaced the plastic with his mouth, laving her mistreated flesh with his tongue, helping to stimulate her as the blood flow resumed.

"That wasn't as bad as I expected, Sir," she said. "Thank you."

He slowly released his hold. "I do like it when you're respectful."

The mouthy little brat stuck out her tongue then offered a quick explanation, "Sorry, Sir. My lips are dry. Must be the altitude."

"On second thought, perhaps I'll be focused on my own pleasure. I'll let you stroke me off, and I'll ejaculate all over your breasts, then I'll feed you my cum. Then I'll fall asleep."

"You really do have a sadistic streak, Sir."

"Little sub, you haven't even begun to suspect the depths of my desire to torment you."

She shuddered.

"Keep it up and you'll find out." He captured her right hand and moved it to the apex of her thighs. Without warning, he removed the second clamp. Once more, he used his mouth to soothe her ache.

"If that's the treatment I get after you clamp me, feel free to do it anytime."

"My pleasure." And it was. He loved the feminine taste of her and the way her nipple lengthened as he sucked. He used his tongue to press the elongated tip against the roof of his mouth, then gently bit her as he released it.

"Wow, Sir."

He stood and crossed to the leather-covered storage bench at the foot of the bed. He removed a wooden box that had been buried under a comforter. Careful to stay in her sight, he placed the box on a nightstand, then he pulled out several pairs of clamps, some scarves, a small bottle of lube, and a couple lengths of sturdy rope.

"Do you have condoms there?" she asked. "Otherwise, my purse is downstairs."

He looked at her. With her eyes wide, mouth softly parted, naked body, and reddened breasts, she was beautiful. "So you want to fuck?" he asked, his chest constricting. There was nothing he wanted more.

"I want you in me, Sir. Yes."

Suddenly he had difficulty remembering what he was doing. The idea of burying himself balls-deep in her pussy scrambled his brains.

He forced himself to think about her. His needs could and would wait. He'd promised her several orgasms, and that was his priority.

She kept her gaze fixed on him as he selected a pair of Japanese clover clamps. For a moment, he allowed the chain to dangle from his index finger.

"I'm willing to try. *For you.*"

His cock grew much harder.

He returned to her and sucked on each of her nipples before attaching the rubber-tipped metal clamps.

She lifted her butt off the bed. "It burns, Sir."

"Use your safe word, or slow word, or settle down." He stroked between her legs, making her wet again. Within moments, she responded to his touch.

"Ah…"

After capturing the chain in one hand, he gave a gentle tug.

"*Damn!*"

Gently, he slid a finger inside of her. "Your mouth protests, but your body sings a different story." He released the chain before sliding back out. "Turn over and put your forehead on the mattress. Extend your hands so they reach the headboard."

Although she moved slowly and with a ferocious frown, he didn't hurry her.

To protect her skin, he wrapped scarves around her wrists before tying them together. Keeping a careful eye on her, he listened intently to the sound of her breathing. Her muscles were relaxed, and she inhaled softly.

After securing the length of sturdy rope to the lowest beam of the headboard, he stepped back to survey his handiwork. "Fabulous." What could be more perfect than a beautiful woman tied in place for him?

She tugged on the bonds, as if testing them. As he'd suspected, they held her in place.

Michael tugged his shirt from his waistband and began to unfasten the buttons, from the bottom up, and she turned her head to the side to watch.

After shrugging out of the material, he tossed it in the direction of the closet.

"Sexy, if you don't mind me saying so, Sir. And nice tattoo."

"Thank you." It was a good thing the artist had had talent. The night his father had passed, Michael had consumed too much, and in honor of the man's memory — and his own commitment to the land — he'd had an eagle tattooed on his right biceps. "Now to see to you, Sydney."

He stroked her ass. "You're not even a bit pink from your earlier spanking."

She wiggled her hips as if in invitation.

He rubbed her, gradually increasing the friction. Then he smacked her, hard.

"Mmm." The word was all but a sigh.

He spanked the other buttock as well. As she relaxed, her spine became supple, and she pressed her cheek onto the mattress.

As he continued, he used his right hand to unbuckle his belt while he stroked her with the other.

Wordlessly turning herself over to him, she moved back and forth.

"Are you ready to come already?"

"Yes. Yes, Sir, I am. *Please*."

Her plea was almost his undoing. But since he wanted her to wait a little longer, he stopped touching her and finished removing his belt.

Doubling it over, he asked, "How about a taste of leather?"

"More than a taste would be nice."

He gave her a few gentle slaps, searching for a rhythm they'd both enjoy. At the Den, he'd learned a bit about her.

She could tolerate hard hits—in fact, she seemed to enjoy them the most. It would take a minute to get her there, though, and he forced himself to be patient. While he wanted her red and sore, he also wanted her to recover quickly. He had other plans for her.

With every third hit, he applied a little more wrist. And he rained the leather kisses over her buttocks and the backs of her thighs. Her tiny whimpers drove him on.

"God, Sir!"

That she became so aroused by an erotic belting appealed to him. He couldn't wait to use a flogger and a paddle on her.

For a moment, he paused to tease her pussy.

"Now, now, now," she chanted.

"Almost." He stepped back and resumed the spanking until her ass was red.

"I'm going to come without you touching me." Her fingers were interlaced, and she strained against the rope binding.

Where she'd been soft, she was now tense. He'd never kept a woman waiting for so long, and never had a sub been more deserving.

Michael threw aside the belt and slid three fingers inside her then back out.

"Sir!"

He didn't respond. Instead, he relentlessly finger-fucked her.

Screaming, she rode his hand, and he kept at it, driving her orgasm, not ceasing until she was twitching wildly and sobbing into the sheets.

When she went limp, he stroked her spine with his fingertips. "Now, little sub, I'm going to fuck you thoroughly."

Chapter Four

Shattered.

Sydney was completely and utterly shattered.

She collapsed into the mattress and dragged in several breaths. Even though she'd played with a number of Doms and had had a serious D/s relationship, she'd never experienced anything like this.

"Are you all right?"

"Fine," she mumbled, wrinkling her nose as she struggled to regain her bearings, aware of him moving around the room.

Master Michael had kept her on the edge for at least an hour, and before he'd allowed her a release, he had demanded that she give everything she'd had to offer. The man wasn't satisfied with her surrendering her body. He insisted she expose her innermost secrets as well.

When he'd left her alone for a short period, he'd uncovered a fear she hadn't known she had.

Until tonight, she hadn't been this vulnerable. She'd always been in control of scenes — setting the ground rules.

But Master Michael, with his gentle yet devious ways, went beyond simple whip-wielding. He'd succeeded in pushing her into a submissive mindset, something she'd always resisted.

After unfastening her, he rubbed circulation back into her wrists and shoulders.

"Stay as you are. I'll be right with you," he said, his voice rich and husky. "Not more than thirty seconds, I promise."

Only after she nodded did he walk away.

She squeezed her eyes shut and focused on the splash of running water hitting porcelain. Then there was silence.

Breathing deep, she attempted to compose herself before dealing with him again.

Most times, after being satisfied, she'd thanked the Top, then headed home and back to her life. But tonight, with Master Michael, she was content to stay, at least for the immediate future.

And honestly, now that she'd seen Master Michael's bare chest and the tattoo that matched the brand she'd seen on the sign above the ranch's entrance, she wanted him naked and inside her.

His restraint amazed her. Though he'd had an erection for hours, he'd focused his attention solely on her. No doubt he had mad bedroom skills.

More than that, though, he'd backed up his arrogant statements. The orgasm *had* been worth waiting for. It had curled inside, an incessant demand that his strokes and ministrations fed, and when he had shoved her over the edge, the physical sensation had ripped its way out.

She wasn't sure how much time had passed when she felt him sit on the mattress behind her. He was a big man, and the mattress was forced to yield to him, just as she had been.

"You'll feel a little dampness," he said.

He ran a cool washcloth over her back, across her shoulders. He lifted her hair to wipe her nape. Next, he lightly daubed her heated butt cheeks. She'd never been much for aftercare, preferring her own company and a shower, but this was luxurious.

"Shouldn't have any marks tomorrow from my belt."

"Then maybe you should have used it a little harder." She turned her head to look at him. His eyes were narrowed, and she wondered for a second if she'd gone too far.

"You do like to wander into dangerous territory."

"You knew that from the beginning, Sir."

"Yeah. I did."

After he helped her to turn over, he bathed her front, even beneath her breasts, though he didn't remove the clamps. "So are you going to fuck me? Or is this good night?" she asked, repeating his earlier question.

He wadded the washcloth, then tossed it in the direction of his discarded shirt. He'd already removed his belt, and now she watched, transfixed, as he removed his boots and socks, then unfastened the metal button at his waist before lowering the zipper on his jeans.

He was already fully erect, and she arched her eyebrows when she realized he wasn't wearing underwear. "Commando, Sir?" He didn't seem the type. She'd expected tighty-whities or, at the least, boxers. Perhaps unfairly, but she'd judged him to be a bit staid, too polite.

She had another surprise when he was naked.

His balls were shaved, and he only had a small patch of closely trimmed pubic hair. "You, Sir, are totally hot." Her rear and the backs of her thighs still felt seared.

She was beginning to notice the ache in her nipples again. The clamps hadn't bothered her while he was playing with her, but now she was beginning to experience real discomfort. If he didn't give her some attention soon, she'd crawl out of her skin.

He stroked his dick a couple of times.

"You were serious that you want to torment me."

"Both of us," he said.

He opened a drawer and removed a condom. He ripped it open and placed it on his cockhead. "Your turn," he said.

"Sir?"

"Roll it down me."

"Are you serious, Sir?"

"Use your mouth."

"I've never done that before."

"Happy to be your first."

No doubt she'd underestimated him.

He knelt on the bed and cradled her cheeks between his strong palms, offering support, but also giving her no chance to pull away.

She opened her mouth and tentatively closed it around him. Since she was somewhat perplexed about how to actually accomplish his task, her motions were awkward. Still, this was enticingly erotic, and the idea of pleasing him made her giddy. He massaged her scalp as she worked, and he offered no criticism.

"You're doing well," he said, as she used her tongue to work the latex past his cockhead.

For a moment, she pressed the tip of her tongue against the spot under his shaft where she knew he would be the most sensitive.

He tightened his grip on her head. Encouraged, she drew her mouth up a bit then went down again, unrolling the condom a little farther.

"Maybe this wasn't such a good idea," he said around a gasp.

Gamely, she continued to try to figure it out, using only her lips as she worked the latex into place. Knowing it was driving him mad helped her enjoy it more, and she took extra time on the areas where he involuntarily jerked.

As he thickened, she increased her tempo.

"Enough," he finally said, the word nearly a growl as he pulled away from her.

She looked up at him.

Her in-control, take-charge Dom had his jaw clenched. His rich green eyes were narrowed, and perspiration dotted his brow.

She smiled. It hadn't taken her long to bring him to the brink. "I was just getting the hang of it, Sir."

"Oh, I want a blow job from you, and no doubt it will be world-class, but now is not the time." With a wicked grin, he tugged on her chain.

She jerked at the sudden burn. "Sir!" It had taken only seconds for him to regain control.

"I want you on all fours."

At least in this position, her breasts weren't pressed against the bed, and she was grateful for that small mercy.

"I've been fantasizing all night about having my hand in your hair as I fuck you from behind."

The image filled her mind, obliterating all thoughts.

"And I'm going to put a finger up your ass."

He hadn't phrased it as a request. She knew she could refuse, but the idea had a wicked appeal to her.

He grabbed lube from the nightstand drawer, then placed the bottle on the sheet before positioning himself behind her.

Simultaneously, he slapped both of her ass cheeks.

The unexpected action shocked her. She might have toppled over, but he was there, his hands on her hipbones, steadying her. "Damn, Sir." The momentary explosion of pain receded, lancing her with arousal.

Because he'd spanked her earlier, the sensation seemed magnified.

"Are you getting ready for me, Sydney?"

"More," she said.

"More of what?"

She thrust her hips back toward him in silent plea.

Thankfully he didn't make her beg. "That's a good little subbie," he said.

He tapped each cheek then spanked her harder and harder still, tanning her hide the way she'd craved, needed.

On and on, he went, until her thoughts swam. Her breaths were no longer shallow. Instead, they were long and further apart as she surrendered to pleasure.

Nothing existed but the sensual connection of skin on skin.

Before she was ready, he was rubbing her scorched rear.

"Are you with me, Sydney?"

His gruff voice came from a great distance, then he placed both his hands on her back, grounding her. "Yes, Sir," she whispered obediently.

"Your responses are perfect."

"No, Sir. It's you." She meant his treatment of her was the perfect thing, and she hoped he understood that because her tongue suddenly felt too big for her mouth.

Without responding, he parted her butt cheeks.

"Lift your rear higher for me."

She maneuvered, but the position forced her breasts down. His ass-warming had distracted her, but now she was hyperaware of the clamps again. After tonight, she might opt out of having her nipples tormented.

Momentarily, he played with her pussy, making her slicker. His delicious spanking had already prepared her for him.

Master Michael placed the tip of his cock against her and began to ease his way inside, making her suck in a breath. He pulled back after the first couple of shallow strokes, driving her mad. "Sir!"

"So wet," he said. "Patience."

He might as well have asked the earth to stop spinning. She arched her back, trying to encourage him along, but this annoying man moved at his own — glacial — pace. She told herself not to be frustrated — after all, he'd made sure their time together was memorable — but damn, she was ready to have his entire cock in her.

"Give up the struggle."

Since he offered no other choice, she attempted to school her mind.

He rocked his pelvis, going deeper with each thrust.

Sydney forced her fingers apart. And when she took his advice, the slow fuck became more enjoyable.

"That's it," he said.

She became aware of all the sensations, the way his length filled her and the way his girth stretched her.

Once more, his work-hewn hands were on her buttocks, parting the globes. His thrusts slid her breasts back and forth on the mattress, and the resulting pain shot straight to her pussy. On its journey it seemed to transform into pleasure, and an orgasm began to unfurl. "Sir, that's… I'm struggling for control."

"Take your climax," he told her, his voice enveloping her. "From here on, you don't need permission."

His earlier denial made his change of heart more empowering, and his words unleashed her.

He continued his unhurried pace.

It was enough.

She arched her back more, flattening her breasts, and offering herself to him. He sank in deep, and he moved his grip to her hip bones, holding her in place.

"Come," he whispered. He pulled back then surged forward.

She cried out as the orgasm pulsed through her.

"Ride it," he instructed.

She shuddered against him, prolonging the thrill.

"That's it," he whispered. "That's it…"

Once the shocks had subsided, the sound of something wet reached her, and she suspected he'd squirted out a dollop of lube. Reflexively she squeezed her lower body. Then he pressed something cold against her anus.

"Open your ass for me."

Helplessly, she drummed her fingers on the bed.

"I mean it."

He reached beneath her to pinch the side of her breast, then the bastard took advantage of her shift to insert the tip of his finger into her rectum. "It will be better than you're expecting," he promised.

She had her doubts.

Master Michael was focused on the pursuit of what he wanted. He moved his left arm beneath her hip bones to support her weight as he eased his cock into her pussy and slid a finger in and out of her rear.

"Imagine what it will be like when you have a fat plug there."

Frantically, she shook her head. "No way, Sir."

"I love it when you tell me no, little sub." He laughed. "Makes your inevitable yes all the sweeter."

Her temporary Dom put a finger all the way up her, seating it to the knuckle. Then, as she gasped, he fucked her with it, twisting his finger as he pushed in. He stuffed her, leaving her feeling overly full.

Still, the sensation wasn't nearly as bad as she'd feared, and within less than a minute, her normal thirst to experience something new reasserted itself.

"What do you think, Sydney?" Instead of waiting for a response, he did her, hard.

Pain from the clamps, combined with the exhilarating thrill of the anal penetration and the pounding from his thick dick, created a dizzying rush of excitement that she'd never experienced before.

He left her breathless.

She cried out an orgasm, but he kept going, never acknowledging or slowing down. As a Dom, he overwhelmed her. She was grateful for his arm beneath her, supporting her, since she wasn't sure she could have held herself up.

She'd thought the orgasms up until now had been exquisite, but this was beyond anything she'd hoped for.

"Damn," he muttered. "Your pussy is tight on me. So, so good."

Then he was at her rear again, forcing her sphincter wider as he added a second finger. "I can't take that much," she protested.

"You can. You will."

She did, and she was grateful for it. Going beyond her self-imposed limits was more incredible than she'd thought possible.

He continued his relentless onslaught, and she came again and again until it became like an out of body experience.

It seemed an incredible amount of time later when she felt a change in his rhythm. A sense of feminine power crept over her when he gave a guttural moan. "Come, Sir," she said. "Deep in me. Give it to me."

With the arm he had beneath her, he powerfully lifted her lower body off the mattress, owning her as he gave a final few jerky motions before pulsing inside her.

"So hot, Sir."

"*Fuck.*"

As he convulsed in her, she smiled. *Who is dominating whom?*

He held her for several moments before slowly withdrawing his fingers and cock from her. Her heartbeat started to return to normal.

Eventually she exhaled a shaky breath. "Well, Sir…" She left the sentence unfinished as she had no words.

"Stay as you are," he said. "Just a few seconds."

Before she had fully realized that he was gone, she heard water running in the en suite. He was back right away with a washcloth to cleanse her. Then he pressed the warm towel against her rear, soothing the ache there.

"Your ass is presented so prettily. Maybe I'll keep you in this position for a while longer."

"That's a horrid suggestion."

"Excuse me?"

"Horrid, *Sir.*"

He chuckled, proving he'd taken no offense.

Then he helped her onto her back. "Now for the clamps."

Michael Dayton was sinfully handsome. His face was all hard angles, and his bright green eyes missed nothing.

Once more, very deliberately, he took hold of the chain and yanked.

The pain paralyzing her, she whimpered. He placed a hand on her mound, slapped her hard, then masturbated her to another completion. "*God!*"

"Turns out I like the unexpected as much as you do," he explained with a wolfish grin.

She narrowed her eyes at him.

"You may thank me at any time."

Her manners had been remiss. "Thank you, Sir." How much she meant the words surprised her. She had figured his climax had signaled the end of their encounter, so the additional orgasm left her dazed.

Only then did he sit next to her to remove the clamps.

She appreciated the paradox of him. Big and strong, but gentle and caring.

Like he had earlier, he alleviated the anguish of the blood rushing back in by immediately putting his mouth on her flesh and gently sucking. "Thank you for your consideration, Sir."

"I'll always take care of you, Sydney." He dropped the clamps on the nightstand. "Would you like a shower?"

She hesitated. This was the moment she'd dreaded. They both knew he wasn't just asking if she wanted a shower. He was inviting her to stay. She wasn't big on the morning after. Yet she was reluctant to leave him.

Patiently he waited, never pushing her.

Rationalizing that she'd be fresher tomorrow for the drive back, she replied, "Yes. I think I would. Thank you, Sir."

"I was hoping you'd say that."

Before she could respond, he scooped her from the bed.

"I can walk," she protested, but the words sounded weak, even to her.

"No doubt."

Other than that, he didn't acknowledge that she'd spoken. He carried her into his bathroom.

"Good grief," she exclaimed when he placed her feet on the tiled floor. "This isn't what I expected."

"I took out a bedroom so I could have a little space."

"A *little* space?" she repeated, looking around. "I've stayed in hotel rooms smaller than this. Recently, even." Though his en suite was huge, it was still in keeping with the rest of the house. Thin planks of aspen or pine—she wasn't sure which—angled across the walls. A sandstone vanity had dual sinks with wall-mounted faucets. The room had several mirrors, one full-length. And oval-shaped princess-looking mirrors above the sinks actually tilted.

Wooden shelves held thick towels and even a few candles.

His large shower was tiled in glass. But the focal point of the room was a picture window that occupied the space above a soaker tub. "Do you bring a lot of women here?" she asked. It bothered her how much his answer suddenly mattered.

"The tub is for me. Nothing better for sore muscles."

"You didn't answer my question."

He folded his arms across his chest. "Does it matter?"

It shouldn't.

After all, she wasn't looking for anything other than a thrilling ride, and he was a Dom — a damn good one. No doubt subs lined up for his attentions.

"No woman, except my sister, has been in this house since my ex walked out." He brushed his thumb pad across her lips. "Would you like me to run you a bath or start the shower?"

She frowned at him. "Doms aren't supposed to do that kind of thing."

"Being a Dominant doesn't mean you're an asshole."

In her experience, it sure as hell had.

"Every person in a D/s dynamic gets to define their own relationship. I don't anticipate you'd ever stop being who you are. Nor would I want you to. Similarly, I demand respect, courtesy, and communication. And I'll give you all of that in return."

When she'd hooked up with Lewis, she'd been young and naive. In the beginning, she'd thought the lifestyle was about play parties, being tied up, getting her kink on.

But once his collar had been locked around her neck, everything had gone horribly wrong.

Master Michael was a rugged individual with his own ideas, something she might have once been interested in, but that now terrified her.

She'd never be a twenty-four seven sub again.

"Bath? Shower? Or I can use the back scrubber as a paddle."

The long piece of wood hung from a peg in the wall. The implement looked like an oversize hairbrush, and it had definite potential for a harsh spanking.

Still, she didn't move.

"Right, then," he said.

Her mouth fell open as he grabbed the scrubber.

"Bend over the bathtub."

"Are you serious?"

He smacked the back end of it against his left palm, making her jump.

"Bend over the bathtub."

"My butt is already sore, Sir."

"You will regret making me repeat myself."

She debated using a safe word, but she wanted the experience. There was no doubt he'd seen that in her eyes.

Assailed by nerves, she slowly moved into place, her fingers forming a death grip on the tub's edge.

"Wait."

"Sir?" She pushed herself upright and turned to face him.

His eyes had a gleam she didn't recognize. A part of her was frightened. A bigger part of her made her stand her ground.

"Stand up straight and spread your legs." He moved his hand much lower on the handle and turned over the scrubber so the bristles pointed up.

"Oh, no. No way." She shook her head. "Absolutely not, Sir."

"*Tur-tle*?" He broke the word into two syllables — on purpose, she was sure, returning her earlier goading. "Say it."

"No."

"Then safe word or spread your legs and put your hands behind your neck."

She looked at the pokey points, then at his face.

His eyes held a devilish, but not malicious, gleam.

Reassured, she did as he demanded.

"Don't hump it like a naughty little subbie."

"As if, Sir." She kept her head tipped back so she could look at him.

He dropped his gaze to her crotch.

She gulped as he touched the bristles to her tender pussy. For the first time, she wasn't sure she could follow his command.

In an achingly gentle motion, he moved back and forth.

"*Oh!*" Despite her trepidation, she liked this. She rose up, giving him greater access.

"I hope you learn to trust me," he said, his mouth near her ear.

He exerted a small amount of pressure but continued to stroke her with exquisite slowness.

An orgasm teased her, remaining just out of reach. "I'm shocked, but I might be able to come."

"What do you need for that to happen?"

"Maybe a little more stimulation."

"Before or after the paddling on your ass?"

"Sir! This isn't instead of a spanking?"

"No," he said. He reached his free hand between her legs and spread her labia. "This is in addition to the spanking. Like whipped cream with an Irish coffee."

At his increased pressure, she slammed her heels onto the floor. "Yow, Sir!"

"Come any time."

She leaned forward into him, and he adjusted his stance to support her. Lost, she closed her eyes. Everything tingled.

Bending her knees, she rocked back and forth.

"You're humping it, you naughty girl."

She was gone. Trembling, she climaxed.

He moved without her realizing it, wrapping an arm around her waist. "You're an insatiable wench."

"You bring it out in me."

He pulled the implement away, leaving her aflame in the most fabulous way.

Before she was thinking straight, he turned her back around and bent her over the tub once more.

"Hold on tight. You'll need to." His tone held a diabolical note. "Keep your legs together. I'm going to start just above your knees and work my way up. If you need to flex, do so, but as soon as you can compose yourself, resume the position I specified."

Fighting the delirium caused by his words, she braced herself.

"Repeat what I said."

She looked over her shoulder.

Gently, he tucked strands of her hair behind her ears. "You said, Sir, that I should keep my legs together." How could he be so perfect? There was a tenderness in his tone that was at odds with his stance and the fact that he held the punishing wooden brush.

"You'll start at the bottom and work your way up. If I get out of position, I should get back in as soon as I can."

"Close enough." He lowered his hand.

The first spank seared. The second was a lot more powerful. The third, on a fleshier part of her leg, was higher and harder.

He knew how to give her what she wanted. How to inflict pain with deliberate intensity. How to keep her guessing.

The one under her buttocks forced her to lift up. She closed her eyes, waited for the pain to settle then re-gripped the tub. While he wasn't letting her be in charge, he allowed her to set the pace.

"Last one."

She tightened her cheeks, expecting it to blaze. She waited and waited. But it didn't come. Finally, it dawned on her. He was being patient while she did as he instructed.

With great determination, she loosened her muscles. Only then did he lay the brush to her.

She sucked a breath through her teeth.

"*Now* your ass is a pretty shade of pink."

"It matches my pussy then, Sir."

"So it does." He helped her stand and turn around. "Cool shower or a warm one?"

"One without bristles," she said, dubiously eyeing the brush.

"Perhaps you shouldn't have let me know how much you dislike it. I may keep one in every room."

She considered a snappy comeback then thought better of it. Her rear burned. She wasn't sure her skin would survive anything more. "A warm one, Sir."

He moved across the bathroom to turn on the shower. After checking the temperature twice, he looked at her calculatingly before lowering the adjustable showerhead. "Your shower, ma'am. Feel free to use anything in there."

"This is luxurious," she said, stepping into the oversize glass enclosure.

At her condo, the showerhead was small and attached to the wall above the tile. She spent most of her time moving around beneath the pelting water, trying to rinse off soap or shampoo, and catching a chill wherever the uneven spray wasn't hitting.

"Can I scrub your back?" he offered.

"Hell, no," she muttered.

"I didn't quite hear you."

That had been her intention. "I said this is perfect as it is, Sir."

"That's what I thought."

Steam billowed in the stall. She watched him move around the bathroom, clearly comfortable with his nakedness.

"Washcloth?"

"Yes, please."

He handed one in, along with a fresh bar of soap.

"I figured you'd want something unscented."

"Thanks." She wasn't sure she'd ever been in the same bathroom with a man before. When she and Lewis had cohabitated, she'd taken over the guest bathroom. But this man, apparently, didn't believe in giving or expecting privacy. The thought unnerved her.

He draped a great big towel over the top of the glass door. Did he think of everything?

When he left the bathroom, she sighed and hurriedly washed herself. She was grateful he'd given her this bar. It was bad enough that she'd be sleeping next to him, inhaling his masculine scent. If she used his soap, at least a hint would remain on her skin even after they parted. And the last thing she needed was to be going out of her mind with reminders of him.

She used his shampoo and wished he had conditioner. The outdoor spanking followed by him wrapping his hand in her hair had made a mess of her locks. It would take forever to detangle it all.

After reluctantly turning off the shower, she wrapped herself in the towel. He'd left an unopened toothbrush on the counter. It was scary what an exceptional host he was.

In the bedroom, he'd put away the toy box, arranged the pillows, and turned back the blankets. And he was still distractingly naked. As he drew the blinds he told her, "I'm going to take a quick shower."

"Do you have a T-shirt I can borrow, Sir?" Anything of his would swallow her, and she liked that idea.

"You won't need one. I'll keep you warm."

"I don't like to sleep nude."

"Because?"

"I was in a hotel in Belize that was evacuated in the middle of the night, so I've learned to wear something to bed."

"Sounds reasonable."

"So, can I borrow a T-shirt?"

"No. But I'm willing to compromise. I'll get you a T-shirt, and you can hang it on the bedpost. If you wake up cold or if we have a fire, it will be right there."

She sighed. "There's no dissuading you when you've made a decision, is there?"

"If you wanted to be with a man you could push around, you wouldn't have come home with me."

"That's a warped kind of logic, Sir."

"Regardless, I'm right." Without another word, he headed into the bathroom.

She watched him go. She couldn't remember having been around a man so annoying...and damn it, intriguing.

He left the door open, and the distant rush of water filled her senses. *No.* He definitely didn't believe in privacy. But after all they'd already shared, what was left?

She used the end of her towel to squeeze excess water from her hair, then finger-combed the strands the best she could. There was a brush in the console of her car, along with a bag filled with extra clothes, a pair of hiking boots, and some toiletries.

Occasionally, she took impromptu trips, and once, while she'd been walking across a river in Wyoming, she'd slipped off a rock and fallen in the icy water. Having extra clothes and shoes had been a lifesaver.

Sudden silence filled the house, meaning he'd turned off the shower.

Less than thirty seconds later, he entered the bedroom with a towel wrapped around his waist. His hair was damp, making it look darker, and a few drops of water clung to his chest.

How was it possible that he'd satisfied her so completely, and she was ravenous again?

"Drop it." He nodded toward her towel. "*Please.*"

Damn you. His politeness disarmed her, and his quick smile was irresistible.

Obediently, she released the fluffy material.

As he snatched it up, he gave a possessive growl. "Goddamn, Sydney. You'll be lucky if I ever let you wear clothes again."

He stalked to the closet, returning with a plain black T-shirt, which he hung on the bedpost. "Which side do you want?"

"The one closest to the door."

"Easier to escape?"

Letting the silence speak for itself, she pressed her lips together.

Her sexy Dom climbed into bed and said, "Come here."

She hadn't spent the night with anyone since Lewis, and this was suddenly, overwhelmingly too much.

"I bite," he promised.

Master Michael understood her, clearly. If he could make her smile, he would win.

Moving slow, conscious of their nudity, she climbed into bed next to him. "I don't snuggle," she warned him, hugging the edge of the mattress.

"*Didn't*," he corrected, dragging her back against him and holding her tight. "You didn't snuggle. Now you do."

He was hard and unyielding, complex, and faultlessly transparent. He'd seemed willing to negotiate and soothe her if it made sense, but if he believed she was being unreasonable, he'd state his case and wait for her capitulation.

In his arms, she felt safe and protected. That thought made her stiffen her body. She had been on her own since she was young, and she didn't need to lean on anyone.

"Stop your struggle, little sub."

He moved so that he could position his semi-erect cock between her buttocks. His thighs were against the backs of her legs, and he held her tight.

It had been a hell of a night.

A coyote howled in the distance.

No way would she feel at ease tonight, and she'd be lucky to get any sleep.

But, shocking her, the next thing she knew, the watery light of predawn was filtering through the slats in the window blinds.

She hated to admit that Master Micheal been right — he had kept her warm all night. Needing a few minutes to herself to sort through her turbulent emotions, she eased herself away from him.

"Sydney," he mumbled. "Stay."

"I'm not leaving," she promised with a whisper. Unable to help herself, she turned and eased a curled lock of dark hair back from his forehead.

He appeared so different in the daylight, and in sleep.

His brow was relaxed, as were the hardened planes and chiseled angles of his face. His skin was golden from time outside beneath the Colorado sun, but right now the tiny lines grooved next to his eyes were less pronounced.

In his relaxation, his lips were slightly parted, and a jolt went through her when she remembered what he'd done to her with his beautiful mouth.

That thought was quickly followed by the realization that he'd exerted a dominant power over her that no one else ever had.

Restlessness churning, she climbed from the bed and reached for the T-shirt hanging from the bedpost. Then she noticed his discarded long-sleeved shirt on the floor near the closet. Giving in to temptation, she padded across the room to pick that up instead.

Near the doorway, she paused, glancing back at him. She thought he might have one eye open slightly, then decided that wasn't the case.

So as not to disturb him, she tiptoed down the stairs.

Sydney exercised every day, yet her muscles ached. He'd kept her in unfamiliar positions for a very long time. Not regretting a single moment, she smiled.

In the mirror of the powder room, she noticed a few stripes on the backs of her thighs, and she traced one with her fingertip. Last night, he'd given her exactly what she'd asked for.

Generally, the morning after sceneing, she didn't spend time thinking about the previous evening. After all, it was rarely worth the effort.

But with him...

Her pulse thundered.

Every moment was special.

In search of coffee, she wandered to the kitchen and found a pound of ground beans.

As the brewer slowly dripped into the pot, she wished he had a single-serve unit like she did.

Since she lacked the patience to watch it splat, she rooted through the cabinets until she found a mug she could carry outside. Then, tired of waiting, she pulled out the carafe and filled her cup.

A single sip of the dark brew told her why it was usually served mixed with half a cup of steamed milk.

Desperate to make the beverage taste better, she walked to the fridge. Though he had a half-gallon bottle of unopened milk, there wasn't a single container of anything with hazelnut or vanilla like she preferred.

Wrinkling her nose, she pried the lid off the glass bottle and almost swooned at the sight of the pure cream on the top. For a moment—well, less than a moment—she debated saving the treasure for him.

But then she greedily poured it into her cup. She hadn't seen something like that since she'd been overseas as a child. Ranch living clearly had some advantages.

Fortified with a more palatable brew, she slipped into the sandals she'd discarded last night, then headed out the back door.

The morning sunlight blazed down, unobstructed by a single cloud.

She saw the land in a way she'd missed last night. Off to the left were several buildings. One looked like a barn, but others she didn't recognize. A corral was in the distance, though she didn't see any horses.

In front of her, a vista swept out to distant mountain peaks, some over twelve thousand feet tall, a few soaring higher than thirteen thousand feet.

She called the picturesque town of Evergreen home and had seen a lot of the planet, but this sight took her breath away as nothing else had. The adventurer in her wanted to explore. A walk would definitely be good for her unsettled mind.

Enjoying the peace and solitude, she made her way down the path and wondered how she hadn't twisted an ankle last night. Without Master Michael's assistance, she would never have made it.

She opened the gate and delicately picked her way through the dirt and gravel to her car. After taking a sip of the coffee that was much sweeter because of the addition of stolen cream, she placed her cup on the roof then opened the back door and reached inside for her duffel bag.

The moment she curled her hand around the strap, she was shoved from behind and went sprawling across the back seat. Yelping, she pushed herself backward and turned, ready to fight, either Master Michael or someone else. He'd mentioned having ranch hands, hadn't he?

Her heart thundered.

No one was there.

Then she heard a pitiful bleat.

She looked down to see the smallest goat imaginable. It looked like a baby. A kid, or whatever young goats were called. Then she recalled Master Michael telling her it was some sort of miniature.

Collapsing against the side of the vehicle, trying to steady her racing heart, she looked around, embarrassed, hoping no one had witnessed her attempt at self-defense against a tiny creature.

The thing cocked its head to the side and bleated again.

"Nice goat," she said, moving away from the car, crisis over.

It moved in again.

"Uh…"

It butted her hand then looked up at her with wide, unblinking eyes.

Good God. A tiny terrorist was imprisoning her.

She didn't know much — strike that, she knew *nothing* — about four-footed animals. Since it wouldn't have fit her parents' lifestyle, she'd never been allowed to have pets, not even a goldfish.

When she attempted to take a step, the creature surged forward again. "Back off, you little menace."

It did, but only long enough to ram her again.

At a loss, she reached out and touched its head.

Chewie — if she remembered the name correctly — bleated once more, but this time at a higher pitch.

Looking around, hoping for someone to rescue her, she scratched behind its ear.

The goat turned its head, giving her better access. Then it made a ridiculous noise, like a laugh. *Who knew it could do that?*

"Aren't you supposed to be in a pen or something, rather than wandering around?" The miniature animal shoved its head at her again, evidently because she'd stopped petting it. *Could things be any more bizarre?*

Still a little intimidated, she maneuvered until she could climb back into the vehicle. The tiny little thing tried to follow her.

With one foot, she attempted to keep it out.

But her sandal came loose, and the thief absconded with it. "Damn it! Bring that back!"

He — or she — dropped it. Then it laughed, picked up her shoe, and high-tailed it out of there. "Get back here, Chewie!"

She exhaled in exasperation when the petty criminal picked up steam.

Ranching, cream or no cream in her coffee, wasn't for her.

Hurriedly, she grabbed a pair of lightweight hiking pants from her bag, worked her way into them then pulled on some socks and boots.

After tossing the remaining shoe forlornly in the bag, she went after the midget. The thing was nowhere to be found. "Damn it."

Trying to pretend the footwear hadn't cost a week's wages, she set out at a brisk pace toward the river.

The walk helped burn off the frustration. Some of her friends used yoga or breathing to calm themselves.

Physical exertion was the only thing that brought her solace. Scaling a mountain was significantly more helpful to her than a day at the spa.

The irritation returned when she remembered she'd left the coffee cup on top of the car.

Rather than going back for it, she allowed the sound of water to lure her.

As she stood at the edge, the river rushing over rocks, an eagle soared overhead, riding thermals, and soaring with hardly a flap.

The wide-open country offered peace to her soul.

Until a familiar and unwelcome bleat split the air.

The goat emerged from between two pine trees. And it didn't have her shoe. "You really *are* a pest." She sat on a large rock, and Chewie joined her. "I was enjoying this until you showed up," Sydney told her.

Innocently, it blinked.

"Fine. You can stay. But I want my shoe back."

It shook its head. Surely the timing was an odd coincidence.

She stayed where she was before finally giving in and stroking the beast's spiny back. The short fur—or was it hair?—was softer than she'd thought it would be. The black and white creature had a few small brown markings and was surprisingly adorable, despite its bad manners. "Don't get any ideas," she said. "I mean it. Stop looking at me like that."

Ears standing straight up, Chewie bumped her hand.

"You forgot this."

At the sound of Master Michael's voice, she jumped.

How had she not heard his approach? With a half smile, she looked over her shoulder to see him standing there holding two cups of coffee. "Bless you," she said.

The goat abandoned her and went straight to him. Clearly even the goat knew who the master was.

He crouched next to her and offered her the same cup she'd abandoned on top of the car. As their hands connected, she glanced away.

Once more, he wore his requisite hat and had on a long-sleeved shirt much like the one she'd donned. He'd rolled back the cuffs, leaving his forearms bare. Faded denim jeans hugged his muscular legs. Even though it was Sunday, he looked ready to work.

"I see you've met Chewie."

"And lost a favorite shoe," she said wryly.

"Expensive?"

"Yes."

He winced. "I'll replace them."

"*Very* expensive," she amended. Then unable to help herself, she laughed. "I don't wear them all that often. I have others."

"I've seen some with spikes on the heels. They were red, as I recall."

"I like red."

"They'd look good on you."

She brought her knees to her chest and wrapped her arms around them. "Maybe I will take you up on your offer of new shoes."

"A woman can never have too many pairs." Chewie wandered down to the water for a drink. "And I'll take you up on yours," he said.

Though his tone was still light, it contained a serious undercurrent. Puzzled, she took a sip of the still warm and very much welcome coffee as she considered him. "My offer, Sir?"

"The one where you get on your knees and suck my cock in apology for leaving my bed without permission."

She jerked her hand, sloshing the coffee. "Ah..."

He took the cup from her hand and placed it on the ground. "Or the one where you pull down your pants, lie across my lap, and beg me to punish you for the same reason."

Breath constricted in her chest. A serious line was drawn between his dark eyebrows. With a squeak, she managed, "Here? Now?"

The confounding Dom countered her questions with his own. "Or the one where I tie you to the fence and flog you?"

His words, his rough-hewn voice, and the lethal promise in his eyes crashed arousal through her. "Do I have to choose?" Her mouth dried. "Or can I select all of the above?"

Chapter Five

All of the above?

Fuck.

With her in his bed — all softness and vulnerability — Michael had been hard all night. Now, his erection was even more demanding. "I'm always happy to accommodate you," he replied.

Her lips parted.

Did my response catch you off guard?

With her quick smile, confident strut, and the way she held her shoulders back, even the occasional flip of her hair, she'd polished her bratty act — the one she showed most Doms — to perfection.

But Michael had glimpsed moments of uncertainty, and once, maybe a trace of fear.

He saw her as so much more than a bottom who yearned for a taste of adventure without commitment.

And the more of her secrets that he uncovered, the more he wanted to reveal.

Studying her, he asked, "Which order would you like to go in? First to last? Or last to first?"

When she didn't respond, he suggested, "We could start with the second option. Having your body pressed against my cock will save you a few seconds on the blow job."

He'd be willing to bet she had no idea how expressive her face was. When something interested her, her lips parted slightly. And that made him want her even more.

Seeing her here, now, in what he assumed was her typical attire, hiking pants and sturdy boots, with her hair ravaged from their sex the night before, wearing no makeup, and dressed in one of his shirts, she hid behind no artifice.

Earlier, when she'd touched his face in bed, he'd considered letting her know he was awake.

He was a notoriously light sleeper, aware of every noise inside and outside the house. But the opportunity to observe Sydney's unguarded moments had been irresistible, despite the hormones urging him to grab her, pin her beneath him, and slake his morning lust.

He'd heard her moving around the kitchen, then smelled the aroma of brewing coffee. He'd taken his time pulling on a pair of jeans and a T-shirt. But before he'd made it down the stairs, the snick of a door closing reached him.

When he'd noticed her leather dress remained artfully draped across the back of the barstool and her purse still sat on the counter, he'd sighed with relief. At least she hadn't left without saying goodbye.

Part of him had expected exactly that. After all, Gregorio had warned Michael about the way she discarded Doms.

Curious about what she was up to, he'd grabbed a cup of coffee.

As a testament to how much he enjoyed having her here, he'd grinned when he noticed she'd taken the cream from the top of the milk.

Barefoot, he'd wandered to the window, where he'd enjoyed watching her interact with Chewie.

He'd always figured he could learn a lot about a person based on the way they treated animals.

When she'd tentatively reached out to pet the goat behind the ears, he'd smiled. Chewie was a decent judge of character, much like some dogs Michael had owned.

Taking his time, he'd headed upstairs to finish dressing. While he'd been putting on his clothes, he'd been mentally removing hers.

Now he intended to do it in reality. "I'm going to kiss you like I fucking own you."

While he put down his coffee and stood, she remained firmly on the rock, unmoving, but not protesting.

Capturing her shoulders, he pulled her to her feet.

Then he dug a hand into her hair and captured her gaze. How easy it would be to lose himself in the blue depths of her eyes. They communicated her true emotion better than anything that came out of her mouth. If she knew what he saw, she'd be terrified.

"Sir, I'd rather we just—"

"Sydney? Use your safe word or shut the hell up." He pulled her between his legs.

Slowly, he brushed his lips across hers. "They're soft."

"I've made a choice. I'll just suck you off." She batted her eyelashes provocatively.

You want to hide from true intimacy, darlin'? He wasn't having it.

Instead, he skimmed his tongue across her upper lip. "Oh! That's…"

He drew her bottom lip between his teeth and bit down with the slightest pressure.

She tipped back her chin.

"Open your mouth to me." He tightened his grip in her hair and unfastened the top button on her shirt to reveal her creamy chest. "I mean it."

The moment she complied, he pressed his tongue to hers, and she moaned, the slight sound of her capitulation galvanizing him. He sought more, wanting her total surrender. She tasted of sweet cream, of morning, of promise.

Michael deepened the kiss, and she responded, rising onto her toes to wrap her arms around his neck, knocking off his hat in the process.

When they communicated like this, from a place of desire, she was completely honest.

Helplessly, she met each of his thrusts, and he reached inside her shirt to caress one of her breasts.

No doubt she was tender from last night, but he didn't want to make her too sore…*for now.* When he flogged her later, he wanted her to enjoy the feel of deer hide biting at her nipples.

With a moan, she curled one hand over his cock. Now he wished he'd dressed in something other than jeans. He adjusted their positions, dragging her closer.

With that, she met his intensity with a ferocity of her own. Still, he maintained control, just as he should.

In incremental measures, he ended the kiss and eased his grip. "I should have done that last night. A dozen times," he amended.

"I don't normally kiss." Her words and expression were both prim.

Along with snuggling. "You do now."

"I suppose that's true, Sir. And since your hat seems to have fallen off..." She moved to press her palms against his chest. "We should get started on my offer." Diligently, she set to work on his shirt, unfastening the buttons and pulling the hem from his waistband.

Enjoying the bold vixen, he allowed her to lead. Temporarily.

When she was done, he shucked the material from his shoulders while she fumbled with the metal button at the top of his jeans.

Then she struggled with the zipper.

"Your massive cock is making this more difficult." A scowl accompanied her protest.

"What do you suggest?"

She used both hands—one to hold the denim taut, the other to release the metal teeth. Then she pushed his jeans down, letting them fall to his ankles.

The sensation of her tongue lapping his cock was stunning.

Kneeling, she cupped his balls with one hand and stroked him with the other, methodically moving up and down his engorged shaft. Then she took him deep into her mouth until he was certain she might choke. But she didn't.

"Damn," he mumbled. Her touch was masterful. She placed a finger on his perineum and a million sensations zinged through him. He'd had blow jobs before, really good ones, but no other woman had been as dedicated to the task as she was.

She moved up to place the tip of her tongue underneath his cock. Eagerly, she continued, adding extra pressure to that sensitive spot near his anus and licking with the lightest of touches.

Constantly she changed the tempo, licking and sucking harder as she tightened her grip. Then she slid up and took his dick in her mouth again.

With tiny sighs of pleasure, she caressed, pulled, cupped. That she was into it, *into him*, drove him mad. "Sydney," he warned, on the verge.

Ignoring him, she tightened her grip, driving his orgasm.

"Darlin'…" He groaned as ejaculate pulsed from deep inside.

He expected her to pull away, letting him spill on the ground or her chest, but she didn't.

Instead, she drew up, holding on to the tip of his cock as she swallowed every single drop.

He cupped the sides of her face, and she flicked her gaze upward. He wasn't sure how it was possible, but it appeared she was smiling while she still had him in her mouth.

Finally, she let go, then licked the last drop from his slit.

"Now I don't have to worry about your hard cock pressing against me while I get a spanking." She wiped tears from her face.

"Don't be too sure of that," he said, getting dressed again. "Come here."

He helped her to stand.

Since the ground was uneven, she took a hopping step to steady herself. He wrapped an arm around her waist then captured her chin and tilted her head back before gently brushing a kiss across her mouth. "Thank you."

"Thank *you*, Sir."

In the distance, Chewie bleated. He glanced over to see the caprine trotting off with his hat.

He exhaled his frustration.

Giving chase would make the Nigerian dwarf think he was playing a game. The best he could hope for was that he'd get it back without any pieces missing. He also knew he was a dreamer. "She thinks she's a dog and she'll eat anything. Hyperactive hellion. I keep hoping she'll grow up."

"I guess my shoe is in good company."

"Should have hung it from a tree branch." He released her chin as he watched one of his most expensive hats bobbing up and down until it and the goat both disappeared.

"At least she wasn't able to steal your jeans."

He raised an eyebrow. "Good point."

"But you could have covered the family jewels with your hat. Since you don't currently have a blazing hard-on, at least it wouldn't stick out." She snickered.

"You think you're funny?"

"Yes, Sir." With a radiant smile, she dazzled him. "As a matter of fact, I do. I'm very comical."

"I think you do need that spanking."

Her smile widened. "I'm sure you're right."

"Incorrigible."

"Yes, Sir."

Spying a boulder, he took her hand and guided her toward it.

"Drop your pants," he ordered, sitting and making sure the ground was solid beneath him so that his boots didn't accidentally slip, sending her sprawling. "You can hold one of my legs for balance since we're on an angle."

"Sir is very generous."

"Was that sarcasm, Sydney?"

"Absolutely not, Sir. That would be disrespectful."

"Your pants," he reminded her.

Beneath his watchful gaze, her hand trembled slightly, delighting him. He loved that he had an effect on her, even when she adopted a blasé demeanor.

"Now over my knee."

When she'd draped herself into position, he admired the sight. "It's hard to decide which position I like you in best."

"You always seem to have my ass sticking up one way or another."

"If you behaved better, maybe you wouldn't always need it warmed." He waited, angling his head to the side. "No response?"

"Ah, that's not really incentive for me to behave, Sir." She kicked her legs a bit.

"Oh, right. The denied orgasm is most effective with you."

She stilled.

"You haven't been that bad, Sydney." The woman was as fierce as she was attractive, and he appreciated her sharp wit.

In this instance, he was clearly the winner — he had the delectable Sydney squirming beneath his hand. "I couldn't be more pleased with you."

He reached between her legs, forcing her to grab his left ankle to stabilize herself. "Your pussy is already damp."

"That's your fault, Sir. It happened while I was sucking you off."

"Did it?" His dick thickened at her words. No other woman had ever said as much. "I'm glad I ignored Gregorio's advice."

"I appreciate a man who's an independent thinker. Now can we get on with it?"

Her ass cheeks were still slightly red in parts, and he delighted in the opportunity to make the rest match.

Without hesitation, he brought his hand down on her buttocks.

"Ouch."

"More sarcasm?" Michael set his jaw. This woman calculated her words for maximum effect, probably hoping he'd lose control. He vowed he never would. Instead, he'd call on his carefully cultivated reserves of patience.

Deliberate, focused on what he was doing, he aimed each of his next three rapid spanks on the fleshiest part of her butt, avoiding her existing marks.

After that, he paused to rub her vigorously.

When she purred her pleasure, he jostled her.

"Sir!"

"Hold on," he suggested.

He grabbed her buttocks and squeezed until she exhaled in an unladylike grunt. He eased off, but barely, before resuming his massage.

"That's... *Shit!*"

After slapping her hard, he fingered her. "Oh, you're even wetter now. You're a perfect little sub."

"I'm not really a—"

"You're *mine.*" Whatever words she used—the facts didn't change.

He tapped his foot to bounce her around and he continued the motion as he resumed the spanking. He caught her a dozen times or more with his cupped hand, making her cry out.

When she thrashed her legs, he teased her pussy once more.

"Sir!"

Again and again, he spanked her. "Are you begging for mercy?"

"*No. No, no, no.*"

Her responses were barely audible over her whimpers.

"Do you remember your safe and slow words?"

"I'm begging for an orgasm, Sir, not for you to stop!"

Rapidly, he moved from spanks to squeezes to teasing her swollen clit.

"Finger-fuck me, Sir."

Had she already learned he could deny her nothing, especially when she was breathlessly pleading with him?

Wanting nothing more than to satisfy her as she'd pleased him, he slipped a finger into her then he pulled some of the dampness backward to lubricate her tightest hole.

She held her breath and clenched her muscles.

"That behavior will not be tolerated." He placed two fingers in her pussy, gathering some more of her feminine arousal. "Open up." He stroked her, encouraging her to lose the tension.

"But..."

"Did that sound like a suggestion?"

"No, Sir," she said miserably, complying with his command.

He kept up what he was doing until she trembled, then he worked a finger inside her ass.

"Argh!"

"That's it." He adjusted himself to trap her legs, upending her a little more in the process, forcing her to put one hand on the ground.

He thrust in and out, pausing occasionally to spank her thighs.

As she started to cry, he pressed a thumb against her clit and continued his relentless pounding of her rectum.

"Oh, Sir…"

"Come for me."

In an instant, she did, clawing his pant leg, feverishly pumping her body. He encouraged her along, drawing out her orgasm until she went limp across him.

Offering soothing, nonsensical words, he withdrew his finger, then helped her turn back over and sit up.

"That was… *Heavens*, Sir." She curled into him in a way she hadn't before. "I feel scalded."

Whether she realized it or not, she was letting down her guard with him, and he cherished that. "That can only mean one thing. You need to cool off. In the river."

"Are you serious?" She glanced around. "I don't have a swimsuit or shorts."

"We have all the privacy in the world out here."

As if considering, she pressed her lips together. "Regardless, we're in the Colorado mountains, which means it's going to be as cold as hell."

"Yeah." He grinned. "Your nipples will stand up and beg for attention. That alone is reason enough for me. Don't tell me you've never skinny-dipped?"

"Of course I have. In a pool and the ocean."

"But not in a river?"

She shook her head.

"And yet you live for adventure."

"I guide white water rafting tours. I've ended up in the water more than once, which is how I know it's frigid."

Still, she didn't say no. Instead she drummed her fingers on her thigh. *Have I won?*

"What about that mangy little — ?"

"Dwarf. She's a Nigerian dwarf goat," he told her for the second time. "And she's not mangy. She gets bathed regularly and groomed often."

"She takes baths?"

He liked their easy banter, along with the fact that Sydney seemed to be in no hurry to get away from him. "Either me or Jeb, my foreman, give them to her."

"You do?"

"As I mentioned, Melanie and my nieces don't make it up here often, so I get the honors."

"You could braid her hair and tie it with ribbons, and she'd still be a menace to society."

"Some females are," he agreed easily.

She lanced him with the knife-edge of a glacial stare.

With a grin, he relented. "Present company excluded."

"I can't have your pampered pet eating any more of my belongings."

"We can put your belongings high enough in the branches so that she can't reach them."

"Are you coming in with me?"

"Someone needs to twist your nipples."

"Ah…" Her eyes now took on a glossy, sensual hue. "In that case, yes. It actually does look inviting." She scampered from his lap and bent to pull off her hiking boots.

Obviously once she'd made up her mind, she didn't entertain second thoughts.

She peeled off her socks, shoved them in the boots, then she tied the shoelaces together and looped them over a branch.

"Chewie can climb that rock." He pointed.

"She's a pain in the ass." Shaking her head, Sydney stood on tiptoe and selected a higher branch.

Michael grinned.

No matter how skilled or determined, the goat probably couldn't have reached the first location. He was sure she would try, but he was convinced she'd never succeed. But he was a red-blooded male and he'd wanted to watch Sydney stretch and rise up.

It didn't take her long to take off her remaining clothes, and she hung them on the tree, too.

Without waiting for him, she headed for the water's edge, picking her way over tiny rocks.

Still, she looked upstream before surveying the rest of the river. Sydney was cautious, not nearly as reckless as her reputation suggested.

"There's a little pool here." She crouched to stick her hand in the water. "It's not as cold as I expected."

Hell of a way to start the day, a pot of strong coffee waiting and looking at a beautiful woman — a beautiful, *naked* woman — who'd given him a hell of a blow job and whose ass had been reddened appropriately. He could get used to this, real fast.

By slow measures, she entered the stream. "Damn!"

"Not that warm after all?"

"It's deeper here," she said, forcing out a breath and rubbing her arms. "And because it's so early, the sun's not warming my skin."

She squatted, which was the only way to get herself wet up to the chest. Her nipples were tantalizingly erect when she stood and faced him. "I thought you were coming in, Sir?"

"I am." Just as he'd watched her, she shamelessly studied him as he undressed.

Like she had done, he hung his clothes from pine tree branches.

"Nice butt, Sir."

Her voice held a seductive, feminine purr that turned him on.

He joined her, and before he adjusted to the shiver-inducing shock, the vixen splashed him. "You like to live dangerously."

"It was an accident, Sir." Her twinkling eyes proved she was lying.

Determinedly, Michael made a large cup with his joined hands, and he dunked them under the water. Then he took a step toward her, allowing droplets to fall between his fingers.

"Uhm… What are you doing, Sir?" In her attempt to back away, she stumbled.

Swearing, he dumped the water and reached for her, grabbing her upper arms and righting her before she could topple. "That's better," he said, hauling her against him.

"It is. Thank you, Sir."

Michael adjusted his hold, placing one hand above her buttocks, the other in the middle of her back.

"You saved me." She stood on tiptoes to kiss his cheek.

He turned to slant his mouth over hers.

With a soft sigh, she yielded to him, parting her lips and meeting the thrust of his tongue.

Hungry for her, he demanded her surrender, tasting, taking.

Syndey leaned into him more, looping her arms around his neck. When he ended the kiss, he pressed a finger to her swollen lips. "You look like a proper sub."

"Looks are deceiving."

Are they?

Despite her protest, she didn't pull away.

He set her back from him, just a bit, and looked at her breasts, cradling them before capturing each nipple and rolling them between his thumbs and forefingers.

Closing her eyes, she moaned.

"Are they tender?"

"Achingly so," she said.

He lowered his head and drew one into his mouth.

"Oh, Sir..."

Holding on tightly to him, she spread her legs and pressed her crotch against his leg.

"Only filthy girls hump like that."

"Fine. I'm filthy."

Mine. You're fucking mine. He flexed his knee so he could help her brace against his thigh.

"Yum. I like this," she confessed.

He resumed pinching and pulling her nipples, mindful of using a much lighter touch than he had last night. "Grind yourself against me."

Slowly, she lowered herself, then began rubbing back and forth. "Do I have permission to come, Sir?"

"Since you asked so nice, yes."

A smile ghosted around her lips. Then their gazes met before she closed her eyes and let him take more of her weight.

Wanting to support her, he reached behind her.

This would have been a much better idea on a firmer surface, preferably where he could lean against something. But it was more fun and challenging this way.

As she found her rhythm, she increased her speed.

Michael responded by smacking one of her butt cheeks while digging a hand into her hair.

"Mmm. That hurts," she said.

"Do you want me to stop?"

"Are you crazy, Sir?"

He encouraged her as she ground out an orgasm, leaving his leg slightly damp. "You're a hot little subbie," he told her when the last aftershock had subsided, and she'd straightened her back.

"Thank you." Her words held no gratitude. "But I don't like that word."

Why was it bothering her now? With a frown he studied her. "Talk to me."

Water bubbled past them as her juices dried on his thigh.

"I tried it once. Didn't like it. I prefer to be a man's equal."

He frowned.

She raked an unkempt strand of hair back from her face. "The word sub implies someone's beneath you."

"To me, it certainly does not." He stepped carefully. This discussion vibrated with danger, and realization dawned.

If she believed that, it was no wonder she behaved as a brat, in the BDSM meaning of the word. No wonder she had very carefully drawn lines to keep men at bay and to get her kinky needs met. "Being a submissive, even twenty-four seven, would never diminish a woman I was involved with." He took her shoulders in what he hoped was a reassuring grip. "In fact, to me, it's a position of reverence. There are many women out there, but only one that I'd honor in that way."

She wrinkled her nose. "Not convinced, Sir."

"It didn't seem to bother you when you were riding my leg."

"You're right about that. It didn't. But it's because I see you, this, as a scene, nothing more. I get my kink on, get off then I go home."

"*I see you, this, as a scene, nothing more.*" Her well-aimed words made him wince. "You said you'd tried being a submissive and didn't like it." And the experience had left her wounded.

"It's in the past." With a sigh, she finished, "Which means it's no longer relevant."

"I disagree. You went through something you didn't enjoy, and that affects what we share." He struggled to keep anger from his words. "So yeah. It matters." In fact, to him, it was a big fucking deal. "Now you equate submission with subservience?" he guessed.

"Among other things." Fatalistically, as if it didn't matter, she shrugged. "It wasn't all bad. I learned what I like and what I don't. I got out quick, and unscathed."

The last part, he wasn't sure of.

He wanted to suggest they dress, maybe sit on a rock, or return to the house where they could be more comfortable. But he didn't want to shatter the moment.

"Now I spend time chasing my dreams." She swept her hand wide. "It's not any different from you owning half the state. We've made different choices. Mine are right for me. And I don't have any hoofed pets."

Michael resisted her attempts to divert the subject away from herself. "Who hurt you, Sydney?"

She exhaled.

Five minutes ago, she'd come apart in his arms. And now she was a totally different woman.

"You're not going to quit until you get your answers."

She was one hundred percent right. "Your earlier comment is an important one. That being submissive means someone is beneath you."

Her jaw tightened, which told him all he needed to know. "I'm hoping you'll trust me enough to continue the conversation. I want to understand you."

The water caused goose bumps to rise on her skin. Either that, or it was a result of her emotional vulnerability.

"Lewis. That was his name."

While she sorted through her thoughts, he waited.

"He collared me." She scoffed. "I was young. Naive enough to believe in love and happily ever after. He was my first experience with BDSM." She shrugged. "It was new. An adrenaline rush. As you can guess, I enjoyed it, and I went along with everything he said."

"Because you didn't know anything different."

"And what happened?"

"Exactly."

"After a few months, I got tired of being a doormat, of making him dinner so he could come home whenever the hell he wanted while I waited on my knees. And he didn't want me working outside the house."

Lewis wasn't a Dom. He was an asshole who wanted total control.

Forcing himself to remain silent, Michael waited for her to speak again.

"Once, he locked me in our bedroom in that position for hours. He had a camera on me to ensure I didn't move. I thought it would only be for a few minutes. But it wasn't. Of course I got restless, so I shifted, then a couple of times I stood so I could stretch. I wasn't allowed dinner, and he thrashed me for my disobedience." She hesitated. "The bruises were still there almost two weeks later."

Bastard.

"Then..." After trailing off, she gulped as if steadying her nerves. "The final thing that made me end it..."

Even after that, you stayed?

"He had a party one night at our place—his guy friends came over to play poker. He expected me to be their cocktail waitress, short dress, high heels. I was uncomfortable with the whole thing—I mean, they were vanilla friends, you know? I'd met their wives and girlfriends. It was humiliating."

This time, her pause lasted a full thirty seconds, maybe more.

"Anyway, I accidentally spilled some whiskey, and Lewis snatched the bottle from me, then he grabbed my collar and yanked me over his lap." As if trying to banish the memory, she rubbed her forearms. "He flipped my dress up then he started a horrible spanking. When his hand got tired, he told one of his friends to grab a big wooden spoon from the kitchen. I was screaming the entire time. That only made him madder."

What in the actual fuck?

"So then he's blistering my ass and my legs relentlessly, and I'm reaching back, trying to protect myself, and he's catching my hands, my wrist bones, telling me he knows how much I liked it."

Michael scowled. "Anything without your consent is abuse, Sydney."

"Well, then his friends wanted to see him do it on my bare ass. So one of his friends yanked my panties down and then took out his dick to fuck me. I was frantic." Her breaths came in frantic bursts. "We'd never discussed him sharing me, and I didn't want this guy inside me. When I refused, Lewis was furious, shouting that I was his sub and had to do what he said. On some level, I realized he and his friends had planned this in advance. I kicked backward as hard as I could, catching that guy in the nuts. That caused enough of a commotion for me to get away."

He curled his hands into fists. "I'll fucking kill him."

"It was a long time ago."

To him, it wasn't. Anyone who'd treat Sydney like that deserved to die. After suffering mightily for his crimes.

"Being his sub, wearing his collar meant I was a glorified servant." She cupped her palms and used them to cover her eyes. "Someone to be used any way he wanted, and by anyone he chose."

He ached to comfort her and had no damn clue what to do.

When she lowered her hands, a tear clung to her eyelashes. "I left with less money than I arrived with and a shit-pile less self-respect."

That damnable tear spilled down onto her cheek, and he tenderly wiped it away. "You found the strength to walk away."

"Walk?" She shook her head. "Ran. Left my belongings. Never went back. A friend of mine, Vanessa, put me in touch with Gregorio, and he helped me find a jeweler to cut my collar off. After that, I finally agreed to go to the Den with her. She'd been concerned about my relationship with Lewis for some time." She shrugged. "Turns out she was right. Anyway, I accepted Vanessa's invitation to a Ladies' Night party there, and I've been going ever since. It's safe. Controlled."

No wonder you don't go home with any men.

Forcing a smile that looked fake, she finished, "Is that what you expected to hear?"

He tamped back his rage in order to care for her. "Thank you for telling me."

Her shoulders rolled forward as she expelled a deep breath.

"I'll address you in any way you prefer. And I assure you, I have nothing but the utmost respect for you and what we share."

She flipped her hair back. Now he recognized the gesture as self-protective nonchalance.

"You're not like him." Her words lacked conviction. "I know that."

Do you?

"Lewis and I didn't use a safe word, and I didn't have one for slow."

"With me, you have both, and I encourage you to use them. A relationship—especially a D/s one—requires constant nurturing and refinement. But I also think it's more freeing. With fewer societal constraints, there are more opportunities to be authentic. You ask or state—we negotiate."

"It doesn't matter, does it? In a few minutes, I'll be leaving, and I may never see you again…"

That wasn't what he wanted, and he'd do anything for one more night.

"Before you demand something that I don't want to give."

"Look, Sydney, in a D/s, a *real* D/s, I only have the power that you entrust to me. It's yours to give, not mine to take."

"Sounds like a fantasy."

"Lewis was an abusive shithead. A true Dom looks after your needs, puts your best interests first. He'll nurture and protect you."

"Again, idealism." She scoffed. "Been there, done that. No desire to get on that ride again. At this point, nothing matters more to me than my independence."

"After what you've been through, you're right to be cautious." And he'd still like to come face-to-face with Lewis, anytime, anyplace.

"Look, Sir—Michael—I'm not looking for a Dominant. I want a Top I can scene with, and nothing more."

A loud splash grabbed his attention.

In front of him, Sydney's eyes widened, but before she could utter a word, something plowed into the backs of his legs.

Sydney momentarily steadied him so he didn't slip as he turned. "Chewie."

"Is it safe for her to be in the river?"

"You're more worried about her than me?" he demanded.

"Uhm… About that…" She smiled.

"Goats can swim," he assured her.

"Seriously?"

"But she'll need a bath."

"I look forward to watching."

Which meant Sydney might not be rushing off—the thought gave him some hope.

"And I'm fine, too. Thanks for asking." The goat's arrival had shattered the tension, and he wasn't sure he welcomed that. The conversation had been important, and he wanted to know more about her. "Spend the day with me?" he invited. "We have a lot of things to discuss."

"I can't." She shook her head.

Her teasing tone held no regret.

"I have a pile of things to do at home, laundry, packing. I leave town tomorrow and I'll be gone for ten days."

A story so you can escape? "I'd better make you a hearty breakfast before you go."

"You cook?" Her eyes widened.

"I have a housekeeper who does my cleaning and shopping. Every once in a while, she'll make a meal, and I appreciate it. But my grandfather believed all men should know how to cook." He shrugged. "Probably from being on the range, away from the house so much. He and Grandma made sure I'm self-sufficient. I can manage biscuits and gravy for breakfast, along with bacon and eggs. From the ranch's chickens."

"Fresh eggs?"

"I get a few a day."

"There's nothing better. I like to go to the local farmer's market, but sometimes I don't get there early enough, and they're already sold out."

"Whatever is your preference, I can probably whip them up. Scrambled, poached, fried."

"Is there still some coffee left?"

"I'll brew you a fresh pot."

She opened her mouth then shut it.

"Are you interested?"

"Yes, please. It turns out that I've burned a lot of energy since last night."

"That's two of us."

Chewie bleated.

"Let's get you dry," he told Sydney, exiting the river and offering her a hand to help her over the rocks.

Chewie followed, staying close to see what they were doing.

On the bank, he wadded his shirt and used it to pat Sydney's chest dry.

"The water didn't cause you much shrinkage, Sir."

"Seems to be a constant condition when you're naked." The sun emerged from behind a cloud, and he told her, "Turn around."

Once she had, he dried the rest of her body. When he was finished, he gave one cheek a quick pinch.

With a yelp, she faced him.

"Payback for the shrinkage comment," he informed her.

She wrinkled her nose. "I suppose that's fair. And speaking of fair, can I dry you?"

By way of an answer, he offered his shirt.

She rubbed it across his head then shaped his hair with her fingers.

"This one piece likes to curl," she said.

"Bane of my existence."

"It's cute."

"I don't do cute," he said, his words all but a growl.

"Still, it's adorable."

He captured her wrist.

"Adorable, Sir," she amended.

"That's better." With a grin, he released her.

She continued to draw the cotton down his chest. She boldly took his now-erect cock and moved it so she could dry the lower part of his stomach. Then she knelt to lick his balls.

"Damn, Sydney..."

"Oh. Oops. Seems I caused you to get damp again." Looking up at him, she wiped a fingertip across the slit in his penis.

Then she raised the pre-ejaculate to her mouth and licked it off.

It was a good thing she had to leave soon. Otherwise he might not let her go.

Resuming her ministrations, she dried his thighs and shins. "Turn around for me."

It took her a long time to dry his backside, even tracing up the insides of his thighs, over his perineum, and parting his buttocks to daub them.

"Not sure that part was wet."

"Being thorough, Sir."

"Being a temptress," he countered. But he didn't stop her. This kind of brattiness, he liked.

The clouds had drifted away, and the summer sun blazed. Though he'd be dry in seconds anyway, there was no way in hell he was going to stop her.

A minute or so later, she placed her hands on his waist and used him for balance as she stood.

She slid the makeshift towel across his shoulders, taking her time drying them, then his chest. Much too soon, she said, "All done."

Michael turned to cup her shoulders.

Everything about her appealed to him, her windswept hair, compact, muscular body, and red marks — his — on her skin.

In such a short time, she'd gotten to him.

Grinning, she offered back his shirt. He shook it out, and that grabbed Chewie's attention. The pest trotted over, angling her head as she tried to snatch it from his hand.

Sydney laughed.

"Always funny when it's my clothes," he observed.

"Definitely, Sir."

They dressed while Chewie kept an interested, thieving, eye on them.

"She's opportunistic," he warned.

"Cunning is more like it," Sydney replied, hurriedly tying her shoelaces.

He picked up their cups, and they walked back to the house side by side while Chewie trotted ahead of them and kept glancing back. When she approached a big rock, she walked up it, stood on top, and looked into the distance.

"She really is agile."

"You're lucky you didn't find her on one of our vehicles this morning."

"That could cause some damage."

"Mostly she behaves herself."

"Just like me," Sydney replied.

"Yeah." He couldn't help but laugh. "Just like you."

Once they neared the house, Chewie went toward the barn. Michael held open the gate for Sydney, and she walked to her car to grab a bag.

"Mind if I take a quick shower, Sir?"

"Help yourself. Or feel free to take a bath. I'll get another pot of coffee going then I'll bring you a cup."

"Thank you."

By the time he entered his suite, she was dressed, her damp hair curling against her face. How was it possible he was already so accustomed to having her around?

"Can I do anything to help with breakfast?" she asked, accepting her cup with a smile.

"You could set the table. I'm sure you'll find everything you need."

She traced her fingertips across his chest before heading downstairs.

Anxious to spend as much time together as possible before she left, he showered in record time.

When he joined her, she had placed a handful of columbines in a small vase near his placemat. The sight of her leaning across the width of the table to pour orange juice into a glass was even better.

While he fried the bacon, she perched on a barstool and propped her chin on her hands. "This is a treat."

"It's a chore I enjoy."

"I'm not a fan. Lewis expected homecooked meals, and I came to resent his expectations."

"No one likes to be taken for granted." He cracked half a dozen eggs into a bowl, then added milk—sans cream—and tossed in some salt and pepper.

"What are you going to eat?" she teased.

He glanced up. "You've got a healthy appetite?"

"Always, and I'm planning to hit the gym later," she said.

"Do you have a workout bag in your car, too?" he reached into the carton for a couple more eggs.

"Prepared for anything, anytime."

Also the result of your relationship with Lewis?

"I'm never in one place for too long."

"Has it always been that way?"

"Except for that one failed attempt at a relationship." She took a sip of her coffee. "I inherited my parents' love of the world. The story goes that I was conceived in Sydney, Australia. Hence, my name."

"Clever."

"Glad that didn't happen when they were in Kuala Lumpur."

"Right?"

"Anyway, I was born in the United States, but I spent my first birthday in Budapest. My second in London." She picked a strawberry from a bowl on the bar and popped it into her mouth. "From what I've been told, I took my first steps in Geneva. Learned to ski in Utah."

Which explained a lot about her.

"Dad is quite a bit older than Mom, and he'd inherited some money. He worked as a consultant, and that took him all over the world. So she went with him. They didn't accumulate a lot of worldly goods, believing experiences were more important than things."

"Hard to disagree with that."

After biting into a second berry, she picked up the threads of her story. "I think I was unexpected — not unwelcome, but not planned. So their philosophy was to throw me in a backpack and keep going."

When breakfast was ready, she helped him carry the platters of food to the table.

She snagged a piece of bacon before he could serve it. "This might do the trick."

"Trick?" he repeated, frowning in confusion. "What are you talking about?" He pulled back a chair for her.

"You cook. Crispy bacon. Fluffy eggs. And you brew an amazing pot of coffee. It might get me to accept another invitation."

"If I'd known it was that easy..." He took the chair next to hers. "And I was planning to offer to tie you to the fence and flog you to sweeten the pot."

The piece of bacon dropped from her fingertips. "Well, you certainly do know how to capture a girl's interest, Sir."

"That's my intent." He spooned eggs onto her plate.

After taking the first bite, she saluted him with her fork. "This is amazing."

Her pleasure sustained him.

As they ate, they talked about ranch life.

Afterward, she carried their dishes to the sink, then returned with the coffee pot. As she refilled their cups, she regarded him.

"What's bothering you?" he asked.

"How do you keep doing that? Reading my mind?"

"You've got an expressive face." Sitting back, he waited for her to take the carafe back to the kitchen.

When she was across from him again, she said, "I'm curious about what happened to your marriage."

Though he didn't like to talk about it, he wanted to see her again. Gaining her trust was more important than his need to compartmentalize his past. "After we were married, she shifted her expectations about BDSM and sex. What had been fun was now forbidden."

"I see."

"It turns out"—painful as it was to admit—"she wanted the security that came along with marrying me." He took a drink, then slammed the mug down with more force than he'd intended, and coffee sloshed onto the table.

Without a word, Sydney blotted the spill with a napkin.

"Not me, specifically. Any man of means would have done."

She winced. "I'm so sorry."

"It was a long time ago." Still, the painful lessons lingered. "One night, after a couple of glasses of wine, I tried to kiss her. She turned away." That memory burned. "She finally said we wouldn't be having sex ever again, and I wanted children." He looked out the window, surveying a tiny portion of the holdings. "It's a great place to grow up."

"I'm sure it is." So different from the way she was raised.

When he looked back, she was still considering him, head tipped to one side.

"She hadn't told you this before?"

"No. The ending of the relationship was devastating, but she tried to get half of the ranch. It took a lot of skillful financial moves to hold on to it."

Her mouth fell open.

"I believe she was having an affair." He shrugged. "Never proved it, and she denied it. Not that it mattered in the end." But his next relationship would have an ironclad prenuptial agreement. "Mine was the first marriage in family history to crash and burn."

Quietly, she waited for him to go on.

"Last I heard, she has two children."

"With the other guy?"

He shrugged. "Since I never knew whether or not she was cheating, I can't say."

"But she lied about the kids part."

"Maybe not. Perhaps she didn't want children with me."

On his behalf, Sydney winced.

"Are you sorry you asked?"

"No. And I appreciate you telling me. It had to hurt."

"Like you, I'm no longer idealistic. I still want a family, but I'll be a whole lot more careful about my choice in women."

As if a chill had gone through her, she shivered.

"You were honest with me. You deserved to hear the unvarnished truth from me."

She nodded and pushed back her chair. "In that case, this arrangement could be successful for both of us. I'm looking for a Top. You're being cautious about who you get involved with."

Her statement pissed him off, though he was loath to admit why.

Together, they cleaned the kitchen. He loaded the dishwasher while she cleared the table.

"This has been a wonderful experience," she said, drying her hands on a dishtowel. "Thanks for having me out to your ranch."

"You're welcome anytime."

Though she smiled, it seemed more forced than genuine. "And, ah...I need to get going."

Within five minutes, she'd gathered her belongings and headed for the back door.

He joined her, following her down the path.

Chewie grazed beyond the fence, exactly where she was supposed to be.

Sydney used her key fob to unlock the vehicle, then placed her purse and other belongings on the back seat.

Before she could escape, he slapped both of his palms on the roof, on either side of her head, making her jump. "Before you go..."

She frowned.

"Turn around."

"I..."

In his sternest voice, he repeated his order.

Trembling slightly, she did as he said.

Michael moved her a foot or so to the right, then he grabbed her hands and pinned them together at the small of her back.

Once she was captive, helpless, he spanked her delectable butt cheeks several times, hard, until she gasped. Then he placed a kiss on the side of her neck and released her.

Gently, hands on her shoulders, he turned her back to face him. "There's more of this anytime you're interested."

Her eyes opened wide, and her breaths came in ragged little bursts.

"After all, you did select *all of the above* earlier. Which means I still need to tie you to the fence for your flogging."

He wanted her thinking about it, imagining it, craving it. Mostly, he wanted her to come back to him.

Where she belonged.

Chapter Six

The next afternoon, in a fancy Miami hotel suite, perched on the couch, Sydney finished telling her two friends about the wild weekend at the Den, then at Master Michael's ranch.

"Wait, let me get this straight," Leaundra said, standing near the French doors that led to the patio and an ocean view. She had a glass of wine in hand, and her eyes were wide with shock. "You had a mind-blowing night with a hunky cowboy, and you freaking walked away without giving him your phone number? Girl, are you crazy?"

"You're going to have to give us more details," Jacqueline said. She was seated in a high-back chair and was drumming her fingers on the upholstered arm.

The three of them had shared an apartment in college, and they met up once a year to renew their friendship. None of them had changed much.

Leaundra loved men, the idea of being in love, shopping, and dining out. And not necessarily in any particular order. The first time they'd met, she'd said she was only attending school to meet a rich man and marry him. Senior year, she'd found a man who met her requirements. Right after graduation, she'd tied the knot.

Jacqueline, a trial lawyer, was the most successful of them all, at least by worldly goods standards.

"This is going to need more wine," Leaundra insisted, walking across the room to pick up an oversize bottle with a twist-off lid.

Sydney knew the cheap pink stuff probably wouldn't be considered wine by connoisseurs, but in their college days, it had been the only thing they could afford. It was sweet and went down easy. Money wasn't as big of an issue now, but they still bought the same brand — probably more for nostalgic reasons than anything else.

She leaned forward and offered her glass for the refill. "I didn't come here to discuss my love life," Sydney insisted. "I want to hear about Leaundra's upcoming wedding plans."

"I haven't turned into bridezilla this time. Well, at least not so far." She refilled Jacqueline's glass. "I'm hoping I've had enough experience to know what's worth getting my panties in a wad for."

True. Though Leaundra wasn't thirty, this was going to be her third trip down the aisle. At least she'd traded up with each engagement. When she'd first seen the size of the rock on her friend's hand, Sydney had reached for a pair of sunglasses.

"The worst that has happened so far is that his mother dragged me to a cake tasting. One of her friends owns a bakery. But really, matcha and black sesame?" She pulled back, as if appalled. "Green tea flavor for a wedding cake? Who does that?" She shrugged. "But what the hell? I've had vanilla with buttercream frosting before."

"Last time was red velvet," Jacqueline added.

"See?" Leaundra added. "I've been traditional, and it didn't work. So green tea it is. At least it's better than chili chocolate avocado."

"Seriously? Avocado?" Sydney echoed, exchanging glances with Jacqueline.

"I kid you not. This is what my life has become." Leaundra put down the bottle, then returned to her place by the window. "Please, I beg you, let me live vicariously through you."

Obviously getting no reprieve from that quarter, Sydney turned to Jacqueline. "You've always got fantastic stories about perverted judges."

"You're not getting out of this," Jacqueline said. "Later tonight I'll tell you about Judge Samuels and what he was wearing under his robe." She lifted her glass in a mock salute.

Sydney and Leaundra dutifully followed suit. They pretended to clink the glasses together.

After a sip, Jacqueline returned to the topic at hand. "We want to hear about Mr. Tie Me Up, Tie Me Down."

"There's not much to tell. He's not any different from other guys I play with at the Den."

"Well, we like those stories too, right, Lea?"

"Damn straight." She nodded. "But this is significant, and don't pretend it's not. He's the first guy you've gone home with since Lewis."

"He was a loser," Jacqueline added helpfully. "We should have tattooed a capital L on his forehead while he was asleep."

Sydney grinned. There was nothing like hanging out with friends she'd known since her late teens.

"So, about Michael," Leaundra prompted.

"Master Michael," she corrected automatically.

"Hmm." Jacqueline arched a carefully sculpted eyebrow.

"When you went to the Den, did you see that hunky piece of man, Gregorio?" Lea blinked. "I mean, he is single, right?"

"It doesn't matter," Sydney replied, shaking her head. "You're getting married. Remember?"

"Oh. Right. Walking down the aisle. I digress."

"Yes. He was there."

Lea fanned herself.

"He even had a few words with Master Michael about me."

"And he approached you anyway?" Lea asked. "Brave man. I like brave men."

"You like any men," Jacqueline fired back.

Completely unoffended, Lea lifted a shoulder.

"So then what happened?" Jacqueline asked, returning them to the original discussion.

"We played, and after that, he invited me back to the ranch."

"In the middle of nowhere," Lea added. "And you spent the night."

Sydney nodded.

"You met his goat. He cooked you breakfast. And you left without giving him your phone number."

"Correct. And that's the whole story." She squirmed, wanting to move on to a different topic. At this point, Sydney was sorry she'd told them anything at all. But still, her emotions had been in such turmoil since she'd driven away from Master Michael that she hadn't been able to keep the events bottled up inside.

Maybe going home with him was a mistake.

His house was huge, and it spoke of a commitment to something deeper than his own life. He was attached to the land and his family history. And he had an eye on future generations, creating a legacy.

When she'd escaped from the relationship with Lewis, she'd reinforced her choices to carpe diem, seizing the present moment.

Yet, a single night with the sexy cowboy at the Eagle's Bend Ranch had turned her inside out.

Master Michael was a skilled Top. Dominant to his core, and he'd seen through her in ways no one else ever had. And he challenged her. No one else had discovered her fear of being left alone. Most likely it was because she'd never let anyone get close enough to learn any of her secrets.

So why you, Master Michael?

As she'd cleaned her condo and packed for her trip, she'd asked herself that question a dozen times.

During a restless night's sleep, where she'd dreamed of that spanking and his final, deliciously tempting parting words to her, she'd finally admitted the truth to herself.

He was man enough to thrill her, and persistently Dominant enough to read her emotions and shatter her resistance.

She sighed, hating the realization, knowing it left her vulnerable to him.

Intuition blared in warning. But feminine hunger urged her to ignore her more cautious side and play with him a second time, despite her hard and fast rules.

"Earth to Sydney." Lea snapped her fingers.

"Sorry." She shook her head to clear it of the near-constant thoughts of Michael.

"Your story seems to be lacking some details."

"I think that about covers it."

"No, ma'am." She took a sip of wine. "You left out the part where you got the welts on the backs of your thighs. I saw them when we were at the swimming pool."

"You should become a private investigator," Jacqueline said with a raised brow. "If Jack doesn't work out—"

"John," Lea corrected. "This one is named John."

"As I was saying, if this marriage doesn't work out, I'll offer you a job at my law firm."

"Hmm. I may take you up on it. Do I need a license or something?"

"Mostly you need to chase down obscure details and angles and check out people's stories."

"I'm good at that. Eye for details."

"Nosy," Sydney corrected, leaning forward to grab one of the chocolate chip cookies they'd snagged from the lobby at check-in. They'd split the cost of the suite three ways, and that was the only reason she'd been able to afford to stay at such a fancy place.

"So, about the welts," Leaundra prompted.

"Tenacious, as well," Jacqueline observed.

Knowing Lea wouldn't relent—and was likely to circle back after another glass of wine when Sydney was even more willing to talk—she sighed. "At the beginning of the evening, we had a small scene outside at the Den to see if we were compatible."

"Outside?"

"He had me bend over a fence."

"Like your pants were down and everything?"

"My dress was lifted up."

"Could other people see?" she asked.

"Was it okay with you?" Jacqueline wanted to know. Probably as well as Sydney, her friend remembered her fury that Lewis had done something similar to her.

"First, answering Lea... I doubt anyone else could see us properly. It was getting close to dark, and we were away from the main house." Then she turned to Jacqueline. "This was consensual, which makes it entirely different." And there'd been no deliberate humiliation involved. In fact, what he'd asked of her had rocketed a thrill through her. Even from the first moment they'd met, he'd appealed to her thrill-seeking nature.

"What happened next?" Lea leaned forward. "Did he spank you?"

Sydney took a bite of the cookie and washed it down with wine. Surely all the sugar would give her a toothache. "Yes."

"And it was hot enough that you went home with him?"

"That could have been dangerous," Jacqueline pointed out.

Over the years, Leaundra had stood on the sidelines and encouraged Sydney to do crazy things. Jacqueline would recite a list of concerns as long as a legal disclaimer. Before Jacqueline could go on, Sydney held up a hand. "Master Damien vouched for him, and before I left, he told me to call if I needed anything. He even offered to come and get me if necessary."

"Could he have sent Gregorio instead?"

Rolling her eyes, Sydney laughed. Leaundra saved every conversation from getting too serious.

"Were you your normal, bratty self?" Lea asked.

"Hey!" Sydney protested.

"I'm sure she was guilty as charged," Jacqueline added.

"Some friends you two are."

"Chickie, who knows you like we do?" Lea demanded.

No one. Neither had judged her lifestyle choices, and they'd both listened to her sob over the phone when the relationship with Lewis had ended.

"So did he pretend you didn't exist like Lewis used to?" Jacqueline asked.

"Loser," Leaundra added.

"You two should take this show on the road." Sydney took another bite of her cookie. "And his punishment was much, much worse than that."

"Well that definitely means he didn't spank you for misbehaving," Lea observed.

"Worse?" Jacqueline repeated. "What could be worse than sticking you in timeout like he used to do?"

"Orgasm deprivation."

"The beast!" Leaundra put her glass on a nearby table and fanned herself. "Seriously?"

"Most men I know are thrilled if they can make me come," Jacqueline said. "I can't imagine any of them trying to stop the big O from happening."

Sydney finished off the cookie then brushed her hands together. These two were cheering her up. "Honestly, it sucks," she confessed. "So frustrating. Painful, almost."

"So then what?" Leaundra asked. "He has a ranch, surely he knows something about ropes."

"He does." She recalled him tying her to his massive bed. Then her wayward brain once again supplied an image of her being secured to his fence while he used a flogger on her.

"When do we get to the welts part?"

"Those were probably from his belt."

Jacqueline shuddered while Leaundra did a little dance on her four-inch stilettoes. "I want to go to the Den with you again sometime."

"You're getting married." How many times had Sydney reminded her friend of that fact?

"There is that."

"So what went wrong?" Jacqueline asked, more seriously.

Sydney picked up her glass and rolled it between her palms. "Nothing."

"Did you have fun?" Leaundra demanded. "Those welts sure make it look like you did."

"Well...yeah."

"But you did everything possible there is to do in one night? There's nothing left? You used that boy up?"

"Well, maybe not," Sydney admitted.

"Did he put anything up your ass yet?" Leaundra asked.

"Ah..."

"He did! *Damn.* So tell me again why you don't want to see him again? You gonna let some other girl get him?"

Sydney took a big gulp of wine. The thought stung, though it shouldn't have.

Leaundra crossed the room with the grace of a supermodel and pulled up a chair. It was as if her friends were forming a protective half-circle around her.

After taking a small, fortifying sip of wine, she slid the glass on the coffee table. Her friend's persistent questions uncovered a deeper, more terrifying fear. "We're a mismatch. He owns half of Colorado. I own a suitcase and a ten-year-old vehicle."

"Chickie, you're acting as if he asked you to marry him," Lea protested.

"What's the point in sceneing?" Sydney countered. "Nothing can come of it anyway."

"Except a good time. And you should grab as many of those as you can."

"But he wants me to be a submissive."

"And you just want a good spanking." Leaundra grinned, always telling it as it was.

"What does that mean, really?" Jacqueline asked. "I don't understand all this bondage, spanking, discipline stuff. If it's like the shit you went through with Lewis, you're right to run away."

"It's not all like that," Lea said.

Surprised, she looked at her friend. Though she'd visited the Den with Sydney, she didn't know that her friend had experiences beyond that.

"I do a lot of reading." As she smiled, Lea batted her fake eyelashes. "So anyway, tell us what Master Michael expects."

Maybe she should have asked him for further clarification on what submission meant to him.

When she didn't answer right away, Lea started guessing. "Housework?"

"He has a housekeeper."

"That's a point in his favor. Does he want you to do all the cooking?"

"I thought he made breakfast," Jacqueline said.

Sydney laughed. She hardly needed to participate in this conversation. "He did. And it was yummy."

"I'd marry any guy who cooked for me," Leaundra said.

"You're going to." Jacqueline rolled her eyes.

"See?" Lea looked at the cookies, then glanced away and refocused on Sydney. "He doesn't seem to expect service, right?"

"Actually, no. And he was a very good host."

Lea grinned. "So maybe he wants you kneeling naked in the living room when he gets home from riding the range." Then she frowned. "Or whatever it is that cowboys do all day."

Sydney had no idea what he did, either.

"Anyway, you're always the one who tells me that relationships, especially lifestyle ones, are all about excellent communication."

At Lea's pointed words, Sydney winced.

But in her usual way, Leaundra didn't linger on her statement, something Sydney appreciated. "And Doms are supposed to be caring, aren't they?"

"That's what he said yesterday morning. Something about having my best interests at heart." She wrinkled her nose. "Forgive my skepticism."

"I know!" Lea went on, her eyes twinkling. "Jacqueline, you could draw up a contract for her. You know, with all the juicy details in black and white. And I can review it for you."

"Hold on," Sydney protested.

"Give her some negotiating tips, and this way, as we work on it, we get to know all the kinky things Syd is into."

She'd known Lea long enough to realize she was at least halfway serious. "Absolutely no freaking way."

"Like anal." Lea was undeterred by Sydney's protests. "Or paddles. Ohh…wax play? Are you down for that?"

Sydney shook her head. "Enough."

"And we can add a rider that you want to be treated like a princess. No service or anything like that for you."

"I'm sure I'll figure it out." Before she could change the subject, Jacqueline leaned forward.

"Honey, you spend too much time thinking about the future and worrying."

Sydney scowled at her friends over the rim of her glass.

"We all know that Lewis —"

"Loser," Lea interrupted.

"What a shithead. And more than anyone, I urge you to be cautious."

Sydney nodded.

"But sometimes we — and I'm also talking to myself here — we let the bad experiences ruin the joy of the moment," Jacqueline continued. "You're always looking for the next big thing. What if, just for now, you focused on today? If you see him again and have a good time, great. If you don't dig him or he turns out to be a jackass, me and Lea will kick his ass."

Lea pretended to sharpen her fingernails into tiny knives. "For sure."

"But don't throw away the chance for a good time because you got a crazy idea that fucking leads to being collared — or whatever you call it in the lifestyle — or worse, marriage."

Sydney and Lea both gasped. Generally it was Leaundra who made that kind of outrageous comment.

"What she said." Leaundra grabbed a cookie, then sighed and put it back uneaten. "I've got another wedding dress to fit into."

"I've already told you I didn't give him my phone number."

"He made it clear he wanted to see you again, so stop worrying about what if. Figure out a way to contact him."

"Or, wait." Lea snapped her fingers. "Since I'm a private investigator in training, I'll call Gregorio and chat him up."

"*You're getting married,*" Sydney and Jacqueline insisted simultaneously.

"There is that." Still, she eyed a chocolate chip cookie.

"And while we're on that subject, you could listen to me, as well," Jacqueline said, leveling her best courtroom gaze at Lea. "Just because a guy is good in the sack, you don't have to marry him."

This time, with a deep sigh, Lea gave in, grabbing a treat and taking a big bite out of it.

Then, thankfully, the conversation moved on to less fraught topics.

"I want to hear about the judge," Leaundra said, after devouring a third cookie.

"You'll never believe it. I didn't."

Intrigued, Sydney and Lea both gave Jacqueline their full attention.

"This comes from a court clerk. I usually dismiss gossip, but this is so damn good, I listened to every detail. For once, I don't even care whether the clerk's story is reliable or not."

"Tell us!" Lea urged.

"We all know the judge is a cyclist. He'll even ride to the courthouse on occasion. Evidently he's been known to wear cycling shorts under his robe, instead of trousers."

"Is he hot?" Lea demanded. "Those tight things show off the important stuff."

Sydney rolled her eyes.

Without responding to Lea's question, Jacqueline went on. "Apparently when he took off the robe in chambers, he forgot he didn't have shorts on."

"Get *out!*" Leaundra exclaimed. "The judge was naked from the waist down?"

"No. He was wearing a G-string type of arrangement."

"Type of arrangement?" Sydney prodded. "What does that mean?"

Jacqueline's lips quivered as she tried to fight back a grin. "Uh…trying to be delicate here. It had a pouch to hold the boys. And the other section was anatomically accommodating. Meaning the material stretches as you grow."

"Do tell," Leaundra encouraged.

"I guess he was filling it out, well, not all that impressively. He said it looked like a lime green worm."

"A cock sock!" Leaundra exclaimed.

"Oh my God, no." Sydney laughed. She'd seen a lot of interesting outfits at the Den, but nothing quite like that.

"If I'd seen his worm, I'd need therapy," Jacqueline said. "I'd never be able to argue a case in front of him again."

They chatted for a few more minutes before Lea announced she was famished — even after devouring a total of four cookies—and suggested they head downstairs for dinner.

This time, they enjoyed expensive cocktails poolside as they ate, reminisced, laughed, and spent more time discussing Lea's upcoming nuptials.

"I think I want both of you to be my maids of honor."

"We've each had a turn," Sydney said, pulling a cherry out of her glass.

"Agree," Jacqueline said.

It had cost them each a lot of money for dresses and to host her bachelorette parties and bridal showers. And just because it was the third time she'd waltzed down the aisle, didn't mean Lea didn't want the white gown and all the frills.

"I'm ready to attend as a guest," Sydney said.

"No!" Lea shrieked. "I need my besties."

Jacqueline sighed. "Okay. We'll split the responsibilities this time."

Lea danced in her chair. "Bachelorette party in Barbados?"

"Not if I have to pay half," Sydney protested. "I'm on a strict budget."

"Vegas," Jacqueline said with the same finality she used in court when she said, "*The defense rests, Your Honor.*"

"But we've done that before."

"Well," Sydney pointed out reasonably, "You've also gotten married before."

"We can stay at the Bella Rosa," Jacqueline offered as a compromise.

The newest, hottest hotel and casino on the Strip.

"Fine." She picked up her straw and stabbed it back into her glass. "But I want a bridal shower where my future in-laws live."

Sydney narrowed her eyes suspiciously. "Which is where?"

"Boston."

Of course. One of the priciest cities in the United States. "I can't afford many more of your marriages."

"This one should be the final one."

"Should be?" Jacqueline seized on Lea's words. "What about the whole 'till death do us part' thing?"

"A mere a suggestion," Lea said.

Sydney sighed and exchanged glances with Jacqueline.

"Okay," Jacqueline relented. "Boston it is. But if there's a fourth wedding, someone else has to be the maid of honor."

"Third time's the charm." Lea crossed her fingers hopefully.

Beneath the table, so did Sydney.

After dinner, they strolled around the property then sat on the edge of the hot tub to soak their feet. Even though she complained of blisters, Lea refused to relinquish her dozens of designer heels.

Finally back in her room, Sydney fell onto her bed facedown.

Before drifting off, she grabbed her phone to shut it off so that no one tried to reach her stupid early — before noon — only to find a text message waiting.

It was from the Den, asking for her permission to share her phone number with Master Michael.

She grinned.

Her one-night stand was definitely determined.

Jacqueline's words tumbled over in Sydney's mind. *"...Don't throw away the chance for a good time because you got a crazy idea that fucking leads to being collared — or whatever you call it in the lifestyle — or worse, marriage."*

And even Lea had a point. All relationships, especially BDSM ones, needed excellent communication. She only wished she could be as forthright about her emotional needs as she was her desire to be spanked and flogged.

Feeling wildly, stupidly giddy, her hand trembling, she typed her answer. *Yes.* He'd gone to some trouble to track her down, and she appreciated it.

It wasn't until the following night that she received a message from a Colorado area code with a number she didn't recognize. She was grinning as she opened it.

There were no words, just a picture...of the stilettos Master Michael had promised he'd buy her to replace the ones his goat had absconded with. He'd positioned the red shoes on top of a box, and the studs that ran up the heels made her heart miss a beat.

Sydney was astounded, first by the fact that he'd remembered to replace her shoes, and she also appreciated that he hadn't called and interrupted her vacation.

As she was looking at the screen, another text came through. This one had a picture of Chewie standing on a rock. There was a sign around her neck. Sydney had to zoom in to read the writing. *Sorry I was baaaaaaaaad.*

Sydney grinned. Master Michael had a terrible sense of humor. But it had obviously required a lot of work and creativity to get the photo. She had no idea how he'd gotten the four-footed, eating, thieving machine to stand still for so long.

She waited and waited, staring at the screen. Nothing else came through.

* * * *

The next morning, at the crack of ten a.m., the first thing Sydney did was look at her phone. No texts, calls, or emails.

But Master Michael successfully managed to make sure he occupied her every thought.

Dropping her phone beside her, she flopped her head back onto the pillow.

Someone pounded on her door. Nursing a bit of a hangover, she groaned at the obnoxious sound. "Go away!"

"Let's go!" Leaundra shouted back. "We're waiting on you for brunch. We're starving, and the mimosas are waiting."

She groaned. After last night's consumption of cheap pink wine, nothing sounded worse.

"And we need time for shopping! Get out of bed before I come in there and get you."

Sydney scooped her hair back from her forehead. "Ugh."

"Be ready in ten minutes."

How the heck did Lea manage to sleep so little, consume too much alcohol, and still have boundless energy?

"*Syd?*"

"I'm coming!" She climbed from the bed.

One time, during their college years, Lea and Jacqueline had stormed her room and dressed her, done her hair, and applied makeup. When they'd finished, she'd looked something like a fashion doll. The only thing they hadn't done was pour her into one of Lea's ridiculously short dresses.

If she wasn't ready in ten minutes, Sydney had no doubt that Lea and Jacqueline would repeat their torment — safe word or not — and enjoy every moment as they cackled their way through the process.

With one minute to spare, she was ready, hair pulled back into a ponytail, a coat of mascara on her eyelashes, wearing leggings, a T-shirt, and a ballcap that she could use to block the annoying sun from her face.

"Are you a vampire?" Lea demanded when she emerged into their living room.

"What?"

"You're pale, and there's no way you'll catch any sun unless you show some skin."

"I'm fine, thank you for your concern." She scowled and snatched up a cookie remaining from last night's raid on the check-in counter.

After brunch, and having given in to the champagne cocktail that Lea had ordered for her, the trio headed toward some local shops.

Their first stop was a high-end lingerie store.

While Leaundra looked for a white garter belt and stockings, Sydney found a black pleated micromini latex skirt that would look fabulous with the new shoes that Master Michael had bought her.

She also purchased a bolero jacket made of the same material. It had a thick silver zipper and plenty of buckles.

"You're looking like a chickie who wants to get some when she gets back to Colorado."

"Does this mean you're going to see him?" Jacqueline asked.

"I..."

"Did he contact you?" Lea demanded.

"Yes." Grinning, unable to help herself, she showed them a picture of Chewie and the new, replacement shoes.

"Holy shit. If it doesn't work out—"

"*You're getting married,*" Sydney and Jacqueline interrupted Lea.

"I'm just saying."

"Don't," Jacqueline warned.

In the end, Sydney also paid for Lea's lingerie. "It'll be my gift for the bridal shower."

"Thank you!" Lea kissed Sydney's cheek.

It would save her from buying a more expensive gift later because she'd run out of time to shop. Now she just had to land another gig in order to pay her credit card bill.

Toward the end of the day, while they were enjoying Italian food at a highly rated restaurant, Sydney checked her phone.

Nothing.

Alone in her bedroom, she laid out her two-piece outfit on the bedspread, snapped a photo of her ensemble, then sent the image to him.

Afterward, she and the girls took a moonlit stroll along the beach.

By the time she returned to the hotel, he'd responded, with a picture of his own in which he'd superimposed the shoes over her skirt and jacket.

They still hadn't discussed seeing each other.

The night before her flight home, he sent a message showing a snapshot of a flogger hanging from the fence in front of his house.

And it wasn't just any whip. It was a red one, the same shade as her new shoes. And, God help her, the same shade as she hoped he would turn her skin.

A shudder chased its way through her body.

Suddenly she wished she didn't have to guide a multi-day hike along the Continental Divide when she returned to Colorado. *Damn it.* He was making it difficult to resist him.

For a million reasons, she shouldn't return to the Eagle's Bend Ranch. He was a Dom, not a Top, and he eventually wanted to remarry and have children. And she would never be a woman who wanted that.

But still, a wayward, wicked part of her was desperate to see him again.

Rationalizing that as long as he agreed that they were just sceneing, no harm could come from playing with each other, she replied with her return date, and she added she wouldn't have cell signal for much of the upcoming time.

He answered that he was looking forward to seeing her whenever it worked out for her.

Her body tingled, making her wish the hookup would happen tomorrow.

A couple of days later, after she and her friends parted ways at the airport, Sydney traveled back to Colorado, becoming more excited for the future with every passing mile.

She only spent about twelve hours at her Evergreen condo, just long enough to wash her clothes then pack for the extended hike.

Sydney ended up spending the next few days being somewhat of a glorified cook and pack mule. Her clients were younger than she was and were on their honeymoon. They were focused on each other, and three was definitely a crowd. For the first time in years, she found herself lonely for the type of easy companionship that the newlyweds shared. And honestly, part of her time with Master Michael had been like that.

What would it be like if she enjoyed more time like that with him?

At night, she knew the couple was trying to be quiet, but the tent walls were thin, and the mountains were otherwise silent. She spent hours tossing and turning on her cot, fantasizing about Master Michael forcing her to yield to his will.

Not soon enough, the excursion drew to a close.

Under a cloudy afternoon sky, they returned to their vehicles at the trailhead.

The appreciative couple had tipped her a shocking amount of money. The envelope of cash would pay off her credit card and put her in a much better financial position to survive the lean period between the end of summer and fall activities and the beginning of the ski season.

She generally led some autumn mountain trips to see the aspen trees change color, but after the first good snow or wind event, that ended. As long as the weather held, she could still arrange biking or hiking, especially at Moab.

Often, she headed south and looked for other work, but this money would allow her to take an unplanned vacation.

She cranked up the music, trying to drown out the idea of having extra time to spend with Master Michael in late fall. After all, she hadn't heard from him in days. And that caused even more crazy thoughts to collide. What if he had gone to the Den last weekend and found someone else to submit to him?

How had she gone from wanting a one-night Dom to fearing that he was seeing someone else?

When she was finally in cell phone range, she exited I-70 near a small coffee and ice cream shop.

The notifications screen was all but bare. Leaundra had left a voicemail with the tentative date of her wedding, a year in the future.

Sydney had a handful of emails, including one from the Den with a list of upcoming activities.

She also had a message from her friend Vanessa, asking if she was going to be attending an upcoming event at the Den where a new entertainer — singer Zephyr 'Zeph' Rockwell — would be welcomed into the club.

At one time, rocker Evan C had been used to provide the entertainment, but after he'd been an ass to Master Alexander Monahan's new sub, Master Damien had revoked the star's membership.

Along with several other people, Sydney had cheered the decision.

But that was the end of her messages.

There was nothing from Master Michael.

With a disappointed sigh, she dropped her purse on the console then headed inside for a mocha latte drizzled with raspberry syrup.

Figuring that Murphy's Law would be at work and that she would have missed his call while she was getting her drink, she picked up her phone.

Still nothing.

Exhaling her frustration, she dropped her head against the seat back.

Then, with her phone close by, Sydney finished the drive home.

Back at her condo, she dragged in her backpack and went to toss it on the bed. But the outfit she'd bought in Miami was in the middle of the mattress, waiting. In her haste to meet the newlyweds, she hadn't put it away. Now the sexy pieces seemed to taunt her.

She wanted to wear them for Master Michael.

The harder she fought to keep thoughts of him out of her head, the stronger the memories became. It was as if she could feel his belt scorching her skin. The welts that had adorned her buttocks and thighs after her time at the Eagle's Bend Ranch had long since healed, and she craved new ones.

Tamping down her desires, she hung the outfit in her closet, then shut the door.

Afterward, she unloaded the car and stowed the camping equipment in the garage.

Even after she had spent a ridiculous amount of time in a much-needed warm shower, the damn phone remained silent.

Now what?

She reminded herself that a modern, empowered woman would contact him.

After stalling another hour, she grabbed her phone and scrolled to his contact information. Her heart thundered. Why did a simple telephone call matter so much?

Finally, gathering her courage, half hoping she'd get his voicemail, she touched the green icon.

"Welcome home, Sydney," he said by way of greeting, his rich, gruff voice spilling into her ear. "Does this mean you want your pretty little ass reddened?"

Chapter Seven

Master Michael's sexy, dominant purr melted her from the inside out, and she collapsed her shoulders against the refrigerator.

"Glad to be home?"

Colorado was a great base, but she'd always considered it a temporary place to stay while she decided what she wanted to do next.

This time, though, she'd been happy to return, no matter how small and unimaginative her home was. She'd told herself it had nothing to do with seeing him again, but she knew she'd been lying to herself. "I am."

For a moment, she paused. It would be easy to fall into an inane conversation. When he'd answered the phone, he'd called her Sydney, rather than by the nickname he'd used during their time together.

"Thank you for asking, Sir. I spent a few days in Miami with my girlfriends from college, then I guided a pair of honeymooners on a hike of the Continental Divide. They couldn't wait for me to pitch the tents at night, and it took them a while to get up in the mornings. I had a lot of free time."

"Same for me. I occupied myself by looking at your new shoes and imagining you in them."

Her breath vaporized. "I was thinking about that flogger."

"It was custom-made for you. I have others, but I wanted you to be able to endure a long, long session."

She allowed the appliance to take more of her weight. "I noticed it matches the outfit," she said, aiming for a casualness she was nowhere close to feeling.

"Always an added bonus." He allowed silence to gather for a few seconds before speaking again. "I'm glad you called."

Her shoulders loosened as tension unwound. How did he always know the right thing to say? "I didn't know if it would be okay."

"My Sydney, I'm on the porch drinking a glass of wine and looking at the fence."

Her heart missed its next beat.

"I wasn't sure when you'd be back, and I also suspected you needed time to sort through your thoughts. I wasn't going to call you, but I was hoping you'd contact me."

So he'd been waiting for her to make the next move. She appreciated that he wasn't trying to crowd her. By calling the Den and getting her contact information, he'd reached out and let her know he was interested in her.

"Did you masturbate while you were gone?"

What? His question caught her off guard, so much so that she answered without hesitating. "No." She pushed herself upright and paced the kitchen floor. "I was too tired when I got to bed in Miami—there's quite a nightlife."

"And on the hike, the couple didn't inspire you?"

She imagined his smile. "That's not the right word. I was frustrated more than anything."

"Tell me why," he encouraged in that seductive, thrilling voice of his.

When he spoke to her in that tone, she'd do anything for him. "I want to have a real experience, not just a fantasy."

"I can certainly arrange that."

Her insides turned molten.

"When are you available?"

She wanted to say *now, if not sooner,* but she tried to act nonchalant. "I'm fairly flexible at the moment, except for my upcoming mud race."

"You mentioned that."

"It's challenging and fun, and since we do it to benefit one of my favorite charities, I never miss a year. The part where I crawl beneath barbed wire is my favorite."

"Playing with you will force me to be creative."

Right now, things seemed perfect. She spun around. Maybe Jacqueline had been right. Sydney spent so much time thinking about the future that she often robbed the moment of its pleasures. "I have no complaints, Sir. So far."

"I've said before that you like to live on the edge."

She laughed. "True story."

"How's tomorrow for you?" he asked.

Yes. Yes, yes, yes, yes, *yes.* "Sounds good."

"You're welcome here, or I am happy to come to you."

"Thanks for the offer, but I prefer to drive up." As always, she wanted the ability to leave when she desired.

"Of course."

"What time would you like me to arrive?"

"How about early afternoon? Do you remember the code for the gate? Or if you want to call when you're in Winter Park, I'll meet you somewhere and we could have lunch."

While that sounded tempting, she was anxious to scene. "Thanks for the offer, but I'm good. I remember the combination."

"Would you like me to text the specific directions?"

Since it had gotten a little confusing after leaving the main road, she appreciated the offer. "That would be great, Sir."

"Bring the new outfit. Oh, and Sydney?"

"Sir?"

"Tonight? Don't masturbate. I want you aroused and frustrated when you get here."

His voice, so masterful, chilled her. Until this moment, she hadn't been thinking about touching herself. Now the idea consumed her.

"Please acknowledge what I said."

Are you serious? "But..." Knowing she was going to see him ratcheted her desire up to a whole new level. "It's been ten days."

"Then a few more hours won't matter a bit."

She sighed. "Of course you're right." Her own words gave her an illicit thrill. She insisted she wasn't a sub, but when he gave her commands like that, part of her melted, as if doing what he said—even outside a scene—were the most natural thing in the world. "I won't masturbate, Sir."

"You have no idea how much your obedience pleases me."

"Thank you, Sir."

After the call ended, her skin seemed to hum with energy. Knowing she had to burn it off or go crazy, she changed into running shorts and shoes, then put on a sports bra and lightweight top. Finally, she pulled her hair into a ponytail before exiting the condo.

To warm up her body, she started with a gentle jog down the street before crossing over and heading toward Evergreen Lake.

A path encircled the picturesque forty-acre lake, and she entered on the dam side. She zoned out as she turned up the dial on her pace. It didn't take long for her to regulate her breathing and work up a sweat as she neared the Lake House. Sydney hardly noticed the other pedestrians or bicyclists, or the elk and deer grazing in the brush. She startled a rabbit at one point, but that barely distracted her.

Finally, more than twenty minutes later, breathless, she slowed to a walk for the trek back to her place.

Once she'd cooled off, she took another shower, then after changing into pajamas, fell onto the bed.

The thoughts she'd been trying to outrun—those of Master Michael—plowed into her, in rich, vivid detail as she recalled him spanking her at the Den, claiming her in his home. And now that he'd ordered her not to touch herself, there was nothing she wanted to do more.

After tossing and turning for an hour, noticing how needy her pussy felt, she threw back the sheet in frustration and climbed out of bed.

She grabbed a blanket and went onto the patio to stare at the sky in her version of meditation. Instead of counting sheep, she counted stars. She got to the high five hundreds before managing to harness her thoughts.

When she reached the mid six hundreds, she started to drift off. Sometime before dawn, she woke up chilled and made her way back inside to bed. By the time she reawakened, the sun was beating through her window, warming her up.

After frying a couple of eggs, drinking half a pot of coffee, and updating her website, suggesting some creative late-summer outings, and adding a lovely testimony supplied by the newlyweds, she hit the shower.

As she stood under the spray, contemplating her trip to Master Michael's ranch, she was suddenly unnerved.

Last time, she and Master Michael had spent time at the Den before making the journey to his place. This time, it was daylight. Though she knew his expectations, she was less certain how to behave. Should she wear her outfit? That seemed a bit much given that she would arrive in the early afternoon.

Shorts seemed too casual. And at his elevation, the air could be chillier than it was down here. Immediately she discarded the idea of a dress that would demand sandals. After her experience with Chewie and trying to navigate the uneven terrain, she knew how ridiculous heels were.

A trip to a working ranch demanded boots and jeans, and probably a hat of some kind. Except, she was going there for one purpose—to get her butt spanked.

With a sigh, she threw an assortment of options in an overnight bag—not that she was planning to stay more than a few hours. She simply wanted to be prepared. Or that was what she told herself.

Following a lot of consideration and some amount of anguish, going through her drawers and flipping aside numerous hangers, she opted for a form-fitting hiking skirt. Then she pulled on a lightweight summer shirt with a black bra beneath. Because she knew she was seeing him, her whole body was already sensitized.

After adding her sexy new outfit to her bag, Sydney slipped on a pair of sturdy flat sandals meant for trekking. They were serviceable enough for his rugged environment, but also comfortable enough to drive in.

When she climbed behind the wheel and lowered the windows to let out some of the daytime heat, she sent him a text message to let him know she was on her way.

The drive took forever, something more to do with her excitement and anticipation at having her sexual desires fulfilled than the actual miles involved. She was glad the road demanded her full attention. At least it kept her from obsessing.

Mostly.

Views from Berthoud Pass stole her breath, and Winter Park was streaming with summer visitors. As she passed through the lush green, high-mountain valley, she glimpsed occasional clumps of wildflowers.

Once she left the main road, her pulse picked up a few extra beats. She knew it wasn't from the altitude since she hadn't had a single problem when she was standing on top of the Continental Divide.

As she braked to a stop near the gate, a tall, lanky man of indeterminate age slid off a utility vehicle.

She entered the property, then kept her foot on the brake as he ambled over.

"Welcome to Eagle's Bend. I'm Jeb, the ranch foreman." He touched the brim of a well-worn cowboy hat, its creased leather discolored, perhaps from numerous hours beneath the relentless mountain sun.

"Michael asked me to keep an eye out for you." He extended a calloused, weathered hand in her direction.

The gesture was considerate of both of them. "It's nice to meet you. Thank you."

"It's a pleasure. I'll let you be on your way, ma'am."

In her rearview mirror, she watched him pick up a two-way communication device, say something, then hop back on the motorized vehicle, taking off in the direction of the bunkhouse.

Master Michael was waiting near the fence, one boot heel hooked behind him on the lowest rail, with a look so sexy it was probably outlawed in half the world. His ever-present hat was angled slightly forward.

Jeans rode low on his slim hips, and as usual, his shirtsleeves were folded back to the elbow. He appeared at ease, lord and master of all he surveyed. And right now, he was looking at her.

Adrenaline tripped through her.

As she parked beneath a tree, he pushed away from the fence.

When he reached her vehicle, he opened her door and offered his hand.

Her heart fluttered as she accepted.

She couldn't imagine Lewis ever behaving with such elegant manners. Had she judged Master Michael, and maybe others, too hastily?

"You look fabulous," he said.

"I..." She pulled her hand away and nervously smoothed the front of her skirt. "Didn't know what to wear."

"This is perfect. You did bring the outfit that's kept me up nights?"

"I wouldn't dare forget it, Sir. It's in my blue duffel bag."

"I'll grab it," he said, opening the back door. "Anything else?"

"No. Everything I need is in there."

He nodded.

"Jeb met me at the gate. Nice man."

"He's been on the ranch since before I was born. Couldn't manage without him." After closing both doors, he indicated that she should precede him to the house.

Before heading down the path, she glanced around. "Where's the petty thief?"

"Chewie is annoying the hands who are checking the fence."

"Better them than me." But she didn't mean it. She had already developed an affection for the miniature nuisance.

"I'll take your bag upstairs," he said as they entered the house. "Would you like to go with it?"

She laughed. "Was that your subtle way of telling me to change my clothes, Sir?"

"Actually, I was asking if you needed to freshen up. I was going to invite you to join me for a glass of lemonade."

Lemonade? She blinked. *What about sceneing?*

"I thought it was polite to allow you to settle in before ripping off your clothes and bending you over."

"Screw politeness. Sir."

He pushed the brim of his hat back a little, far enough that she had a better look at his sizzling green eyes. "But now that you mention it…" He dropped her bag on the kitchen floor. The resulting thud echoed through the open space.

Under his scrutiny, she grew warm.

"What kind of panties are you wearing?"

Oh, yes. He was one hundred percent Dom. This was what she'd craved. "Boy shorts, Sir."

"Like the first night?"

"Yes." And as she recalled, he'd pocketed the panties and never returned them.

"What color?"

"Pink." She smiled. "And this particular pair is my favorite." The edges were lacy, making the stretchy material serviceable, but also cute. "Are you planning to add them to your collection?"

"That's a hell of an idea."

His footfalls resounded off the hardwood planks, and her heart thumped a terrific tattoo.

"Raise your skirt for me."

Her hands suddenly trembling from nerves, from excitement, she did as he said.

"Be my good girl and turn and spread your legs as far apart as you can."

Not knowing what to expect made her delirious. She hadn't been here two minutes, and already he'd taken control instead of spending half an hour on inane pleasantries.

Then in a great surprise, he took hold of her boy shorts and yanked them up hard between the crack of her ass, making her gasp from the shock.

"That's better," he said. "Your buttocks are beautiful, unblemished by a single mark."

It had been too long.

"They won't look that way when you leave."

A thrill danced through her. This was what she wanted. "I figured as much, Sir."

"You're going to stay in position for me, aren't you?"

Before she could respond, he reached one hand in front of her to capture the front of the fabric.

He worked the material back and forth between her folds, abrading her most sensitive area. Having no option, she began to move in time with him.

"You're getting your panties damp, naughty girl."

"Yes, Sir."

He increased the friction, and she began to whimper.

Staying in place became more and more difficult as he worked his magic over her. "Oh, Sir… Sir, Sir, *Sir!*"

"Did you masturbate?"

"No, Sir! I promise."

"Then this has to feel maddening."

"It does. Very much so, Sir."

"How long has it been since you came?"

How did he expect her to think? "When I was here last, Sir. Not since."

He all but lifted her from the ground, making her squeal.

"You must want an orgasm."

"I do. Please. Please, Sir."

"You're compliant when you think you're going to get what you want, aren't you?"

In this moment, she'd agree to anything.

Abruptly, he released her, leaving her maddeningly on edge.

In frustration, she squeezed her eyes shut.

"Stay where you are."

Though her pussy throbbed, she followed his order.

"That's it."

Please, please spank me.

But he didn't. Instead, he left her panties where they were, wedged tightly between her legs, and lowered her skirt back into place.

"Are you serious right now, Sir?" she demanded when he stood in front of her.

"One hundred percent."

She pulled her hair back into a momentary ponytail before once again dropping the strands.

"I think I invited you to join me for a lemonade."

Had she ever met a more annoying Dominant? Especially since the only thing she wanted was some impact play and a dozen or so climaxes.

"Feel free to freshen up, if you wish." With a devilish smile, he stroked her cheek before picking up her bag and carrying it up the stairs.

Her whole body vibrating with need, she followed him to his suite.

After placing her belongings on a closet shelf, he faced her. "I'll be on the patio, and I expect that your panties will be in this same position when you come outside." Intimidatingly, he folded his arms. "Do I need to stay here and watch you to be sure you don't do anything to...alleviate your discomfort?"

"Maybe, Sir."

"In that case..." He planted his feet shoulder-width apart.

From other Doms, that kind of sass would have earned her a spanking. But he wasn't a man she could goad, and she didn't like it. "Actually, uhm... I'm good. You can believe what I say, Sir."

"By your own admission, that may not be true."

Because she couldn't keep her mouth shut, she'd gotten herself in a predicament. She should have known better. After all, she'd told her friends that he tortured her by withholding what she wanted most.

Stubbornly, he even followed her into the bathroom.

Wishing she'd had even a few minutes of privacy, she finished drying her hands.

"Shall we?"

Managing to keep her mouth shut this time, she nodded and followed him back downstairs, then outside where a tray waited.

There were two tall glasses and a pitcher filled with the refreshing-looking lemonade. Off to the side was a board topped with olives, cheeses, and meats. "You've thought of everything."

"I know how long the drive can be."

With old-world manners, he waited until she sat before taking his chair.

Deciding she might as well relax because the damned Dominant was going to move at his own glacial pace, she kicked off her shoes and sat back, feet curled beneath her, and surveyed the landscape. "This is a totally different view than the one from the front of the house," she observed. "Far fewer trees." Since there were no buildings, it was much more serene.

"The river convinced my grandfather to buy, but he built the house over here so that he could take advantage of all the vistas, and this has a beauty all of its own. May I pour you a glass of lemonade? It may be a bit tart for your taste, but it's refreshing."

"You made it yourself?"

"It's from my grandmother's recipe. And it's one I enjoy."

"You definitely know what you like, Sir. I'm getting that message loud and clear."

"About time," he fired back pointedly.

With a tiny sigh, she accepted the glass and took a sip. "Oh my God, it's wonderful. Tart, as you say, but sweet at the same time. Best lemonade I've ever had."

"I keep trying to convince you to trust me with your well-being, Sydney."

"As you know, Sir, that's something I have little interest in giving. Nothing personal." Though the admission made her a little uncomfortable, she wanted to be straight with him. "I came here for one reason."

"You'll get that. And I'll eventually earn your trust."

Which was suddenly getting a little too complicated for her.

"Challenge accepted?"

Since it wasn't a bet she could lose, she nodded.

"Please stand, turn away from me, lift your skirt, bend over, and grab your ankles."

Since the patio was on the opposite side from any of the ranch's buildings, they had privacy. Happily, she slid her drink onto the table then stood, her back to him, and slowly pulled up her skirt.

Since he'd been such a torment, she took her sweet time getting herself into the position he required.

Master Michael left her there for long moments, the sun kissing her skin, a gentle breeze cooling her between the legs.

Slowly, he stood and came up behind her to slide a finger beneath the elastic of her panties then between her labia. "Your pussy is so very wet. I might think you enjoy me withholding orgasm."

She exhaled her frustration. "It's anticipation of completion, Sir."

He continued to move back and forth until she swayed in time with his touch. "You've got a beautiful body, Sydney."

"Thank you, Sir."

"So responsive." He grasped her underwear in much the same way that he had earlier in the kitchen, see-sawing the material harshly over her clit.

Holding her ankles was nearly impossible as he abraded her pussy. She wanted to stand up, to face him, ride his thigh like she had in the river.

Deftly, he brought her to the brink.

Wondering if there was any way she could manage a small orgasm without him knowing it, she squeezed her eyes shut.

Right then, he snapped the elastic waistband of her panties, and the tiny prick of pain distracted her from the imminent climax.

"You're close," he said.

"Yes. Yes, Sir." *Very*. She lifted her heels off the ground, unsure if he would really continue to withhold what she wanted, or whether he was testing her.

"Good." He moved faster.

Her legs began to quake. "Oh, oh, Sir. Oh!"

"Would you like to orgasm?"

"Yes! Please, Sir."

He stopped.

She let out a shaky, vexed sigh. Tears stung the backs of her eyes.

"You're my good girl, Sydney," he murmured. "You're not arguing with me."

He couldn't possibly have any idea how difficult that was for her.

Shocking her, he caught a handful of her hair at the root. But because of the way he held her, it didn't hurt.

"Stand."

Master Michael helped her, but before she could face him, he kept his hand where it was, preventing her from moving.

"Now kneel for me."

Again, he was there to help her.

"Legs a little farther apart," he said, finally releasing his grip on her hair.

Her skirt still around her waist, she complied. Desperately she wished she could look at him so she could decipher his expression. But everything he did was intentional.

Her skirt hung askew, and a gentle breeze cooled her heated pussy.

"Thank me."

"For what, Sir?"

"My attentions."

"But I didn't get to —" She shut her mouth. "Thank you, Sir."

"I'm not ready for you to come yet."

"Anything you say, Sir." He was behaving much more like a Dom than a Top… And it was as annoying as hell.

He moved around to stand in front of her, his crotch at eye level.

"Now you're going to suck my dick," he told her. "And you're going to do a good job of it."

That she liked to do. She fumbled with his belt, then the fastening on his jeans, and he offered no help, seeming to enjoy watching her struggle.

After finally freeing him, she greedily sucked his cockhead into her mouth. She loved the clean taste of him and his intoxicatingly male scent.

Since he was already semihard, it took no time to get him fully erect. Power pulsed through her as she aroused him.

Master Michael pumped his hips a bit, forcing her to take more of his length. Then as she shifted to get a better angle, he withdrew.

Puzzled, Sydney sat back on her calves and frowned up at him. Was he really going to spend the whole night frustrating her?

"You're great at that." His eyelids were partially lowered, and from that she knew that he, too, would prefer they continue.

"I am happy to finish you off, Sir."

"I'd like that…later. There's something unutterably rewarding about a state of denial, isn't there?"

"I've been told it's uncomfortable for men."

"It can be," he agreed.

"So then…?"

"I don't ask you to suffer anything that I'm unwilling to endure."

His response surprised her. A thought like that would have never entered Lewis's head.

As she watched, Master Michael stroked his cock a few times, then readjusted himself, zipped his pants and re-fastened his jeans. "Your new shoes are in the bedroom closet."

"Would you like me to model my new outfit?"

"Later."

"Sir?"

"For now, I'd like to see you only in the shoes."

Eagerness shot through her.

"I don't want any article of clothing getting in the way while I flog you."

The sexy, rough tone to his words almost made her come.

He offered his hand to help her back to her feet, and she took it.

"They're in a box on a shelf near your bag."

"Yes, Sir."

"Meet me back out here, wearing just the shoes. You've got three minutes."

Which was barely enough time to dart up the stairs and manage everything he'd asked.

"If you keep me waiting..."

The words — threat — hung between them. He didn't need to finish his statement. He might not spank her, but he most certainly would withhold her much-needed orgasm. "I'll be right back, Sir."

"You're down to two minutes and forty-five seconds."

Chapter Eight

Contemplating her, Michael watched Sydney hurry away.

Gregorio and Damien had both been right — the lovely Sydney Wallace was a challenge. But when he'd called the Den to get her contact information, Damien had reacted favorably, suggesting she might be worth the effort.

Both men interacted with all the club's members, and the house's atmosphere lent itself to intimate discussions.

Damien had said he suspected she had a tough outer shell to protect herself. Gregorio believed she acted like a brat so that she could collect more spankings without ever opening herself up emotionally. Not that he blamed her. After all, he had been the one to find her a jeweler to cut off her collar. Gregorio had confirmed Damien's hunch. Sydney's reputation was a carefully constructed protective veneer.

Since she'd left, Michael had spent a lot of time thinking about her and considering the best way to approach and ensnare her. He'd ordered the flogger and new shoes for her. That may not have been his best idea. The very thought of seeing her in them constantly diverted blood from his brain.

He'd contacted her while she was traveling, but only a few times. Though he'd intended to pique her interest, he hadn't wanted her to feel cornered and skitter away.

He'd made plenty of mistakes in his marriage regarding his expectations. His work since, with horses, had taught him a few things about patience. Even when he wanted to rush things—especially then—he forced himself to take a mental step back.

The day his divorce had become final, he'd grabbed a pricy bottle of Bonds whiskey from the liquor cabinet. As he'd downed his third shot, he'd vowed never again to fall deeply in love without taking his time, getting to know someone on every level.

And yet that would have been so easy with the delectable and determined Sydney.

He'd never connected sexually with a woman the way he did her. She wanted him to cover her skin with leather kisses and devour her in bed.

The trouble was, she didn't want anything more.

Michael was a man of the land, entrusted by his ancestors to protect and care for it. And she was a woman of the world, living for adventure.

And eventually, she'd move on to a new Dom, or someone better for her—a Top.

Unfortunately, she was already starting to matter to him, and he'd enjoyed all the time they'd spent together—at the river, drinking lemonade, showering, cooking.

He'd caught glimpses of the vulnerable woman beneath her pain, and he wanted her heart and soul laid bare to him, to earn the trust that she'd vowed never again to give.

A loud squeal rent the air.

He grinned. Evidently she'd found the shoes. Her unbridled joy made him smile. Truthfully, he'd do a lot to keep her happy.

While she was still occupied, he grabbed the flogger and a ball gag from a box he'd put together. He laid both on top of the table.

Last night, he'd spent the better part of an hour cutting rope to the length perfect to secure her to the wooden fence. Now he took all four pieces and placed them side by side.

When she rejoined him, shoulders pulled back, chin angled, blonde hair spilling over her shoulders, his mouth fell open.

He prided himself on the fact that he had a hell of an imagination, but with Sydney it hadn't been nearly wild enough. "That's a hell of a getup, Sydney." *My girl. My sub.* The tall red shoes with spiky metal studs on the heels made her calves appear extraordinarily shapely. The full-frontal sight of her nearly did him in.

She'd put a touch of scandalous gloss on her lips, making them appear fuller and more kissable. Her small pink nipples were pebbling beautifully under his scrutiny, and her bare pussy drew his gaze toward the juncture of her thighs. The whole package, including her compact, athletic body, made him glad to be male.

"Do you like the shoes, Sir?"

"*Fuck me,*" he said.

She grinned saucily. "I think that can be arranged."

Now who is in control? "I'm going to give Chewie an extra carrot tonight," he said. "I'm glad she absconded with your sandal."

"I'm definitely not complaining, Sir."

He severed the connection of their gazes so he could focus on something other than his physical response to her nakedness. "We need to check off the last box on your 'all of the above' answer from the last time you were here. It's time you were tied to the fence, Sydney."

Her lips parted and she swallowed a breath. "Yes, Sir."

That was the tone he needed from her — aroused and compliant.

"Now?" she asked.

"No. Since you'll be totally tied to the fence, unable to get away, we have a few things to discuss first."

"Okay."

"I'll be using rawhide as rope, instead of easy-release handcuffs. It will take longer to bind you and longer to get you out, especially if you panic."

"I won't panic, Sir. I've been tied before." Then her gaze landed on the flogger. "Is that the one you sent me a picture of?"

"Would you like to hold it?"

"Do you mind, Sir?"

"I ordered it for you. It's yours." He picked it up and offered it to her. "Like the shoes, you're welcome to take it with you."

"It's beautiful. I love the color!"

"I thought it might suit you."

She took the hilt and shook it, scattering the falls. "The strands are thicker than I'm accustomed to seeing."

"It's made from deer hide," he explained. "The pain is meant to be thuddy rather than stingy. I think you'll like it. I'll be able to use it on you longer than I could with any other flogger I have."

"But I'll still get marks, right?"

"Do you want them?"

"Yes," she said. She met his gaze with her open, readable blue eyes. When she looked at him like that, she had no artifice.

The raw hunger inflamed him.

"Please," she added.

"I live to serve," he told her with a quick grin.

"Thank you, Sir."

The sincerity in her voice and the simmer of desire in her eyes were all the reward he'd ever need.

She offered him back the implement, then she looked at his makeshift toy box. "Uh, is that a gag?" she asked.

"It is."

"For me?"

"Is that a problem?" He watched her reaction. The fact that she'd taken one step away telegraphed her nervousness, but she hadn't refused outright, or used a safe word, meaning she wasn't distraught. "We're outside. I want you to be able to completely let go without worrying. Though no one will rescue you, regardless. I thought you might be more comfortable if your voice is muffled. But I'll still be able to hear your sobs."

Without speaking, eyebrows knitted together, she regarded him.

"I don't think it's going to look very flattering, Sir."

Wryly, he said, "Other than the aesthetics, do you have any issues with being gagged?"

"No, Sir."

"Good. Because I think it's hot when a submissive drools all over the place."

She crinkled her nose.

"If you don't want to wear it, you have a safe word that will always be honored."

"I…" She didn't finish.

"Tell me your slow word?"

"Turtle."

It was the first time she hadn't broken it into two mocking syllables. Progress. *Welcome* progress at that. "And your safe word?"

"Everest."

"Would you like to use either?"

"No." Determined finality rang in her words.

"Nothing matters more to me than your well-being."

"Right now, I'm fine. Just…"

Waiting, he arched an eyebrow.

"I'll do anything if it gets me an orgasm."

"You'll earn it."

She exhaled, expressing her emotions.

"Are you being a brat?"

"No, Sir. That was me agreeing with you." She smiled brilliantly. "I understand your confusion."

Turning away so she didn't see his smile, he picked up a scrap of fabric that was nestled at the bottom of the box. He extended the remnants of the red cotton bandanna toward her. "I want you to hold on to this. Since you'll be gagged, it will take the place of your safe word. Drop it and the scene will immediately stop, and I'll remove the gag. If you need to be released from the bondage, I'll see to it right away. I'll have safety scissors in my back pocket."

She nodded. "I understand."

"Any questions?"

"Only one, Sir."

He waited.

"Can we freaking get on with it?" Once again, she delivered a bright, sunshiny smile to take the heat out of her words.

"You do understand that impatience won't get things to move faster?" He waited for effect. "And it will make me go easier on you."

"You, Sir, are a terrible spoilsport."

He captured her chin in his hand. "Would you like to be tied up and flogged, or would you prefer to suck my dick all afternoon?"

Although she couldn't move her head, she managed to look down at his waistband purposefully. "As always, all of the above, Sir."

Christ. So much for being the rule-maker. Or issuing a pseudo-threat. It seemed he was the one at a constant disadvantage. "Let's get on with it." He released his grip on her. "Your back to the fence."

"Yes, Sir." Despite the ridiculous height of the shoes, she executed a beautiful, flawless pivot, then headed down the concrete path.

He wouldn't tell her, but it had been recently poured, just for her.

Captivated, he watched the sway of Sydney's hips as she purposefully moved to the fence. *Hot damn.*

If she were his, he'd constantly keep her in those shoes, hire out all the chores, pay a business manager, and spend all day playing with her as his sex toy.

The thought was impossible. In winter, she'd need different shoes.

After snatching up the temporary toy box, he walked toward her. *That* wasn't easy when all he wanted to do was take her inside and throw her beneath him.

She'd already spread her arms wide and legs apart, and she was facing him, watching him, waiting for him.

He had to remind himself he was the big, bad Dom.

Michael kept his gaze focused on her, and she never glanced away. "We'll do the gag last," he informed her.

"Anything you say, Sir."

"You may or may not get to orgasm."

"I..." She opened her mouth for a moment. Resolutely she closed it again. "Yes, Sir."

He raised a brow and waited.

"Whatever pleases you, Sir."

"That time it sounded as if you meant it."

"I do."

His chest constricted. In this moment, he'd have done anything he could to satisfy her.

After removing his hat, he hung it from a vertical post.

"You make the littlest things seem so sexy, Sir."

He knelt in front of her and looped the rawhide strips around her right thigh several times before securing her to the wood behind her. "How's that?"

"Unyielding, Sir."

"Too uncomfortable?"

"Isn't it supposed to be?"

He shook his head and looked up. "Absolutely not. I don't want you focused on the bondage, I want you surrendered to the moment."

"Honestly, Sir, it feels fine. I would tell you if it didn't. I promise."

"Good. I want to be able to land a strike or two on your pussy."

"*Oh?*" She pursed her lips before breathing in and exhaling a jagged breath.

"Now your wrists."

Afterward, he rechecked all the bonds to ensure she was properly affixed. Though he didn't want her to pull away and get injured, he also needed to be sure her circulation would not be compromised.

Satisfied, he took a step back. "Beautiful." And she was. She seemed serene, more so than she generally did. Being tied up suited her.

On some level, he understood that. Her struggle might provide her with a physical release. And that gave her tacit permission to let go emotionally. For someone like Sydney, that was probably true freedom. He was glad to take her on the journey.

Holding up the gag, he returned to her. "Is there anything you need me to know?"

"No, Sir."

"Every part of you is available to me?"

"It is, Sir."

"I will not go near your face or your neck," he said.

"Thank you, Sir. That's thoughtful."

"Now open your mouth." He inserted the ball between her teeth. Since there was only a small part inside, he commanded, "Wider."

She waited a moment, stalling, but he outlasted her.

When she relaxed slightly, he forced it in a bit farther, then told her, "Tip your head forward slightly." Getting her hair out of the way of the buckle was a challenge. "Sorry," he said when he accidentally pulled a few strands.

"It's all right," she mumbled, or at least that's what he thought she'd said.

He adjusted the fit so the straps wouldn't slip. Now it was perfect. She wouldn't be able to properly form any words, and her cries would be stifled. "Damn, you are a sexy woman, Sydney."

Normally he'd like her mouth to be free, but it really was a turn-on seeing that big device forcing her jaw apart. "Do I need to adjust anything?"

She shook her head.

After placing the scissors nearby, he picked up the flogger and shook it out, much like she had done earlier, only he did it with more of a snap to his wrist so the strands jumped. "Your entire body is mine."

In quick succession, she blinked several times.

He trailed the leather strands across her shoulders, then between her breasts, making her shudder.

"I'm going to give you some time to get used to it. I will warm up your body with a number of strokes before increasing the pressure. I know you want some welts. I'll try to make sure you get them, but I also don't want you bruised or too sore for me to use you in other ways."

Her breathing increased.

And when he ran his hand over her pussy, he found she was already damp. "Nice," he said.

Intentionally, he masturbated her with his fingers for a few moments then dragged the hilt of the flogger over her clit.

Jerking, she strained against his bindings.

He kept his gaze on her, tuning into her breathing and her expressions. It was as if the rest of the world fell away.

Michael placed the end of the dampened flogger against her pussy. "Be a good girl and fuck it for me."

He held it still and reached around her to give her rear end some support while she tried to work it inside her.

By wriggling, she took a small amount of the handle.

He eased it out. then slid it in again, a little farther. "Shall I use it on you as if it were a dildo?"

The words she attempted were garbled.

"This is a very pretty pussy, Sydney," he told her while he crouched in front of her.

She moaned.

"Right now, this moment, whose is it?"

Silently she thrust her pelvis toward him.

As a reward, he gave her more of the handle as he looked up at her.

Her breasts were lovely, and her nipples were extraordinarily hard. Her legs quivered, and the pleading in her eyes made the blue luminous.

He leaned in and licked her clit. To her credit, she didn't try to sneak in an orgasm, though she probably was figuring she could get away with it because she couldn't ask permission.

Michael was careful, making certain she didn't come from his tongue and ensuring she was lubricated enough for him to fuck her with the makeshift toy.

Once he had it all the way inside her, he licked her faster and faster as he filled her.

Her body shook from silent sobs.

He'd be willing to bet she'd never wanted an orgasm like she wanted one now. He planned to make it worth her wait. "That's my girl," he told her. "Hold off. Do it for me."

She went rigid and she sucked in her stomach. Obviously she was struggling fiercely because he wanted her to.

He pulled out the flogger and moved his head away.

When he stood, her eyes were closed, and he smoothed a fingertip over her cheekbone.

Only then did she look at him.

"Oh, yes. You please me very much, Sydney. Thank you."

The gag couldn't completely muffle her cry as she relaxed her body. Unlike earlier, her body was pliant.

Was she trusting him, putting his demands ahead of her adrenaline-fueled desires? "Are you ready to continue?"

She nodded.

Gently, he began to use the flogger, the strands caressing her skin. He wielded the implement with precision, whipping her breasts then moving back so he could catch her nipples with the tips, making her jerk.

He watched for signs of distress, but she still clasped the piece of fabric. Pleased, he adjusted his stance and continued, using both back and forehand motions across her body.

As he worked, she relaxed into her bondage.

Michael stepped back a little to get a fuller swing.

When it landed, Sydney made a little sound, like a whimper, but when he studied her face, there was no pain there. Rather, her forehead was relaxed.

For long minutes, he continued the flogging, adding more force at times, occasionally hitting her with the broad side of the lashes, then varying the pace so she would never know where the strands would land, or how hard the impact would be.

On a soft sigh, she closed her eyes once again.

He moved up and down her body, landing the leather on her breasts, wrapping the lashes around her waist, flicking between her legs to sear her.

Though she pulled against her thigh bonds, she held on to the fabric.

Realizing she was releasing her resistance, he increased the velocity slightly, leaving crisscrossed lines on her flesh.

Her head lolled to the side.

Michael considered asking if she was okay, but she appeared serene, deep inside herself. If so, he wanted to let her linger there for a while longer.

Captivated by the moment, and her, he went on, marveling at the way she responded, her body swaying as she absorbed his punishing kisses.

You're so damn beautiful.

For several more minutes, he continued. Then, when he believed she couldn't attain any greater heights of pleasure, he stopped. "You've done well, Sydney," he said, keeping his voice barely above a whisper.

If his guess was right, she wasn't yet starting to come back to him. "I'm going to start releasing you, and it will take a few minutes. Just continue to relax." He placed the flogger on top of a post before bending to untie her thighs.

Her skin was a beautiful shade of pink.

In admiration, he traced a couple of his marks. She was made for this.

His cock, which had been semi-aroused since they'd come out here, now hardened completely.

Slowly, he reached behind her to unbuckle the gag, and she didn't react at all. "Open your mouth a bit for me, if you can." He took hold of the ball and eased it out, then placed it with the flogger.

Though she flexed her jaw, her eyes remained closed.

He removed the restraint from her right wrist and massaged her skin and her shoulder as he lowered her arm to her side.

Since she'd yet to speak or interact other than to physically respond, he used a normal tone of voice as he asked, "How are you doing? Can you move?"

She made soft sounds and the barest of motions.

As she worked her way back to him, he continued to free her and work the circulation back into her body.

"Almost done." He dropped the last strip of bondage into the box, and she slowly brought her right hand to her face to push back strands of hair.

"Hey," he said softly when she fully opened her eyes.

A tiny smile played at the corners of her lips. She blinked, looking as if she were waking up from a drugged sleep.

"I'm going to carry you to the patio," he said sweeping her off her feet.

With a gentle exhalation, she turned her head into his shoulder, and he savored the silky feel of her long hair on his cheek and her feminine curves against his body.

While still holding her, he sat, then leaned forward for a half-finished glass of lemonade. "Can you drink a little of this?" he asked, offering her the beverage.

She accepted and took a few sips.

When he put down the glass, she once more snuggled against him. He smoothed her hair, cradled her, saying nothing as he luxuriated in the feel of her.

"That was..."

He waited.

"Sensational. I had no idea. You can do that to me anytime."

If she was willing, he had a number of other things in mind.

After a couple of minutes of shared silence, she squirmed a bit and looked up at him. "I'm..." Her unfinished sentence hung between them.

"You're what?"

"Nothing. Never mind. I don't want to overstep my bounds, Sir."

"Say whatever you want, Sydney. Always."

"I'm so aroused. But I'm content to wait as long as you say, Sir. I think I understand more now, about what you were talking about earlier. At first I didn't, but..."

"Go on." Did she realize that waiting, longing, subjecting herself to his dominance could transform her experience?

Had she learned that he could be trusted to nurture and care for her, that all her deepest desires would be met, and that all men were not like the ass who'd collared her?

"It's not about the orgasm... I'm struggling to express what I feel." She curled one hand into a fist. "I want you in me. The connection."

So did he. "There's no hurry. I don't think you've ever been that far gone before." But hopefully this time wouldn't be the last.

"When you're ready, Sir, so am I."

After holding her until she began to push away from him and stretch, showing him that she really was back with him, he carried her inside. Shockingly, her shoes had somehow managed to stay on, and they aroused him all over again.

In his bedroom, he managed to pull back the comforter and toss the pillows on the floor, even with her still clinging to him.

Gently, he lowered her onto the bed then grabbed the toy box and placed it on the nightstand.

Sydney stirred, rolling onto her side to watch him undress. "Your cock is hard, Sir."

As it's been for days. "You're not the only one who's been deprived for more than a week."

"Have you really?"

"As I've said, I don't expect anything from you that I'm unwilling to do."

"You haven't jacked off since we were together last?"

"Not even once." Which might have been somewhat of a record for him. He was a sexual man, and he generally started his day by masturbating in the shower.

He donned a condom. Even though he'd enjoyed it when he'd had her use her mouth to roll it down him, he didn't want to wait that long.

"Shall I keep the shoes on, Sir?"

"Only if you want to drive me wild."

"I'll take that as a yes."

Though the idea appealed, he calculated the damage the spikes might cause his body, especially since he didn't intend to be gentle with her. "Unfortunately, the shoes will have to go for now, no matter how much I'd rather leave them on you." He pulled off one and tossed it in the direction of the closet, wincing when it smacked into the hardwood.

"I guess they're also a weapon, in a pinch," she mused.

The second shoe, he removed a bit more respectfully then tucked it under the bed. "Roll on your back and put your feet flat on the mattress," he said. "And let your knees fall to the sides comfortably." When she did, her body became available to him, as if in invitation. "You're still red," he observed, tracing some of the marks with his thumb.

"Thank you for doing that for me, Sir."

"My pleasure." In every way, she was perfect. "How are your arms? Shoulders okay?"

"Fine, Sir."

"Good. Then grab the headboard."

Eyes wide open, she complied with his instructions. In under a minute, he had her cuffed in place.

Her breath caught.

"I'll help you into position, but I want you to put your knees over my shoulders."

He knelt between her legs and lifted her hips since he knew she wouldn't be able to get a lot of leverage herself.

When she was where he wished, he took his shaft in hand and placed his cockhead at her entrance. Then he captured her gaze as he caressed her clit.

"Sir!"

After her experience outside, he wanted to be sure she really was ready for this. And when she rocked her body in silent demand, he knew she was. He'd never been with a woman this free, this voracious, and she fed his appetite.

He stroked himself as he inserted his cock into her. As he surged forward, his shoulders putting pressure on the backs of her legs, she moaned slightly. "Too much?"

"Stretching my hamstrings and my pussy, Sir. It feels good. Please don't stop."

Now that his cock was buried in her, it would take all his resolve to pull out.

"Fuck me, Sir," she urged. "I want to feel it."

Hell yes. She was his woman. And after this, she'd know it.

He placed his hands next to her head so that he could balance his weight. She was obviously in excellent physical condition, but the angle and the fact that he outweighed her by a good eighty or ninety pounds meant he couldn't collapse on top of her, despite the temptation.

After starting with a few long, slow strokes to get her ready, he fucked her hard and deep, making her gasp.

He craved release as much as she did. But this angle and the incredible sensations gave him another idea.

Calling on all superhuman restraint, he pulled out.

"Sir?"

To her credit, she looked at him with a frown of puzzlement, rather than frustration. "Give me a moment," he said. "Keep your legs spread, with your feet flat on the mattress."

"You're making me nervous."

"Good. We both like it when that happens." He pulled out a small glass butt plug from his toy box.

"Ah…"

"Turtle?" he asked, his back to her as he squirted lube all over the smooth elongated oval shape with a fat base to keep it from getting lost.

When he faced her, her brow was furrowed. "Taking your cock in that position is difficult enough, Sir."

"You can use a safe word or a slow word any time you need to." He suspected she wouldn't, even if it was just because of pride. "We had a discussion that first evening at the Den about your limits. You didn't mention it. I want to be sure before we go on."

Her scowl made her look utterly adorable.

Since he valued his hide, he didn't say so to her. "I'll make sure you're prepared as I insert it." And he would watch for signs of real discomfort, not just uncertainty.

"I don't suppose it matters that I don't want that up my ass?"

"Not at all. Lift your legs straight up."

It took her so long to obey that he was beginning to doubt she intended to.

Behaving as a no-nonsense Dom, he sat on the bed, put his back to her leg then leaned back a bit, forcing her into a stretch and keeping her in place.

Since she was not going to cooperate easily, he intended to use his power to force her compliance. The angle he'd selected exposed her anal whorl. "This will be easier on you if you open up."

Stubbornly, she kept her muscles contracted.

"It's going in, my girl. Like it or not." He teased the glass between her pussy lips, running the smooth surface back and forth until her clit hardened.

She exerted pressure against him as she wordlessly sought more.

"So, so perfect," he told her. He ran the plug a little lower, teasing her ass.

"I…"

"It's okay to like it," he promised her. "This is barely bigger than my finger, and you took that fine." He placed the end of the oval barely inside her rear, then pulled the toy away. Again and again he repeated the motion, each time pressing the plug in a little deeper. When he reached the thickest part, she mewled.

To distract her, he smacked her pussy then drove the plug the rest of the way in.

"That's—"

"In. All the way. Would you like to continue to protest?"

She exhaled fully.

He took hold of her legs and placed her feet back on the sheets. "I'll give you a moment to adjust to the feeling."

"It's a little cold, Sir."

"It will warm up. Now, if you'd like, you're welcome to come at any time while I fuck you." His cock was still hard, and he hadn't removed the condom.

"I'm not sure I'll be able to with the pressure."

"Of course, it's your choice. But if you don't, it may be some time before I offer you another opportunity. The plug stays."

She wrinkled her nose.

Once again, he moved between her legs, maneuvering her into position, her legs over his shoulders, and pressed his cockhead against her opening.

"Oh!"

He gave her a moment to use one of her safe words, but when she didn't, he pulled back before surging forward again.

Fuck. She was correct about the tight fit.

As he finally sank all the way into her, she gulped for air. Her channel was slick, and the pressure from the plug was nearly enough to make him come. "Are you still doing all right?"

"Holy hell's balls, Sir."

His thoughts, exactly.

"I'm... Do me."

Knowing it pleased her, he lowered himself a bit more, and she whimpered.

"I've never experienced anything like this." Though she seemed to struggle to accommodate him, she didn't protest. "You might have suggested I not skip my yoga practice, though."

He kissed the top of her head before relentlessly impaling her time and again. There was nothing soft or sensuous about their joining—it was turbulent and dangerous and as hot as fuck.

With every thrust, she cried out, and he had to force himself to think of her pleasure before selfishly taking his own in her hot body.

"I think... I..."

"Come, Sydney. All over me."

She used her knees against his shoulders to dig in and raise her pelvis to slightly change his angle. "Sir!"

"That's it." He rocked in and out at a frantic pace, and she screamed as her body convulsed.

As she thrashed, he gritted his teeth long enough to reach up and release her cuffs.

Instantly, she grabbed on to the back of his neck as she rocketed through another orgasm. God, he loved pleasing this woman.

Her contractions drove him toward his flash point.

He went still, then a hot pulse shot through him as he climaxed in long, powerful spurts.

"Sir, *Sir!*"

He moaned, and her body convulsed again. "*Give it to me,*" he demanded, shuddering with her once again, the final seed surging out of him.

Afterward, struggling to catch his breath, he rolled to his side to pull her tight against him.

She didn't protest.

For several minutes, until their breathing returned to normal, he held her.

"That was…"

"Yes?" he asked.

"Spectacular, Sir."

"No worse for wear?"

"Deliciously sore everywhere, Sir."

That, he liked to hear.

"I think I need to make you some food," he said. "After a shower. Let me take out that plug for you."

"No, thanks," she replied, turning her head so she could face him. "I'll manage it."

"Embarrassed? After everything we've done?"

"That's a little personal, Sir. Don't you think?"

"All the more reason for me to do it. On your stomach."

"Uhm…"

"Tur-tle?" he asked.

"Damn you. You know I can't use a slow word now, Sir." She narrowed her eyes. "You did that on purpose."

"Then the sooner we get this over with, the better." Before she could argue any further, he flipped her over. "Lift your hips off the mattress."

"I'm glad you can't see me blushing."

He spanked her right below her buttocks. "Enough stalling."

Yelping in shock, she offered her ass.

"Better." He grasped the base of the plug. "Now bear down." Once she had, he was able to remove the toy. "Not so bad, was it?"

"Says the Top. You try being the sub."

"I'm clear on our roles," he told her, lips quirking into a smile. "And you should be, as well." Climbing from the bed, he went into the bathroom to rinse and sterilize the plug and dispose of his condom.

By the time she joined him, the shower water was warm, and steam filled the room.

"Some of those marks are going to last a few days."

She looked down at her body. "Good." Like he had done, she traced a couple of the more prominent ones.

He entered the shower unit and invited her in.

"Most men don't share their shower." She looked at him.

Once again, he was unexpectedly struck by her bright blue eyes. The orgasm had drained his testicles, but the sight of her naked, wet body and slightly parted lips was enough to knock him in the solar plexus. "I'm not most men," he reminded her.

"That's becoming obvious, Sir."

"Is that a good thing?"

"Scary."

Maybe for him, as well.

Earlier, he'd had the unexpected, but not entirely unwelcome thought that she belonged to him.

Odd for a man vowing to protect his heart.

Claiming a woman who spent most of her time away from home, looking for adventure, wasn't a smart move.

Too bad he was no longer thinking with his brain.

Michael lathered the soap and washed her breasts and stomach before moving his hand between her legs. "Turn around," he instructed, moving his hands over her back and shoulders.

She braced her palms on the tiles, surrendering to his ministrations.

Continuing, he bent to cleanse her buttocks and legs.

"Thank you, Sir," she said when he detached the showerhead to rinse her off. "That feels so good. My muscles were a little more cramped than I thought after being tied up. I could stay here all day."

"I'd let you," he said.

He reached for one of the towels he'd tossed over the glass door and offered it to her as he helped her out of the enclosure. "I'll finish up, then I'll be right behind you."

A few minutes later, he joined her in the bedroom.

"Uh, I wasn't sure what to put on," she said. The bath towel was still wrapped around her, and her bag was on the edge of the bed.

Without her saying anything else, he understood the depth of her question, and more, he recognized it as a pivotal moment.

He could tell her to put on the outfit she'd bought in Miami. Or he could tell her to wear the clothes she'd had on earlier. Either way, she was looking to him to define the moment and asking if he wanted her to stay longer.

That she hadn't made the decision to immediately run gave him great hope. "I want you to be comfortable," he said, drying his hair with a towel, aiming for casualness he was suddenly nowhere close to feeling. "You're welcome to help yourself to one of my shirts or a robe, if you'd like. But make no mistake. It doesn't matter what you wear. It won't stop me from fucking you senseless on the kitchen table after dinner."

Chapter Nine

Sydney exhaled a shaky breath. How did he always know the exact right words to say?

Master Michael walked into his closet, and when he came out, he was wearing a pair of faded jeans and seen-better-days boots. He'd put on a navy T-shirt that showed off his biceps that made her imagination serve up all kinds of naughty scenarios. Anytime she was nervous, he defused the feeling and lightened the atmosphere.

"I'll start dinner," he offered.

After applying a coat of mascara, then dressing in her skirt and top from earlier, she looked for her hiking sandals and couldn't find them. Belatedly, she recalled she'd left them downstairs while they were having lemonade.

Barefoot, she headed down the stairs.

The house stood empty, but the patio door was open, so she went outside and saw him sitting in the same chair he'd occupied earlier.

"Steaks are marinating," he told her. "I poured you some wine."

As she sat, she accepted the glass.

"I hope red's okay," he said. "If not, there's a chardonnay in the refrigerator."

"This is perfect." She had a feeling this wasn't going to be like drinking the fermented fruit juice she'd had with her friends. "Thank you…"

One eyebrow raised, he considered her.

It didn't take a genius to understand that he expected her to use formalities, even if they were not in the bedroom. That chafed, but at least he was clear in his expectations. "Thank you, *Sir*."

"Salud." He lifted his glass toward her.

The first sip sang across her senses. It was rich and full-bodied, definitely not like the wines that came out of a jug. "Holy cannoli. What is this?"

"Zinfandel. Not at all related to white zin."

After the amount she'd consumed in Miami, she'd definitely never confuse the two. "It's almost a meal in itself." And the alcohol in the drink went straight to her head. At least she wouldn't be tempted to have a second glass.

"Is it acceptable?"

"I bet the bottle has a cork, even."

He frowned, as if he had no idea whether or not she was joking.

"I like it." She wrinkled her nose. "I think."

"I can get you something else," he said, standing.

"No, Sir. *Really*. I was teasing." She leaned over to grab the shoe she saw sticking out from under her chair. But she didn't see the match. "Where's the other one?"

"Crap." He helped her look before giving up. "The gate was open when I came back out. Were they expensive?"

She smiled. "Very, Sir."

"I may have to get a second job. Or maybe I should get her a companion? Another nuisance to entertain her?"

"Are you kidding me? And have more of them?" she asked, pretending to be aghast. Then she shrugged. "I *have* been thinking about a new wardrobe. I could accidentally leave out all my things, one at a time."

"You may not like all my replacements."

"You did pretty well on the red shoes."

"At least she didn't get away with the flogger."

"That's happy news."

After another sip of his wine, he lit the grill. "Would you like to eat out here? That way we can use the kitchen table for fucking."

Her mouth dried.

Once they'd cleaned up after dinner, she learned how serious he was.

"Go change," he said. "I've pretended to be a gentleman long enough. My inner Neanderthal is done being polite."

She looked at him.

"Move it, my girl. Now."

"Yes, Sir." Hurrying her along, he slapped her rear.

Upstairs, she quickly stripped. Then all thoughts vanished when she caught sight of herself in the mirror.

There were a few faint red marks on her skin, most of which she suspected would be gone by tomorrow.

Small indentations remained on her thighs and wrists from his bondage. The reminder of being tied to the fence and flogged beyond reason thrilled her.

She paused.

At some point while she'd been outside, bound and gagged, subjected to a dozen strands simultaneously lashing her body, she had stopped thinking.

Now, she tried to remember everything that had occurred. He'd been striking her belly, and an unusual peace had washed over her. Right after that, they'd made eye contact, then...

Nothing.

It was as if she'd drifted away.

She couldn't remember what had happened between then and the moment he'd instructed her to open her mouth so he could remove the gag.

Once he'd loosened her arms, he'd swept her from the ground and carried her to a chair. This meant he'd somehow unfastened her legs without her realizing it.

Was it possible she'd reached subspace? She'd heard about that magical place, something she'd believed was nothing more than mythical fantasy. In fact, when she and her friend, Vanessa, had been having a discussion about it a year or so ago, Sydney had insisted it was a chupacabra, the legendary creature of folklore that people had heard of, but no one had ever seen.

But now...?

All she knew was that she'd felt groggy, as if she'd been in a deep sleep or had been plunged into an alternate reality.

The orgasm afterward, with the plug, had left her speechless.

As annoyed as she'd been prior to that, she hated to admit that he'd been right to keep her on edge. When she'd finally come, the sensation had been more intense than anything she'd experienced before.

Master Michael had taken her to unexpected, dizzying sexual heights. Every moment they spent together made her crave more.

As she shimmied into the skirt and zipped the jacket, she heard him moving around downstairs. He could wield a flogger and a spatula. Could a man be any more perfect?

After slipping on her heels, she checked her reflection to be sure her hair looked presentable.

When she descended the stairs, he was waiting for her near the table, his belt and four strands of rope in hand.

"Christ," he said, eyes darkening a shade. "I knew the outfit was going to be hot, but I had no idea."

"I hope your inner Neanderthal is pleased?"

"Oh, yeah. Very much so." Slowly, he nodded. "Right now, I have two questions. Do you want your butt reddened to match your front, or would you like me to just shove my cock inside you?"

His words, along with the way he raked his gaze down her body, from her eyes to her toes, made her shudder. The comment had been bluntly sexual, but his questions held a serious note. "As usual, why choose?"

"I was hoping you'd say that." He nodded. "Unzip that jacket. I want your breasts flat on the table."

Desire slammed into her.

Like the expert he was, the moment she was in position, he secured her in place.

"The height of those shoes puts you in the perfect fucking position." He growled the words as he dragged her skirt up over her buttocks.

Before she was mentally prepared, he smacked her ass with the leather, making her cry out and tug against the restraints.

"Would you like the gag?"

"No, thank you. I'd rather fucking scream the house down, Sir."

"Do it," he said.

Unfortunately, he backed off, warming her with a few gentle spanks. "One or two lasting marks are fine," he said. "But I don't want your ass black and blue."

Turning her head to the side, she sought his gaze and challenged him. "What if I do?"

"Too bad. I'd rather do this numerous times than have to wait between sessions."

Since she would soon be taking a couple of college guys on a mountain biking expedition, she would have loved a reminder of him to take with her. "Refusing to break your toys, Sir?"

"You're much more than a plaything to me, Sydney."

After several more swipes, he finally belted her hard enough that breath whooshed from her lungs.

When she lifted her chest, he placed a strong hand between her shoulder blades and forced her breasts back onto the table.

His deliciously harsh actions made her lose herself.

This kind of scene was exactly what she'd hoped to find when she went to the Den. Who knew that a gentleman cowboy would be the one to satisfy her?

The strapping continued, and he even caught her behind her knees. She roared out her anguished pleasure. In reward, he repeated the motion in the same spot.

Overwhelmed with gratitude, Sydney started to sob. To his credit, he kept going, the rhythm soothing her and making her pussy wet.

Then his massive, sheathed cock was at her entrance.

Instead of taking her slowly, he parted her and shoved in with a single impaling stroke. The scratch of denim on her thighs told her he hadn't even bothered undressing.

He put his hand on her nape, immobilizing her as he repeatedly took her.

It stunned her that he was ready for sex so soon after they'd finished, and that it was this rough fulfilled her.

"Come for me, Sydney."

Master Michael used her body so completely that she was lost. When he reached beneath her to squeeze one of her breasts, she bucked, granting him deeper access, and when he took it, she screamed out her orgasm.

Bracing himself, he cupped her shoulders, then he moved inside her with short, quick motions before releasing a telltale guttural moan that signaled his climax.

He thrust a few more times, with a little less depth, before digging his fingers into her flesh and surging forward in a powerful motion.

She adored his primal, driving culmination.

Once they were done, they both stayed in the same position, together, connected, his fingers lightly on her hips. Surprising herself, she didn't want to instantly end it.

Contentment unlike anything she'd ever experienced washed through her, bringing tears to her eyes.

At least a full minute later, he released her bindings. "Will you be okay if I leave you for a moment? I want to grab a washcloth. You'll be able to hear me, and you don't have to stay in one place."

His thoughtfulness touched her. "I'm fine." Even if she wanted to, she wasn't sure she'd be able to move right now.

He left her in her puddle of emotion, her thighs sticky.

This, what she had with him, was exactly what she'd been seeking.

Less than a minute later, he returned and pressed a cool cloth between her legs. Always, after a scene, he cared for her. She was already coming to appreciate that about him. "Thank you, Sir," she murmured.

After helping her to stand, he used a second washcloth to wipe the tracks of her tears. Though some Tops offered post-spanking comfort, Master Michael went above and beyond.

"I smeared the finish on your table," she said as he turned her to face him.

"Fair's fair. I wrecked your makeup. And Christ, that's hot."

"Is it?"

"It means you surrendered. There's nothing more rewarding than proof of your tears." He lowered the washcloth.

For a moment, she wondered if he might kiss her, and she wondered if she would let him if he tried.

He smiled, leaned down, and softly said, "How about a fresh glass of wine?"

"I can finish the one I was already drinking."

He shuddered. "I won't hear of it. After sitting outside for so long, it's oxidized."

"Really?" She was clearly no connoisseur. "I thought that some people decanted red wine."

"A much more controlled process."

"Honestly, I'm not sure I'd know the difference."

"My preference. Indulge me?"

"In that case, thank you." He shot her a cocky, inviting smile that she found it impossible to resist. "Do you mind if I take a quick shower?"

"Not at all. Or, if you want, feel free to soak in the bathtub."

Though that was tempting, she wanted to spend more time with him, so she opted for the quicker option—standing beneath the water's spray for just long enough to be reinvigorated.

After dressing in one of his T-shirts and a pair of leggings that she'd brought with her, she rejoined him.

Neither seemed to have any need for any major conversation, and, over wine, they watched the sun begin its descent. "This is a beautiful spot."

"I couldn't agree more." He slid his wineglass onto the small table.

Considering him and the vast, empty distance, she asked, "Do you ever get lonely out here?"

Instead of immediately responding, he faced her, his hands pressed together, seemingly considering her question. "It's an honor to sit here, and an obligation to the past, and the future. As for being lonely…" He shrugged. "There's peace here. One that was ruined when I thought I might lose some of the land. Harsh lesson, but it taught me it's better to be alone than with the wrong person."

His ex, no doubt.

"How about you?" he asked.

"Me?"

"No desire to put down roots?"

"As you said, it's better to be alone than with the wrong person. The relationship with Lewis made me regret my choices." She thought back to her life with her parents. They'd moved every year or two, looking for new experiences. And all of their vacations had been exciting. "There's too many places to explore, so many adventures that are still on my bucket list."

"Such as?"

"Climbing Everest."

"I should have guessed." He grinned. "What intrigues you about that?"

"The challenge, right? Standing at the highest spot on the planet, a place so few people have ever been."

"So what stops you?"

"It's been a combination of the time and financial commitment. With acclimatization, ascent and descent can take a couple of months." She took a tiny sip of her wine. "And while I'm away, I'm not working in my business."

"That makes sense. What else is on your list?"

"This is one I don't tell a lot of people." She smiled. "Seeing penguins in the wild."

"Penguins?" he repeated.

"You know, those adorable creatures that look like they're wearing tuxedos."

"I know what they are," he replied wryly.

"Did you know that the emperor penguin can dive to about sixteen hundred feet. And some species can swim up to twenty-two miles an hour."

"Seriously?"

"Fairy penguins are the smallest of all of them." She grinned. "The African penguin used to be known as the jackass penguin because they seem to bray like donkeys."

"No way." At least he didn't sound bored.

"And many mate for life."

His eyes turned the color of the forest at dusk. "*Now* I'm finding your trivia interesting."

With a laugh, she rolled her eyes. "Is that all you think about?"

"When you're around?" He perused her. "Yeah."

Flashing back to the kitchen table, her insides turned molten.

"Along those lines, are you staying the night?"

By way of an answer, she tipped her glass in his direction. "I'm ready for a refill."

"I'll take that as a yes. And we can build a fire out front, if you'd like."

"That sounds wonderful."

Twenty minutes later, they were seated in chairs around the firepit, and logs crackled and hissed. Master Michael had brought out a bag of marshmallows and several long skewers to toast them.

When Jeb, the foreman, neared on his side-by-side utility vehicle, Master Michael waved the man over. Evidently not to be left out, Chewie trotted alongside him.

Master Michael scratched behind the goat's ears before she wandered away to forage. A few minutes later, apparently seeking a new diversion, she jumped on top of an enormous boulder. Sydney watched in fascination as Chewie looked around, bleated, walked down the far side of the rock then trotted around and did the same thing again. The rock was craggy and had to be three feet tall. "What did you feed her?" she asked.

"Shoes?" he suggested.

Laughing, she popped another marshmallow on a long, thin stick.

Jeb was telling a story about Master Michael learning to work with horses.

"Takes a lot of patience and dedication," Jeb explained. "Establishing trust. Spending time with it, grooming it, asking nothing in return. Are you interested in this?"

"Absolutely." Through the years, she'd done plenty of riding, but on older, gentle horses. Until now, she'd never even considered the amount of skill having a quality horse required.

After finishing her treat, she lanced another with her skewer.

"Only then can you start to get it accustomed to a harness and lead rope before moving on to a bridle and saddle. Requires consistency and repeatedly using the same cues and signals."

She was so engrossed in Jeb's explanation that she forgot to constantly turn the marshmallow. Seconds later, the confection burst into flames.

Frantically she pulled it out of the fire and blew on it. The outside was charred, and the inside was a gooey mess. Happy, she sank her teeth into it. "I'm not sure I've ever had anything that tastes better."

After putting her metal rod down on a rock, she sat back, sipping her wine, and listening intently as Jeb told stories of Master Michael growing up on the ranch.

For a few minutes, she was transported back in time, picturing him as a kid, then a young man.

"How long have you been here?" she asked Jeb.

"A lot of years." He nodded. "Hired by Mr. Dayton a couple of months before Michael was born. Watched his first steps. Was here when he wrecked his truck for the first time, as well as the second."

"Enough of that," Master Michael warned, eyes narrowed.

"And then there's the time a horse bucked him off at a rodeo and he fell into a pile of — "

"You looking to get fired?"

"A bale of hay," Jeb finished, sporting a wide grin. "Wouldn't ruin your reputation in front of a pretty lady."

Both men laughed.

An hour later, with the bag of marshmallows empty and the moon riding high in the sky, Jeb said he'd extinguish the fire if she and Michael wanted to head inside.

As he closed and locked the door behind them, Michael swept his gaze over her. "I've got a couple of suggestions about how we should unwind."

"Do tell, Sir." She moved toward him to trace her fingertip down his chest, letting it rest on his belt buckle. "Do tell..."

* * * *

Almost three weeks later, as she crested Vail pass in her trusty SUV, headed back from Utah, Sydney cranked up one of her favorite open road tunes.

Calling on all of her resolve, she'd intentionally kept up with her regular life. She ran the always-challenging mud race and had just finished guiding a four-day trip to Moab that had included climbing, hiking, and mountain biking.

But as the trip had drawn to a close, she'd had greater and greater difficulty concentrating on anything other than how soon she could return to Eagle's Bend Ranch.

Her preoccupation with Michael and his land was starting to bother her.

But turning up the music even louder didn't help her banish thoughts of him.

As the vehicle's tires devoured the miles between them, memories of their time together stroked through her mind like strobe lights.

She loved the new adventures he dreamed up, sex in the outdoors, a bare-bottomed spanking while they hiked, being secured to his fence, framing her in a window as he flogged her, taking her again and again to the edges of subspace.

Other times were companionable as they stargazed or took a horse out for a ride under the full moon.

In the mornings, she'd watch the sun crest the horizon, or drink a cup of coffee on the patio while Michael worked in his office.

Sitting outside next to a campfire was becoming a regular occurrence, as was chatting with Jeb and learning more about ranch life.

Every moment together was better than the last...

And Michael was beginning to matter to her.

No. Absolutely not.

Disoriented, terrified, she gripped the steering wheel tighter.

Sydney couldn't allow herself to fall for him.

In order to preserve her independence, she had to focus strictly on sex and BDSM.

And yet his tempting invitations made that more and more difficult.

Even though she'd promised herself that she would limit her visits, the moment he'd invited her to join him on her way home, she'd accepted.

Her more rational mind urged her to cancel, go home, shower, relax, then get ready for her next job.

But there was no way that would happen.

Like a snowflake melting in the sun, she was powerless to resist him.

About an hour later, she left I-70 and headed west.

The rest of the drive seemed to take forever.

When she reached the ranch gate, Jeb was there, waiting, ensuring she didn't run into trouble.

Each time she visited, she felt more and more at home. While it was comforting on some level, it was terrifying on others, mostly because it meant she was visiting too often. Even while she'd been gone, Michael's land had beckoned, and an unwelcome part of her craved the peace and solitude he'd created and wanted to share with her.

And that was the crux of her sudden angst.

Her parents had taught her to embrace life, to seize as many opportunities as possible. In her relationship with Lewis, she'd shoved her inclinations aside.

It had taken her more time than she would have liked to run away.

And when she'd dumped the pieces of her collar, she'd promised herself she'd live her life on her terms, hitting the road when she chose, spending time with the people she wanted to see, working only for clients she enjoyed.

Her solo trip had been to the Bahamas where she'd sipped rum and enjoyed the sun as she'd healed from her bruises — emotional ones as well as physical ones.

As she drove onto Michael's property, Jeb tipped his hat, and she waved.

Beneath the now-familiar tree, she parked, then opened the back door to get out her bag that she now kept filled with sexy clothes in addition to utilitarian garments.

Since her arms were full, she bumped her butt against the door to close it.

She was walking toward the house when she was yanked to a shocking and sudden stop, then dragged backward.

Breath whooshed from her lungs.

Before she could lose her balance, strong arms wrapped around her, steadying her. Next to her ear, Master Michael whispered, "Welcome back."

"What the hell was that?"

He turned her to face him. "You've been lassoed," he explained, eyes intensely serious. "It's the best way to get the attention of a gorgeous woman and simultaneously remind her who she belongs to."

She wanted to say she belonged to no one, but damn it, when he looked at her like that, her resistance evaporated. "I—"

"Say 'yes, Master Michael'."

"Anything you say, Sir," she compromised. Her heart still raced, but she had to admit she liked his unusual greeting. "That's a hell of a welcome."

"Wait until you see what else I have in mind."

"Oh?" The diabolical Dominant kept her guessing. And she adored that.

He kissed her senseless, devouring her, leaving her gasping.

Then he stepped back and smiled before releasing her from the lasso.

While she showered and changed, he waited downstairs. Then, when she joined him, sashaying into the kitchen on spiky heels while wearing a garter belt, stockings, and leather bustier, she had the pleasure of watching his mouth fall open.

"New?" he asked, sliding a glass of bottle of water onto the counter.

"For you, Sir."

"Thank you." His words were laced with approval and seduction. "I missed you."

"I thought about you," she admitted, taking a purposeful step toward him, playing the diva. "I almost masturbated."

He scowled. "Almost?"

"It was close. So very tempting."

Scowl deepening, he studied her intently. "But you didn't?"

"Of course not, Sir." Provocatively, she batted her eyelashes. "That would be wrong."

"I'd have had to spank you if you had."

"Really? And how would you have done that, Sir?"

"I'd have sat on that chair." He pointed.

"And then, Sir?"

"I'd have taken you over my knee. Like so."

Quicker than she could have imagined, he reached out and snatched her from the ground. He was sitting and had her over his knee in under three seconds, trapping her legs and bringing his hand down on her rear.

Yes. This was her every desire come true.

Hopelessly surrendered, she allowed her body to go limp.

He blazed her buttocks and that tender flesh right below the cheeks.

"Thank you, thank you, *thank you*, Sir."

Before she fully understood what was happening, he picked her up again. "I should go away more often, Sir."

"I think you should never leave."

Her heart lurched to a momentary stop.

But before she could reply, he sat her on the edge of the table, distracting her, allowing her to tell herself his statement was nothing more than heat-of-the-moment ridiculousness.

After forcing her legs apart and pressing on her chest until she was lying on her back, he pulled a condom from his pocket.

"Sir has one thing on his mind," she noted as he dropped his jeans.

His eyes dark, he looked down at her, making her shiver from anticipation. She'd seen him in a lot of moods, but this one, pulsating sexual dominance from the moment she'd arrived, was new.

"Tell me you don't want me to fuck you like you were missed, my girl."

"Fuck me like you missed me, Sir."

Before entering her, he sheathed himself and spanked her pussy half a dozen times, making her gasp. She thrashed her head. *Holy hell.* She wasn't sure what had gotten into him, but it thrilled her.

Holding her ankles, he dragged her forward so that her butt was no longer on the table. She hung suspended, having to count on him to keep her safe as he ferociously ravaged her.

Repeatedly, he slammed into her pussy, shooting her senses into overdrive. "Sir!"

"Tell me, girl. Tell me what you want."

"Oh, Sir! I *need* to come."

"Take it."

She was lost. The pain from the over-the-knee spanking, the slaps to her pussy, the sensation of weightlessness, and the days apart had left her dizzy.

He moved quickly, propping one of her legs on his shoulder. She was still exposed completely to him, and he pushed on her clit.

Sobs choking her, she screamed as she climaxed.

But he was unsatisfied. Voice gruff, he demanded, "Fucking give me more."

Master Michael relentlessly toyed with her as he thrust, forcing her over the edge in another shattering orgasm. On and on he went, holding back his own orgasm as he incessantly sought to break her.

By the time he ejaculated, her pussy was swollen and tender, and a sheen of sweat dotted her exposed skin. "That was…"

"A short demonstration of how much I missed you." He looked down at her, a lock of damp hair falling over his forehead.

She released a shaky breath. "You really know how to roll out the red carpet, Sir."

Even after he'd helped her to stand, Sydney wobbled for a moment before regaining her footing.

"You'll be okay if I leave you for a moment?"

Once she'd nodded, he went into the small bathroom, and when he returned, his jeans were fastened. He looked respectable, but damn it, still so appealing.

After bathing her between the legs, he asked, "Would you like to shower while I pour you a glass of wine and finish making dinner, or would you like to be the sous-chef? Watching you dice and chop while dressed like that is definitely intriguing."

"Oh." At one point while they'd been text messaging, he had mentioned dinner. "Thanks for the offer. I'm sure it would be wonderful, but I need to go home. I have an early-morning flight."

"I see." His eyes turned the color of iced emeralds, snaking a chill down her spine. "I'm a piece of meat to you? A quick fuck between trips? A means to an end?"

Jesus. His awful words landed with the force of a single-tail lash, and she recoiled. "No." Frantically she shook her head. "You've got it wrong."

"Do I?" he countered, arms folded. "You stopped by for a quick lay."

No. It's not like that. "Sir... We have a misunderstanding."

"Do we?"

Sydney rubbed at the goose bumps that prickled her skin, telling herself his reaction shouldn't have surprised her. As they spent more time together, of course he'd make more demands of her. Like Lewis had.

"You show up here whenever the hell it's convenient for your schedule. Get spanked and fucked, scratch your itch, then go on about your life without looking back."

"Michael, please..."

"Clearly my mistake for thinking I was anything more than a goddamn convenience to you." Icy venom dripped from his voice.

Damn it all. "Please..."

He remained unresponsive.

Too late, she recognized they had fallen into a routine, and she loved the hot scenes enough to keep coming back when she shouldn't have. "Sir..." As her worst nightmare played out, Sydney squeezed her eyes shut. "Michael..." Suddenly unsure what to say, how to behave, she tried once more. "We never talked about anything more than sceneing together."

"So that's all you're offering? Or should I say taking?"

Taking? His accusation stung. "That's unfair." She met his gaze then wished she hadn't when she read the combination of anger and frustration starkly reflected in the stormy depths. But worse was the layer of hurt beneath the other emotions.

In that instant, he crushed her soul.

Softly, trying again, she said, "I never agreed to be your submissive, or anything else. I've told you about my past." Frantically, she tried to make him understand. But his eyes had turned flat. "I...I thought you understood where I was coming from."

"Then we have nothing more to say to one another."

"Are you...?" She shook her head, trying to understand what was happening here. "It doesn't have to be this way."

"No?"

She'd waded into an emotional nightmare.

"It's your way or no way, Sydney. Too damn bad if it doesn't work for me. If I want something more than a casual fuck before you wave and jump back in your car."

But she couldn't give him anything more. Unless she risked everything. "Don't do this."

"It's not enough for me any longer, Sydney."

Her insides chilled. Almost always, he'd called her by an affectionate nickname. But now, he'd built some distance between them.

"Go on with your life like you want." Coldly, he hooked a thumb toward the door. "Don't let me stop you."

Her thoughts swam, as if caught in a class six rapid. This couldn't possibly be happening. *Couldn't.* "I..." Raw emotion lodged itself in her throat, and she tried desperately to gulp it back. "I apologize..." Tears burning her eyes at his stinging rebuke—rejection—of her, she dashed up the stairs.

He didn't follow.

At one time, he would have watched her, maybe even given her a spanking to encourage her along, but not now.

Never again.

When she slowly descended the staircase, bag in hand, he was nowhere around.

Her heart heavy, wishing they could talk but also recognizing the futility, she exited his house for the final time.

Hoping against hope that he'd come after her, she took her time crossing to her SUV.

Still stalling, she climbed behind the wheel.

But her Dominant was nowhere to be seen.

When she arrived at the gate, Jeb was there to wave her off. At least Master Michael—Michael—hadn't forsaken her entirely.

As she drove through the exit and lifted her hand in farewell, he touched the brim of his hat. Chewie wandered over to join him and grazed on some weeds.

Using the back of her hand, she dashed away the tears that spilled down her cheeks.

Crushed in a way she never had been before, Sydney accelerated away, staring in the rearview mirror until she could no longer see Jeb or the cloven-hoofed terror who'd suddenly looked up.

Sobbing, she struggled to concentrate on the road ahead of her.

Once she reached Winter Park, she pulled off the road at a popular restaurant where couples ambled in, hand in hand.

A vision of Master Michael, arms folded as he indicated the exit, seared itself into her memory, and her emotions fractured again.

She couldn't breathe.

How would she go on without him?

Chapter Ten

"Call her."

"Who?" Michael looked up from his office computer screen to see Jeb standing in the doorway.

"Don't be a fucking idiot. You know who I'm talking about."

At his foreman's harsh statement, Michael winced. He did know because Jeb mentioned it at least once a day. "I'm busy."

"No, you're not." From a lifetime of familiarity, Jeb entered and dropped into a chair on the other side of the desk Michael's father and grandfather had sat behind.

"I don't recall issuing an invitation."

"I knocked," Jeb offered by way of an explanation.

"Told you I'm busy." Michael scowled. "Working on accounting."

"*Pretending* to work," Jeb countered, taking off his hat and tossing it onto the desk. "Just like you have been every day since Sydney left."

Recognizing the resolve buried in the lines between Jeb's eyebrows, Michael exhaled and leaned back in his seat.

They'd been through too damn much together for Michael to get away with anything. When his dad had died, Jeb had been constantly in sight, from dawn to well-past dusk. They'd spent hours on the range, even more in the office as Jeb had gone over the books and given detailed explanations of the ranch operations.

Though his father had done his best to prepare Michael to take over, both of them had believed they'd have many more years together, so urgency had been lacking.

Without Jeb's steadying hand and personality, Michael would have been more lost than he was.

And then came the debacle with Jane, and he'd barely scraped together enough funds to ensure she went away, leaving the ranch intact.

The ending of that relationship had been filled with emotional drama, and for a time, as he'd struggled to get through it, Jeb had handled all the regular details that ensured a prosperous future.

The man had more than earned the right to say whatever he wanted. Even if Michael didn't want to hear it. *Especially* if he didn't want to hear it.

"Want a glass of whiskey?" Jeb asked, standing.

"No." Last night, he'd consumed far too much. And the night before, as well.

Jeb narrowed his eyes. "Have you finished every drop in the house?"

Dismissively, Michael waved his hand. "No." But it was close. *Closer than it should be.*

The damn truth was, he'd spent the last twelve nights morosely watching the sun go down, glass in hand.

"Don't mind if I do." Jeb crossed to a small cabinet and pulled out the decanter. Without saying a word, he made a show of holding the contents up to the light and noting the small amount of liquor inside.

After pouring two fingers' worth into a crystal glass, Jeb returned to his seat. Then, rather than taking a sip, he held the beverage and regarded Michael.

"You're wasting your time, Jeb."

"An apology is always a good place to start."

For what? Confronting the truth that neither of them had wanted to accept? "No chance in hell I'm calling her. I'm the last person she wants to hear from."

For long moments, the office rang with a silence so loud that his ears burned.

A few seconds later, Jeb quietly spoke, and the impact rocked Michael back in his boots. "Are you in love with her?"

"*Hell no.*" Michael slammed his hand down. "Never doing that again."

Contemplatively, Jeb took a drink.

Wouldn't matter, either way. Sydney had no interest in anything other than an occasional scene or fucking.

Michael needed to shove aside thoughts of her.

After all, he was no longer a man given to bouts of obsession. Instead, he accepted reality and got on with his responsibilities.

Ranching could be brutal. A lot of winters, he lost cattle to the weather. And spring birthing came with its own risks.

He'd grieved for both of his parents, and acknowledged the fact that his sister and her children didn't want anything to do with the land he loved. And he'd survived it all. He'd get past his bruised ego soon enough. "Better I find out now that she's not interested in being up here."

"Hmm."

"What the hell does that mean?" Michael snapped, annoyed.

"I've watched her. Smiling as she galloped on horseback, laughing as you rode the UTV together."

Before Michael could respond, Jeb continued, "Watching the sunrise with a cup of coffee. Making smores over an open fire. Taking care of Melanie's flowerbeds." He lifted a shoulder. "She helped me give the pest a bath."

"She didn't."

"Yeah. And brought in eggs for you a couple of times."

Why the hell hadn't he known about some of those things?

"There were times you were unavailable, and she was at loose ends. She wandered around, asked questions, made herself useful. She wasn't on her phone or bitching about how quiet it is out here."

Unlike Jane. "Don't you have work to do?"

"Nah."

Michael had been afraid of that answer.

His whole life, Jeb had been a second father when his own had been too busy with family and obligations. Jeb had never treated Michael like a pesky kid. In fact, until today, the man had seemed to have endless patience.

"Jesus." Michael fed his hand into his hair. How could he admit this? "She's not interested in a relationship."

"Which is why she drives hours out of her way to see you? Why she treks up here all the time?"

"Sex." *Mind-blowing sex.* "Nothing more."

"You're nine kinds of fool if you believe the bullshit you're feeding yourself. The woman looks at you like your mama looked at your father."

Michael sat back.

The love between his parents had been amazing, to the point the two of them had seemed to exclude the rest of the world. Following his mom's death, his father had become a shadow of his former self.

"Pull your head out of your ass, son. Think about what happened from Sydney's point of view."

He scowled. Jeb knew nothing about Sydney, or Michael's relationship with her.

"Do you recall nothing I taught you about horses?"

The things Jeb had told Sydney returned to Michael.

"Takes a lot of patience and dedication. Establishing trust. Spending time with it, grooming it, asking nothing in return."

"That time with Bandit?"

The rescue animal was now among Michael's favorite horses. Bandit had been on a ranch, neglected for years. By the time the gelding had arrived at Eagle's Bend, he was as skittish as he was ill-tempered.

Bandit had required months of intense work, but now he was solid, with an even temperament. Michael would trust Bandit with the newest of riders. "What's your point?"

"You gave him what he needed."

Like a thundercloud, aggravation closed in around him. "You're suggesting I didn't behave that way with Sydney?"

"Did you?" Jeb countered.

"I never pressured her."

Jeb didn't respond.

"*Expecting nothing in return.*" Right up until that fateful night, Michael had never demanded more than she wanted to give. And once he had...

"Something made her cry when she left."

Shit.

That information was a deep, jagged stab wound.

Michael pushed back from his desk and strode to the window. He could have done without having that image seared into his mind.

Facing Jeb again, he said, "I didn't demand she give up her life."

"Does she know that?"

"Look, it doesn't matter. Better I find out now. Right?" *Who am I trying to convince?* "At some point, I need a wife. And a family." No sense spending time on a woman who didn't want the same things he did.

"On your terms."

"What the hell does that mean?"

"Figure it out. No one likes ultimatums, son."

"Who said I gave her one?"

"Tell me you didn't."

Michael blew out an annoyed breath. How did Jeb know him so well?

"When something matters, you've always been willing to work for it." Like Michael, Jeb stood. "You need to stop brooding and make a plan."

"I'm not brood—"

"Yeah. You are."

Michael didn't respond. The truth stared him in the face, and he hated it.

"You need to get away from here for a while, catch a change of scenery. Take a vacation."

The solace of ranch life was all he needed.

"Do yourself a favor and take a break. Something more than an occasional evening at Damien's place. Or a trip to town for more liquor."

Not that anywhere local carried Bonds whiskey. The expensive-as-shit brand he drank required a special delivery.

"Being away helped you figure out a lot of things."

Much as he hated to admit it, Jeb was right.

Michael had attended school in College Station, Texas, where he'd studied agribusiness and ranch management. During his four years, he hadn't spent much time at home, even over the holidays — something he'd later regretted.

Eventually, however, the majesty of the land and his connection to family had beckoned, calling him back across the miles.

"Eagle's Bend gets in your blood," Jeb observed.

Michael nodded.

"At least it does for the right person." Jeb tipped back his remaining drink, then thumped the empty glass back onto the desk. "Think about what I said."

Jeb reseated his hat, one Michael suddenly noticed was missing a chunk. "Chewie?"

"Pest," Jeb acknowledged with an affectionate tone.

Guess I have another purchase to make.

"She needs a companion. Like you do."

Jeb slammed the door behind him, hard enough to make the door dance in its frame. Long after he'd left, his words lingered on the late afternoon air, repeating themselves in Michael's head.

Alone — and fucking lonely in a way he'd never been before — he stalked to his desk and dropped back down into his chair.

Reluctantly, he conceded he'd handled the situation with Sydney all wrong.

From a place of anger and hurt, he'd lashed out, saying unforgivable things.

One thing was sure as hell, he wouldn't have reacted positively to behavior like that from her.

Early on, she'd confided in him, telling him about her ex and his abusive, demeaning ways. And Michael had responded by saying a true Dominant looked after their submissive's needs, putting their interests first.

And he'd added that a good Dominant not only nurtured, but also protected.

Wincing in self-judgment, he picked up a pen and drummed it in front of him.

When Jeb had challenged him, Michael hadn't wanted to admit that he actually had issued her an ultimatum. But that was exactly what he'd done — behaved in a way that was completely out of character for him.

Then, in the silence of his office, in a place where his ancestors had faced harsh truths and made tough decisions, an inescapable realization seared him.

He was in love with Sydney.

Christ.

Falling in love was never supposed to happen again.

That unstable emotion risked his heart, left the ranch — and his legacy — vulnerable.

But there it was — truth interwoven with reality, and he dropped the pen as his shoulders fell forward.

Even as they'd scened together and he'd invited her to his home, he'd told himself he could confine his feelings to a D/s dynamic.

But the sexual charge between him and Sydney buzzed with as much energy as a mountain lightning storm. It was intense, as immediate as it was scorching.

Over time, that had flared into respect, then affection.

When she was on the property, her passion and infectious laughter had breathed life into Eagle's Bend.

And he was lost without her.

Sydney might believe, honestly believe, that sex was all they shared.

Yet there was no way she could have faked her joy at being here, with him.

And when he'd thrown down his parting words, she could have countered, made a promise to come back another time and stay for longer. Anything to have given him a glimmer of hope.

But her expression had been stricken.

To her, after Lewis, there could be no greater threat than falling in love again and risking her very precious freedom.

Throwing down the pen, he surged to his feet and returned to the window, this time to stare out.

Fuck it all.

Jeb had been right on a lot of fronts. Michael hadn't been patient, hadn't even told her how he felt. And when something mattered to him, he *was* willing to work for it.

You're mine, Sydney.

And he was goddamn well intent on proving it to her.

Chapter Eleven

"Open the door!"

At the pounding and the shout of her friend Vanessa's voice, Sydney groaned. She wanted to spend the entire day in her pajamas, curled up on the couch beneath her favorite blanket, watching endless hours of home improvement shows.

When she stayed where she was, Vanessa switched to the doorbell, pressing on it incessantly. "Your car's in the parking lot, so I know you're in there!"

She rolled her eyes.

On some level, she shouldn't have been surprised that Vanessa had driven all the way from Denver to Evergreen at such a ridiculous time on a Saturday morning.

After all, Vanessa had called last night. When she'd asked how Sydney was, she'd burst into tears. The effort of forcing them back for so long had become too much, and Sydney had collapsed into a puddle of grief and loss.

They'd been friends for too many years for Vanessa not to have ridden to the rescue, like she had when she'd helped Sydney figure out how to get Lewis's hated collar cut off.

They'd made a pact to always be there for each other — and they both meant it.

"Don't make me go get your landlord for a well-being check. I will. And you know it."

With a massive sigh of frustration, Sydney tossed aside the cozy throw and padded to the entryway.

She pulled open the door just as Vanessa was getting ready to start thumping on the wood again.

"I could have been out for a walk or a run. Maybe riding my bike."

Vanessa shrugged. "Of course you could have been. But you've probably been sleeping like shit. So you would have gotten up early and done that and now you're back to moping."

"I don't mope."

"Yes, my friend. You most certainly do. You are a world-class moper, in fact. If it were a competition, you'd win a gold medal."

Still blocking the entrance, Sydney brushed her damp hair back behind her ears. After her early-morning run, she'd taken a quick shower. But instead of dressing, she'd changed back into her comfiest PJs.

"Since you didn't invite me in, I guess it's a good thing I'm not a vampire."

"What?"

"You know, vampires can't just enter your home. You have to invite them inside. But since I'm human, that means I can barge right in, whether you want me to or not."

Sydney shook her head as Vanessa did just that, pushing past her with the force and determination of a bull charging at a red flag.

"I'm guessing you didn't have breakfast yet."

After expelling a breath between her pursed lips, Sydney closed and locked the door.

Vanessa moved aside Sydney's blanket and the pile of pillows that she'd made into a tiny nest, then she snatched up the remote control as she plonked herself down on the couch.

"Could you be any more obnoxious?" Sydney protested.

"Oh, yeah. Absolutely. In fact, I haven't even gotten warmed up yet. Just wait and see."

Sydney didn't doubt her friend, not for a minute.

Vanessa pressed a button that took her to the television's home screen and scrolled until she found a true crime channel.

Then she propped her feet on the glass coffee table.

Annoyed beyond words, Sydney swatted Vanessa's legs, but, stubbornly, she refused to move.

With a heavy sigh, chased out of her comfortable spot, she sat at the far end of her own couch.

"So did you?" Vanessa demanded, her gaze glued to the screen in front of her.

"Did I what?"

Rather than answering, Vanessa said, "Yep! This is what I was looking for."

Anything but this. "I hate shows about murderers."

"Yeah. I know." Vanessa shot Sydney a wicked grin. So she'd picked it intentionally.

"Other than to punish yourself with exercise — or to go to work — how long has it been since you left this place?"

Sydney glanced around. "What's wrong with my condo?"

"It's not awful, but I mean, c'mon. Even you have to be sick of looking at these same walls."

"As a matter of fact, I like being here."

"Sure." Once she'd started the show, Vanessa turned up the volume.

When she'd insisted she could become even more obnoxious, she'd been right.

"Must be bad," Vanessa shouted over the racket as she glanced around.

She knew what her friend meant. Her home was immaculate. She'd dusted and vacuumed twice yesterday. Swept and mopped three times.

"Not even an empty container of ice cream is in sight. Which answers the question you keep avoiding."

Trying to keep up, Sydney shook her head.

"You haven't had breakfast. And I'm guessing you didn't have dinner last night, either. So we'll have a real meal, junk food — of course ice cream — and alcohol. All of that is on today's agenda."

"No. Thanks, though. But I'm good."

Creepy music spilled from the television's sound bar, rocking the walls and shaking the floor. The last thing Sydney needed after hardly sleeping for two and a half weeks was nightmares of someone trying to break into her house.

But Vanessa was even more diabolical. She'd selected an episode about murders that happened in the Rocky Mountain wilderness. "Oh hell no. Nope, nope. *No,*" she insisted.

"We're spending time together." Vanessa narrowed her gaze at Sydney. "So we can either get the hell out of here or we can watch this. There's a whole bunch of episodes. Twelve, at least."

A full day's worth of fear-inducing shows?

"I'm happy either way. I love this shit. And we can just order in some food in while we enjoy each other's company."

"Look, Ness, I appreciate what you're trying to do —"

"Not what I'm *trying* to do. What I *am* doing. The only choice you get is whether we have a happy time together or a miserable one. Either way, you're stuck with me."

After wrestling the remote control from her friend's death grip, Sydney turned off the TV. "With the way I'm feeling, I don't need your version of merry sunshine around here."

Vanessa grinned, a big, fat, happy smile. "Well, you got it anyway."

The fact Sydney glared daggers at her didn't alter Vanessa's demeanor.

"I got a bonus at work, and I need to spend part of it on something frivolous. So after all that food, we'll do some shopping. Have lunch, then go to a bar and get the largest beer they have and drink it while we cry in our figurative pretzels."

When she didn't answer, Vanessa was undeterred, and went on. "I'm looking for a sage bundle. You know, something I can take to work with me. I've got a new coworker who is as annoying as hell, and I'm hoping that burning some can banish his energy."

"You say sage can get rid of someone's energy?" Not taking chances, Sydney buried the remote between the seat cushion and the sofa's arm before leveling a pointed look at Vanessa. "In that case, I need sage as well."

Vanessa snapped her chin up in a show of fake indignation. "That wasn't nice."

"It wasn't meant to be."

"You know, Sydney, you'd be a lot more pleasant if you had a big cup of coffee."

"The way you're bouncing off the walls, you've already had more than a few."

"But not an iced one with caramel blended in and whipped cream on top."

Sydney winced. "You just gave me a cavity. I know it."

"Do you want to pick out your own outfit? Or do you want me to do it for you? I'm starving." Without waiting for an answer, Vanessa stood, then skipped down the hall.

"Oh hell no." Frantic not to have Vanessa in her closet, pulling out hangers and tossing outfits on the bed, Sydney leaped up and dashed to her bedroom, snatching a shirt out of midair before it hit the mattress. "Out."

"I'll give you five minutes." Vanessa propped her hands on her hips. "And that includes pulling your hair into a ponytail and slapping some eye cream on to disguise the fact you haven't been sleeping and that you've been crying."

Sydney scowled. "You're the most—"

"Best," Vanessa interrupted. "You mean best. As in I'm the best friend ever. I tell it like it is, and you appreciate it. But thanks for the compliment." She smiled widely. "It's good to know that you recognize how wonderful I am."

"That's not what I was going to say."

"Tick tock."

"I still think you should go away."

In answer, Vanessa sat on the edge of the bed and made a show of studying her well-manicured nails.

It was closer to fifteen minutes by the time they were in the downtown area, near Bear Creek. Even though it was still early, the town buzzed with energy.

Vanessa found the last parking space in front of the Misty Mountain coffee shop.

Sydney swore she gained weight just from the scent of sugar when she walked through the door.

The place was amazing with its bright chairs painted a shade of green that was reminiscent of nearby pine trees. The color theme continued throughout the entire place, including the T-shirts and hats they offered for sale.

Since there was a line, she had far too much time to look at the pastry case.

"I'm thinking about a vanilla bean glazed scone," Vanessa said.

"To go with your caramel whatever?"

"Yep. And this is my treat. Get whatever you want."

Vanessa led her into temptation.

When they walked back outside into the bright sunshine, Sydney had a large Americano in one hand and was carrying a bag stuffed with a triple chocolate muffin. The unholy confection had fudge in the middle and chunks of dark chocolate in the batter, along with milk chocolate chips. Not satisfied with that, the baker had drizzled white chocolate on top. "I'll never fit in my running tights tomorrow morning."

"That's okay." As they walked, Vanessa took a bite of her treat. "We're going shopping. I'll find you something in a bigger size."

Unable to help herself, Sydney smiled. Then she wondered, was it for the first time since she'd played the diva for Master Michael at his home?

She sighed.

Why did every thought—even happy ones—lead back to him?

Vanessa headed for a bench near the river, and she took a seat. "Perfect fall day."

It was. Flowers still bloomed in pots, but the air held a noticeable morning chill. To ward it off, she took a drink of her coffee. "Wow. I think they added an extra shot of espresso to it."

"I bypass every coffee shop when I come to visit you, just so I can stop at Misty Mountain." Vanessa grinned. "Sometimes I even dip off the highway and grab a cup on my way to visit the Den."

The mention of Master Damien's mountain retreat made her sad again, so she reached into the bag and broke off a piece of her muffin.

Staring into the distance, she popped the bite into her mouth.

"Speaking of the Den, I'm planning to go next week with Maggie. She's had enough of her asshole boss, and I don't blame her." Vanessa shrugged. "It's been hard for her dealing with the new owner, especially since it was her family's business, and she pretty well ran it. Now she has to answer to an alphahole. I mean, that can be fun in a club setting, right? But dealing with someone like that all day at work? Who thinks he knows your business better than you do? That's a hard no from me."

"He sounds like a tyrant."

"He is." Vanessa slurped her frozen concoction through a straw. "Maggie would quit, but he has her tied up with a Draconian employment contract. A pair of golden handcuffs. So she's ready for a night out where she can forget about him for a while and get her butt paddled."

Because it was expected, and because at one time she'd understood that motivation, Sydney nodded.

"It's gonna be Ladies' Night. You know how much fun that is."

It was. The best. Lots of sweet mocktails, appetizers and decadent bite-size desserts, and tons of Doms and Tops looking to play. She'd had some of her best experiences at Ladies' Night. "Thanks. But I won't be going there anytime soon." *If ever again.*

Seeing Michael with another woman would destroy Sydney.

And she had no doubt he would return.

Dominance mattered to him. And eventually he wanted a family to pass the ranch along to.

That thought made her world go black.

"Are you okay?"

She shook her head to clear it of the sudden, dizzying sensation.

Vanessa was carefully studying her. "Oh…" Vanessa's eyes widened. "The Den. Is that where you met Mr. Heartbreak?"

Last night, Sydney hadn't shared much about Michael. She'd told Vanessa that she'd spent time with a man she liked, but he'd started to demand too much from her.

On those words, her voice had cracked, the tears had fallen, and she'd been unable to stop them.

She lifted her cup and took a small drink. "It is."

"Anyone I know?"

"Potentially." She broke off another piece of heaven—in the form of the decadent pastry—and popped it into her mouth. As far as therapy went, it was as blissful as it was inexpensive. "Master Michael."

Vanessa's mouth fell open. "The cowboy?"

"One and the same."

"Oh, man. Oh, man." She exhaled. "Now I have to know more."

As Sydney nibbled, the multiple flavors of chocolate soothing her soul, she told the whole story.

Because they were such good friends, Sydney even shared his terrible, accusatory parting words.

"That sounds like bitterness, like he didn't really mean them."

"But…" Having had more than enough to eat, Sydney folded her bag and tucked it inside her purse. Then she washed down the sweetness with a gulp of her Americano. "When I combine his ultimatum with what he said about thinking I should never leave…"

Vanessa nodded. "He definitely seems to want more."

"That was never part of the agreement."

Vanessa turned to face her. "So where are you at?"

Lonely.

"I mean, you have to care about him. Otherwise this wouldn't hurt, right?"

Miserably, thinking of him, of all she'd lost, she nodded, and another stupid lump lodged in her throat.

"So what's really going on?"

"What does that mean?"

Holding her drink between her hands, Vanessa regarded Sydney. "After getting away from Lewis, you took a trip to celebrate, right? The Bahamas, right?"

"You're right." Swimming in the warm Caribbean waters had been both cathartic and wonderful. As she'd relaxed on the beach with a cocktail, she'd regrouped and decided on a path to reestablish her business.

By the time she'd returned to Colorado, she'd been filled with energy and looking forward to a future that she'd enjoyed...right up until she'd driven away from the Eagle's Bend.

"But this time is different. *You're* different. You're staying home, alone. You're not interested in working or socializing. And this is the first time you've refused an invitation to the Den." Vanessa pursed her lips, as if considering what she'd just said. "Well, unless you were out of town. You go through men—Tops—as if they're interchangeable." Barely slowing down to take a breath, Vanessa plowed forward. "And you sure as Colorado snow don't go home with them. Or return repeatedly for more. Which means that something is different."

Sydney frowned. She hated that her friend knew her so well.

"Ergo..."

"Ergo?" Sydney repeated after swallowing back her emotions.

"Honey, you are in love with the man. In a way you never were with Lewis..."

Vanessa kept talking, but her words buzzed in Sydney's head, drowning out the rest of what her friend was saying.

Love?

That couldn't be possible.

She'd spent years vowing that she wouldn't allow herself to experience that mind-numbing emotion ever again.

But there it was.

"Have you heard anything I've said?" Vanessa demanded.

"I..." Sydney faced her friend. "No. Sorry."

"You love him, don't you? It's the only thing that makes sense. Otherwise, you'd be guiding some fall hikes or horseback rides, right? Getting in some final trips to Moab. Planning your winter activities. Or you'd be checking something off your bucket list. Trekking somewhere I can't pronounce. Sipping mai tais on a cruise ship. Buying a ticket to go see the northern lights. But you sure as hell wouldn't be moping around your condo, watching lousy—"

"I've told you I wasn't mo—"

"You were in pajamas and buried under a blanket watching a terrible home improvement show."

"Those brothers are handsome."

Her protest didn't persuade Vanessa. "I literally had to drag your ass out of the house. And find you some clothes."

Though she'd selected her outfit, Sydney didn't bother arguing.

"At any rate, I rest my case." Vanessa slurped through her straw. "You're in love with that sexy cowboy." Then, more quietly, she added, "Have you finally found someone who deserves you?"

"Or maybe he's like Lewis?" Sydney challenged, unsure whether she was trying to convince herself or her friend.

Vanessa rolled her eyes. "Yeah, he sounds a lot like Lewis. I mean, Master Michael goes out and gets drunk all the time, right?"

"As if." This time, it was Sydney's turn to roll her eyes. "An occasional glass of nice wine."

"So he makes you kneel and wait for him while he games or goes someplace and passes out?"

Frantically, she shook her head. She couldn't even conceive of him behaving that way. When they were sceneing, he rarely left her alone. When he did, he always reassured her that he'd be right back.

"Allows other men to touch you?"

"God, no." In fact, when he'd learned what Lewis had done to her, he'd threatened to kill the bastard.

"So..." Vanessa wiggled around. "Tell me again what's so awful about the man that you had to run away."

She sighed. When Vanessa broke it down like that, he didn't sound so horrible.

"The bastard didn't demand you marry him. Did he?"

"No." *At least not yet.*

"Or demand that you stop working and wait on him—and his buddies—and his selfish whims?"

"Oh hell no." If that had happened, she'd be counting her blessings that she'd fled before she'd gotten in deeper, and she might actually be on the deck of a cruise ship this very moment. "But still, V... He wanted more than I was willing to give."

"Isn't a relationship about compromise?"

She leveled a skeptical look at her friend.

"What?" Vanessa took a bite of her scone. "I've been listening to this expert on a podcast. I know way more about how to successfully tolerate someone else's shit now."

They both laughed, and Sydney appreciated her friend's humor. "Does that mean you'd be willing to share your space now?"

"Excuse me." Vanessa cleared her throat. "We're examining *your* life, not mine."

"Uh-huh." Vanessa was nothing if not predictable.

Despite having inherited plenty of money from her grandparents, Vanessa lived off the salary from her job. She'd been engaged and only found out she was with a gold digger when her father had insisted she get a prenup. Now, she went by her middle name and kept her family's wealth a secret.

"What are you afraid of, really?"

"I don't need to tell you, do I?" Sydney asked. After all, no one knew her better.

Still, Vanessa waited.

"Losing my freedom. Getting in so deep that I can't find my way back."

"But, honey, when you left Lewis, you blazed a path out of hell. You've already survived the worst life can throw at you. Haven't you?"

Vanessa's wisdom resonated deep inside.

After a few more seconds, Vanessa softly asked, "So what are you going to do about the situation?" Then she shrugged. "I mean, besides mope. That is your right. But it's not your usual MO."

"I'm not…" She allowed her protest to trail off. Vanessa had a point. Sydney *had* been moving from the couch to her bed, a shadow of the person she'd been even a few weeks ago.

But worse than that, she was adrift.

Even though they hadn't been together for very long, Master Michael, and his ranch, had become an anchor in her life, a place of refuge to regroup and rest.

"You may have to give a little," Vanessa said, sounding wise, and no doubt parroting words from the podcast. "Make choices from your possibilities instead of your fears."

"At some point, I'll repeat those words back to you."

Vanessa smiled radiantly. "At which point I will stick my fingers in my ears and go, la, la, la, la, la."

Sydney laughed.

"Seriously, you should call him."

"Vanessa, I told you. He gave me an ultimatum."

"Oh, honey, ultimatums are merely a place to start a negotiation."

Maybe in some alternate universe.

"Anyway, you've got some thinking to do. And I've decided we need to shop so we make some room for lunch."

How could Vanessa still possibly be thinking about food after a thousand-calorie coffee stop?

Vanessa stood and dumped her empty bag in a nearby trashcan.

After wandering in and out of quaint stores and galleries, they agreed to eat at the Timberwolf Saloon, a locals' favorite with live music.

They ordered a large pepperoni pizza and beer, and within minutes the frosty glasses were slid in front of them.

"So why were you watching home improvement shows?"

At her friend's comment, Sydney tipped her head to the side. "I told you. The twin brothers."

"I think it's deeper than that."

"Do you?" After taking a long drink, she couldn't resist pursuing Vanessa's open-ended statement. "Enlighten me."

"It's about home. Connection."

"I have a place." And certain things probably did need to be updated or remodeled, not that she'd thought much about that until right now.

"I'm talking about *home*. Not someplace you dump your bags before your next trip."

Sydney blinked.

"Isn't that what you have on Michael's ranch?"

Maybe it was. A part of her recognized that being on his land restored her.

The sunrises, sunsets. Trailing her fingertips in the gurgling river. Feeling the wind rippling through her hair. Even Chewie and her ridiculous antics. Talking with Jeb. And her ritual of gathering eggs.

At first, she'd been too nervous to go near the chickens, but he'd introduced her to his ladies — as he'd called them — even telling her the girls' names.

But instead of admitting that she truly was missing Michael as well as Eagle's Bend, Sydney changed the subject. "I still argue that home improvement shows are better than watching gruesome murders. Especially ones committed by people who are still out there."

Right after their food arrived, the band began to play again, making conversation more difficult, something she was ridiculously grateful for.

After lunch, they found a store that carried sage, and Sydney waved it in front of her friend. "Hmm. You're still here."

"Don't worry. You'll be getting rid of me soon."

Which sucked, because suddenly Sydney didn't want to face another evening alone.

Once they'd paid for their purchases, they returned to the condo, but Vanessa refused an invitation to come inside. "I need to get back."

Across the car's console, they hugged.

"Think about what I said."

Her friend hadn't stopped talking all day. "Which part?"

"About compromise. Maybe there's a way for you two to sort it out still."

It was already too late. The cold, unfeeling expression in his dark green eyes had made that clear.

After thanking Vanessa for making the drive and for spending the entire day in Evergreen, Sydney went inside her condo.

As she looked around, the truth hit her.

Vanessa's guess had been correct.

Sydney loved Michael.

And the feeling she'd been experiencing since she'd left was…heartbreak.

Utter, shattering despair.

A pain unlike anything she'd ever experienced rocked her.

A great big, racking sob tore from her throat, and she pressed her fingers to her mouth in a futile effort to mute the awful, wrenching sound as her heart broke all over again.

Chapter Twelve

On the Den's patio, near the firepit, Michael sipped an energy drink, staring into the flames, hoping against hope that Sydney would show up for Ladies' Night and that she'd agree to a scene, or, even better, a private conversation.

This, at least, was neutral ground.

On the other hand, he risked an outright rejection.

She could safe word or refuse to talk to him.

Worse, she might opt to scene with some other Top—someone happy to flog her, fuck her, and let her go.

The thought stabbed his heart and made him clench his jaw.

But who could blame her if she chose someone who wouldn't demand forever from her.

Damien, hair pulled back and cinched with a piece of rawhide, joined him.

"You haven't moved in at least half an hour," his friend observed.

Maybe more. Michael had arrived before anyone else, just to be sure he didn't miss her.

"Waiting for someone?"

They both knew the answer to that. "Is she on tonight's guestlist?"

"Can't answer that, and you know it."

"Won't," Michael corrected.

"Semantics. Either way, result's the same, isn't it?"

"I'd like to get her address from you."

"No chance." Damien regarded Michael. "We helped you once. If you fucked it up, that's not on us."

Michael winced. *Yeah.* He'd fucked it up. Bad. "I can hire someone to find her."

"Your call. I think it would be a bad one, but at least it won't be on my hands." Damien allowed his words to hang on the early fall air, before finishing. "You ever tried an apology? Couldn't hurt."

Mistress Catrina strode from the house, her thigh-high boots reflecting the flames from the torches.

In silence, Damien swept his gaze over the Domme's beautiful features.

Interesting.

In all the years he'd known the man, Damien had kept himself aloof from the Den's guests.

"Enjoy your visit." Though he spoke to Michael, Damien had never taken his gaze from the Domme.

With that, he walked away, toward Catrina.

Even more curious.

Twenty minutes later, Michael was in the same spot, still nursing his now-warm beverage.

"Warned you."

Interrupted from his musings, he turned toward Gregorio, who he hadn't heard approach.

"About Sydney."

"So you did."

Gregorio's single diamond earring flickered beneath the moonlight. "Even if you'd have paid attention, it wouldn't have made any difference?"

"No." Despite the loss, spending time with her had been worth it.

"You tried an apology?"

"What the hell is it with you and Damien? Before events, do you rehearse what you're going to say?"

"Nah. Only with friends who've fucked up."

"Piss off."

"House subs are wearing purple armbands, if you want to scene. And with it being Ladies' Night, Tops are in high demand. Even ones who behave like assholes."

"Thanks. No."

"That's what I guessed." With the barest flash of a smile, Gregorio walked off, striding into the house.

A server passed by, and Michael placed his unfinished drink onto his tray.

Maybe his friends were right. He should try an apology. Trouble was, he didn't really know how.

Near the check-in desk, before he reached the front door, he saw his friend, David. One of the few people who didn't know how bad he'd messed things up with Sydney.

He was wearing a black band around his biceps, indicating he was a house monitor for the event.

"How's the new company?" Michael asked.

David frowned. "That's why I'm here."

Michael studied his friend.

"To burn off some energy."

Seemed Michael wasn't the only one dealing with some shit. "That bad?"

"Worse than that."

"How so?"

"I'm being treated as the enemy, as if I'd acquired the company in a hostile takeover." From a server, he accepted a bottle of mineral water. "Could do with a good, stiff drink, but that's against the rules. Need a clear head."

When offered a mocktail, Michael shook his head. "Thanks. No." Then he returned his attention to David. "The mother/daughter duo isn't grateful you rescued them before they lost the business entirely?"

"You'd think so. But no. Gloria is easier to deal with than her daughter, Maggie. She's a total spitfire. She needs a good fucking spanking."

"That's frowned upon in the workplace."

"Damn shame," David agreed. "I'd be happier, even if she wouldn't be. We'd be enjoying much greater success if we were on the same page."

"And you can't fire her because she's too valuable of an asset?"

"Tied her up with an employment contract. Regrettably, it shackles me to her, as well."

"Tough position."

"Well, as soon as my responsibilities are done, I'm going to find some lovely submissive and blaze her ass, pretending she's Maggie."

Sounded like a good plan. Michael just wished something similar would help him forget Sydney, even just temporarily.

But he was single mindedly focused on her.

Frustrated, confounded, he strode back outside, grabbed his keys from the valet, tipped the woman but told her he'd grab his own vehicle. He needed the walk to banish some of the angst pulsing in him.

Coming to the Den had been a shitty idea.

What Jeb had advised was true.

This would require patience.

And that was the one thing Michael was out of.

Which meant it was time for him to take a bold action that she couldn't ignore.

* * * *

Exhausted, Sydney parked her SUV and made her way to the counter of her favorite coffee shop in Avon, Colorado.

She'd spent two days mountain biking, challenging her physical and mental skills as she tried to exhaust herself enough to get a full night's sleep.

Her awful dreams — of losing someone important because of her fear — had no intention of letting her do that.

The harder and faster she ran, the less she rested, and the more exhausted she became.

And she realized one thing.

Sex and BDSM with Michael had been amazing, mostly because she cared so much. Her feelings for him had given their interactions a more powerful intimacy.

And that insight left her… *Where?*

"Ready to order?" the woman behind the counter asked, interrupting her thoughts.

"Sorry." Sydney shook her head, as if that would clear the cobwebs in ways that time and exercise hadn't. "A large iced latte, please."

"Can I get you anything to eat?"

Sydney glanced at the menu. She'd skipped lunch, and her tummy growled, reminding her of that fact. "Oh, and a chicken club sandwich," she added.

"You get a side with that."

She glanced back at the chalkboard to see her options. Fruit. Salad. Pickle spears. Chips. Or fries.

As if it was any kind of choice with her emotional state. At the idea of greasy, salty, carb-loaded deliciousness, her mouth watered. "Do you have sweet potato fries?" At least that was healthier than the regular variety. *Right?* But if Vanessa had been with her, Sydney would have opted for a double helping of them.

"Absolutely."

Just as she was paying, a barista slid the cup in her direction. "We'll have your food right out."

"Thank you." While Sydney waited, she took a long drink of the much-needed caffeine and found a quiet table in the corner where she dropped into a chair.

From her small waist pack, she pulled out her phone and turned it on.

Where she'd been, testing her skills in the back country near Vail and Beaver Creek, cell phone service wasn't always one hundred percent. And having her phone ring might have been distracting enough for her to wreck her bike.

Seconds later, her notifications populated. One missed call and half a dozen text messages.

Her heart stopped when she saw one from Michael.

For a moment, she believed her mind was playing tricks on her.

But when she blinked and looked again, his name was still there.

Telling herself to delete the message unread, she squeezed her eyes shut.

But resisting him hadn't been possible since that very first summer night at the Den when she'd sashayed past him, trying to ensnare his attention.

Finger shaking, she clicked the icon.

An image opened. Of a…

Penguin.

A yellow-eyed, if her guess was right.

Completely captivated, she scrolled to the next message that had a picture of a home overlooking the water in Dunedin, New Zealand.

And then came a snapshot of an airline booking reservation for two, in January, when it was summer in the southern hemisphere and miserably cold in the Colorado mountains.

Another photo showed a close-up of the details, including Michael's name and hers, along with a private suite on an airline she'd never even dreamed of flying with.

He was offering her the trip of a lifetime — one she'd never be able to afford.

Breathless, she pressed the phone to her heart.

Her mind whirred with his possible meanings.

But only one thing truly mattered. Had he retracted his ultimatum? Or was this merely an enticement for her to agree with what he wanted?

Words flashed onto her screen.

Let's figure this out. Together.

Though she waited, nothing else appeared.

Her food arrived, and she turned her phone upside down to resist the temptation to keep looking through the same set of texts.

New Zealand.

Somewhere she'd never been and had wanted to visit.

Suddenly food didn't matter.

Vanessa's words echoed in her mind. What would Sydney's life be like if she lived from possibility instead of fear?

As she sat there, she also realized that she hadn't been blameless on their final night.

His words had fallen like axe blades.

Yet there'd been truth in his awful accusations.

She *had* dropped by his house when it was convenient for her, never staying long. And she hadn't invited him to visit her.

She'd been unwilling to make any accommodations at all for a relationship—preferring to believe they didn't really have one.

But even a casual friendship required give-and-take. And she hadn't afforded Michael that courtesy.

And maybe Vanessa was also right in her belief that an ultimatum was a great place to start a negotiation.

He'd extended an amazing olive branch. The least she could do was accept the offering.

If they couldn't reach an accord, at least she would have tried.

Preferring to talk to him in person rather than over the phone, she grabbed a to-go container from a nearby counter, packaged up her food, finished her coffee—happier than ever that she'd opted for caffeine. She was going to need it.

Then she headed back to her car.

Gaze focused on the road ahead, Sydney entered the highway, unsure whether she was driving toward her future, or total desolation.

* * * *

Michael prowled his office, pacing back and forth, not even pretending to get any work done.

Since he'd gone to the Den last weekend, he'd obsessed over conversations with Sydney, especially about the things that mattered to her.

Jeb had a point too. Michael rarely left Eagle's Bend.

Sydney's love of travel, combined with the fact he hadn't been anywhere in years had sparked an idea.

Once he'd decided on a course of action, he set it into motion, doing research, calling travel agents, putting together a holiday he hoped would let her know how much she meant to him and the extent that he'd go to keep her happy.

If she'd have him.

More nervous than he remembered being — after all, nothing had mattered this much to him before — he'd taken pictures, downloaded information, then arranged it all in an intentional way, then he'd sent his texts.

He'd followed up with numerous pictures.

And…

He'd received nothing in return.

The read receipts proved she'd looked at them, but she hadn't responded.

What the hell does that mean?

Restless, he strode to his desk and snatched up his phone again.

The damn thing had been silent for hours, and there still wasn't a single notification there.

He'd expected to hear something — anything — from Sydney. But not silence.

Jesus. He had severely fucked up with her.

In frustration, he slammed the device back down again.

Across the room, a full bottle of Bonds whiskey beckoned. Though he was tempted, he resisted its siren's call.

When — *if* — she contacted him, he wanted a clear head. He shoved aside the niggling doubt that said he'd never hear from her again.

After all, he'd bet everything on a damn penguin.

His office phone buzzed, and Jeb's voice filled the room. "You have a visitor driving up the road."

He froze. "Sydney?"

"Yeah. When she left, I didn't change the gate code." Silence crackled, then his foreman spoke again. "Remember, son. No one likes an ultimatum."

Jeb's statement didn't need a reply.

Grabbing his hat and shoving it on his head, Michael headed outside.

He'd learned from his damnable mistake.

Gut twisted, he strode to the end of the path, folding his arms, trying to convey a cool calmness.

She braked to a stop in her usual parking spot.

His inner demon demanded he stalk over to her, throw her over his shoulder, take her upstairs, paddle her ass hard in punishment for the sin of leaving him, and then fuck her until she screamed the truth to the heavens that she belonged to him and would never again leave him.

Instead, he forced himself to remain in place, impatiently waiting for her to come to him.

A moment later, she killed the engine and exited the vehicle. Then, slowly, ever so slowly, she turned to face him.

And rocked his world.

Holy fuck me to hell.

Sydney—his Sydney—was even more beautiful than he'd remembered in his dreams.

Her shorts showed off her shapely legs, and a form-fitting T-shirt hugged her upper body.

Her hair was wild and free, and she'd skipped makeup.

Even from across the distance, he read wariness in her face and hesitation in her pretty blue eyes that he'd once thought were icy.

Now he knew the truth.

It was a veneer, a barrier to protect herself. And unfortunately, she'd needed to protect herself from his demands.

Like an impending storm, tension hung between them, crackling the air.

Instinct urged him to talk to her in a language they both understood best, with a kiss, a spank, an orgasm. Then she'd melt into his embrace and be his forever.

But this was bigger than that. He wanted it all. *Everything.*

Patience.

Cautiously, Sydney took a step toward him. Then, after an agonizing stretch of time, a second.

He was done for.

Fuck patience.

In an instant, he'd reached the end of his restraint.

Michael opened the gate, and in a few strides, demolished the distance until he stood in front of her, breathing her in.

Being this close soothed his inner beast, but it wasn't yet close to tamed. "You came."

"How could I not?" With a tentative smile, she brushed back a lock of hair. "You sent a penguin."

"I listened to you, Sydney." Emotion carved his voice into ragged pieces. "It might not have seemed that way, but I did. Every single word. And since you've been gone, I've had them on constant replay."

With a loud, nasally bleat, Chewie trotted over to Sydney then affectionately butted her.

Smiling, her expression genuine, she petted the goat.

"She missed you." *And so did I. I nearly lost my fucking mind.*

Sydney didn't make any further moves in his direction, but she was still here, and that meant something. "Even though I listened to everything you said, there were things I didn't pay enough attention to, and..."

The thought that he might never have seen her again knocked him in the solar plexus, forcing oxygen from his lungs. "I should never have issued an ultimatum. It was wrong." Struggling for calm, he took a gulp of air. "The truth is, I fucked up, Sydney." He lifted his hat. Then, not knowing what to do with it, put it right back where it was. "Bad."

"Does this mean...?"

"That I apologize? That I'm sorry? Yes. Both." Helplessly, he shrugged. "That I won't do it again...probably not. You mean the world to me, and I'm not perfect. I want you in my life, but I promise you that I will try not to make you feel trapped or smothered."

Slowly, she nodded. "You said some harsh things."

He needed to own his mistakes. "I did." And he'd take back every word in an instant. "I was an ass."

"There may have been some truth to them."

Chewie, evidently bored, ran off to jump on top of her favorite boulder, where she stood, staring at the humans.

Her voice shaking, Sydney spoke. "I was so busy making sure I didn't get hurt that I didn't give enough consideration to how my actions impacted you. And I'm so very sorry for that."

"Thank you." He nodded. "But you have nothing to apologize for. From the very beginning, you were honest about what you wanted." Before that, Gregorio had warned him of the same thing. "As I got to know you more, I learned what your fears were. I pushed you too hard."

With a sigh, she lifted her hair into a ponytail only to drop it again. "The truth is, I've spent years making sure I didn't get involved with any man, and I reacted badly to your ultimatum. I didn't have to do that. I have safe words, and you're not generally an unreasonable man."

That night, to his regret, he had been.

"I panicked because the truth is, you scare the hell out of me, Master Michael."

"Sydney…"

"Let me finish." She shaded her eyes with her hand. When he nodded, she went on. "I care about you, the land." With a tiny smile, she looked around until she spotted Chewie. "Even her. Especially her."

This was a start, a beginning.

His heart, which had been missing a piece since he'd sent her away, slowly began to heal.

"So where do we go from here?"

To my bedroom. "You tell me."

"My business matters to me. Along with my freedom."

"Understood."

For a long moment, she remained silent. "My parents traveled a lot."

He nodded. "I enjoyed planning the penguin trip."

Slowly, she blinked. "You did all that?"

"Surprised?"

"One hundred percent. I know how much effort goes into arranging itineraries."

When he'd started doing the research, he'd thought it would make a hell of a honeymoon trip. Still did. But he didn't want to terrify her. "Since we're there, we could arrange some extra time and take in parts of Australia. Or we can return at a later date."

"Do you really mean that?"

"Jeb told me I spend too much time here, that getting away is good for me."

"But the ranch demands a lot of commitment." Tipping her head to the side, she studied him.

"It does." He nudged his hat back a little. "There are times of the year when it's easier to get away, for sure."

"Like January when it's miserable here?"

"Like then," he agreed.

"But that's also a good time for helicopter skiing."

"You can't do both?"

Her eyes opened wide. *With the first rays of hope?*

Then she gestured expansively, taking in his holdings. "At some point you'll want a family."

And he refused to give up hope that, with a lot of patience, she would be his wife as well as the mother of his children. "I need *you*, Sydney." The admission was wrung from the depths of his soul. "As long as you return to me, we can figure this out." Their time apart had taught him that painful lesson.

"A safe place to land."

"Our relationship should add to your life, not take away from it."

Narrowing her eyes once again, this time in suspicion, she said, "I spend time with my girlfriends at various places on the planet."

"Darlin', I don't want to clip your wings." Her joy for life was one of the things he'd fallen in love with.

"What about my condo?"

"You can keep it, if you want. Or you could consider working from here and get rid of your mortgage."

Her chest rose and fell in quick, short bursts. They'd waded into more difficult parts of the discussion.

Signaling he was open to compromise, he turned his palm up. "I meant it. You need to do what's right for you. It would always be your choice."

"My place is closer to Denver and the airport."

By a whole lot of miles and time. "Where does most of your work occur?"

"A lot in Moab. The western slope. Vail. Back country." She sighed. "But your point is well taken. Most of my trips are to the mountains. In fact..."

"Go on."

"I'm thinking Eagle's Bend could be a good spot for excursions."

"For... *What?*"

"Fall tours of the aspen—on quads or horseback. We can bring in Santa in the winter and have hot chocolate on a sleigh ride. Fill a pond and offer ice skating."

"You want to start a business on the ranch?"

"I know it's a lot."

Her ideas had insurance liability, but they could potentially bring in a lot of revenue, and they might entice her to spend more time with him.

"Weddings in the barn."

He shook his head at the ridiculous notion. "Who gets married in a damn barn?"

She regarded him. "Plenty of couples. Of course, we'll remodel it or build a second one for that purpose. Arbors, maybe, with a view of the mountain range in the distance. It would be a photographer's dream."

"Slow down, darlin'." Though he protested, he couldn't have been happier with her enthusiasm.

"We could even consider dude ranching. No reason we can't think of ideas to turn a profit on the areas that are fallow. Maybe get Chewie a companion."

"I'm willing to consider anything you propose." *As long as you're beneath my lash with my dick inside you.* "Can you stay for a while? Maybe join me for a glass of wine?" *A spanking?* "Or the sunset?"

"Yes." Slowly, she nodded.

His blood surging, he extended his hand toward her. "Welcome home."

She smiled, lighting his whole world on fire.

"You had me at penguins, Sir."

Chapter Thirteen

Home.

Until now — until Master Michael — that hadn't been something Sydney had really understood.

Her parents had moved so often that she'd never had a place to return to for visits or holidays.

Suddenly, he closed the physical and metaphoric distance between them, and she was enveloped in his strong arms, comfortable as well as cared for, and a realization rocked her.

Home wasn't necessarily a place — it was a feeling. Of safety, of security. One like she had when she was with him.

The Eagle's Bend Ranch offered her a sense of belonging.

"I'm going to kiss you."

He didn't ask permission, he took.

Gently at first, he staked his claim, coaxing her response, asking for only what she wanted to give, exploring her as if for the first time.

When he sought more, she responded, moaning, wrapping her arms around his neck, holding on tight, yielding completely, offering everything she had to give as he devoured her.

He tasted of invitation, of promise.

Of forever.

The thought no longer terrified her.

Everything she'd needed to hear when she arrived, he'd said.

That he didn't want to curtail her freedom. That she could keep her condo. See her friends. And he hadn't shot down the ideas she had for the ranch.

If he wanted her to work from here, expanding her business onto his property made sense.

As the kiss went on, his hard cock pressed into her.

From the moment they'd met, the attraction had sizzled, a spark that threatened to combust.

How had she survived while they were apart?

When he pulled back, she didn't want to let him go.

She yearned for connection, shoving away the past so they could more fully embrace their future. *Own me, Sir.*

"How was that?"

Amazing. "Fine, Sir." She smiled coyly. Then she spoke again, issuing a submissive challenge. "For an appetizer."

Smoky haze clouded his eyes as he responded in the way she'd hoped he would, with Dominant determination. "Shall I welcome you home properly, Sydney? The way a brat deserves?"

"Did you have something specific in mind?" Intentionally, she left off the expected honorific.

"Yeah." Fire consumed his eyes. "I believe I do."

They were now back in familiar territory, and with each moment that passed, he chased her anxiety further away.

"Join me in the barn."

"The barn, Sir?"

"Before you turn it into a carnival site, you might want to see my plans for it."

"Oh?" Intrigued, she cocked her head to the side.

With a mysterious grin that knocked her pulse for a loop, he captured her hand.

Apparently once again interested in the humans, Chewie jumped off her perch to follow them.

In the distance, Jeb waved and headed toward the bunkhouse, giving them plenty of privacy.

With each step that they took, her nerves ratcheted a notch tighter.

Finally, he opened the door and gave her a tiny push. "In you go."

Then he turned to seal the entrance and keep Chewie out.

He slid a bolt home with a loud metallic *thunk*. "Now you have no escape from me."

Anticipation made her shiver.

"See what I have in store for you."

"Oh my good God." The place gave her goose bumps, in the very best way possible. "This wasn't what I expected, Sir."

"No?"

He'd turned the massive space into a dungeon, complete with Saint Andrew's cross and a spanking bench. He'd also stacked several bales of hay in various places.

Whips of all kinds — single tails and floggers — hung from the walls, along with an assortment of paddles, tawses, and crops.

Making the place somewhat homier, a couple of rugs were tossed on the polished concrete floor between an oversize couch and a couple of chairs. He'd even thought to add pillows, a few blankets, even refreshments. Really, there was no reason ever to leave.

"Have a look around. Make yourself familiar with all the things I'm going to use to torment you."

She met his gaze, and his eyes were stoked with possessive heat.

"Everything is for you."

Accepting his invitation, she crossed to a small bathroom, complete with a gorgeous glass-tile shower.

Then she wandered across the barn to a set of built-in drawers.

"Open them."

Her mouth dried.

One held ropes and cuffs. Another had an assortment of butt plugs, including an inflatable one that terrified her.

He had vibrators and dildos — including one that was crafted from an enormous piece of glass, long and thick with raised veins. "You've thought of everything."

"I'm sure we'll be adding to it."

She explored the rest of his offerings, opening a cabinet that held alcohol wipes, lubricants, and condoms.

But one thing seemed to be missing. "I don't see collars or leashes."

Master Michael shook his head. "After your experience, I assumed you'd have no interest."

"That was..." Sydney struggled for words. He *had* honored everything she'd said. "Thoughtful, and I appreciate it."

Maybe because he'd been so considerate, the idea of wearing one for him didn't scare her.

"If you change your mind, we can shop together. Or I can purchase a few. Alternatively, I'll give you my credit card so you can choose your own."

Gratitude overwhelmed her.

"If you do, get one with studs on it to match your shoes."

The image rocked chills through her.

"And add a leash while you're at it."

Her tummy plummeted in much the way it had when she'd headed straight down the hill on her bicycle near the Beaver Creek resort.

This—wild, wicked, slightly scary feeling—was what she liked best about BDSM and him.

"You'll be glad to know we have both heating and air conditioning out here to keep you comfortable year-round."

"You're doing this for me, Sir?"

"For us," he corrected. "I know how newness and adventure appeal to you. Coming up with something creative will keep me sharp and keep our relationship fresh. I was hoping you'd have the chance to see what I spent weeks building for you."

She inhaled sharply.

"Anything in particular you'd like to start with?"

"Surprise me, Sir."

"My pleasure." With a hungry gaze, he devoured her. "Strip."

Nervous in a way she'd never been before—maybe because no one had ever mattered like he did, she trembled as she removed her clothes beneath his watchful, intent stare.

"Turn around for me. Let me see every delicious inch that I've been missing."

Mouth dry, she did as her Dominant said.

"Good," he said when she faced him again. "Now go stand beneath that." He pointed to an overhead pulley that hung from one of the rafters.

How had she not noticed it before? Maybe because she'd been so busy taking in everything else. "Ah. I'm not sure what you have in mind, Sir."

"Access to your entire body as I flog you hard for a very long time."

"Oh, Sir." His words made her knees weak.

After lowering the hook, he faced her again, expression set in implacable lines. He crooked a finger toward her. "Come here."

Once she stood in front of him, aware of her nudity and how tiny she was in relation to his overwhelming size, he placed a strong finger beneath her chin and tipped it back. "Here's my promise to you, Sydney. I will try my best to be the Top you need and the man you deserve. I'll spend every day working on both."

The conviction in his voice made her shudder. "I'll do my best to meet my fears straight on. And be a sub to your Dom."

"Oh, *fuck...*" He groaned. "You're so damn perfect, you're killing me."

Had she managed to say the words he'd longed to hear?

"Let's start where we were—with my response to your earlier brattiness." He secured her wrists together then fastened them to the hook before adjusting the height to keep her on her toes.

She was stretched taut, not enough to hurt her shoulders, but enough to ensure she was helpless.

Once she was in position, he nodded and stepped back. "Every bit as beautiful as I pictured."

Her body vibrated with need.

Then, before she was ready, he pinched one of her nipples brutally hard. "You're mine, Sydney."

She sighed.

"Another time, I'll blindfold you and gag you while we do this. But it's been so long since I've heard your sobs and screams. And I want to witness the agony in your eyes."

He knew the words that would undo her. "Thank you, Sir."

Tenderly, in shocking contrast to the way he'd brutalized her nipple, he kissed the top of her head. "What's your safe word?"

"Everest, Sir."

"And slow word?"

"Freaking tur-*tle*." She smiled. "Sir."

"That will earn you a delayed orgasm."

"Yes, Sir." The stuff of her fantasies. When she finally came, she'd explode. "If that pleases you."

"Darlin', I'm besotted enough to lasso the moon for you, if you ask me to." With that, he rolled up his shirtsleeves and removed his hat.

If she hadn't been suspended, she might have collapsed. "Now we're getting somewhere, Sir."

After placing it on a hook, he selected a flogger and took a few practice swings, the long, thick strands of leather cutting through the still, afternoon air.

Then, shaking the hilt so the falls danced back and forth, he returned to her, face set in serious lines. "Open your legs."

He didn't add a please or a pet name. He was all serious and Dominant.

Fear left her momentarily frozen.

"Don't make me repeat myself, or I'll shove my cock up your ass before I start."

How could she do as he demanded when her brain had ceased to function?

"Do it, brat."

Slowly, in a haze, she spread her thighs.

When she had he caught her pussy a few times, making her cry out and respond with a flood of desire. "You've missed this," he observed, inhaling deeply.

"I haven't come once since I was with you last, Sir."

"Do you know what you just did to my cock?"

Trying to see through her haze, she looked at the evidence pressing against the front of his jeans.

"Those words have earned you an orgasm. But you still have a penalty to pay from earlier." He sucked on one of her nipples and fingered her until she jerked against him.

Oh God. She burned for him. "Sir? May I have permission to come?"

"Not yet."

Again and again, he edged her until she was sobbing, so desperate to climax that she was going to explode.

"I've learned my lesson, Sir!" Her legs quivered, and her buttocks were clenched tightly as he continued to demand her responses.

Low and soft, disbelieving, he chuckled. "Have you, brat?"

"I swear." Muttering, she repeated herself, mixed with frantic pleas.

"Now you may."

With more fervor, he continued to play with her, stroking harder, lighting the flame. "Thank you, thank you," she whispered as she climbed higher and higher, closer and closer to a climax. "Yes... *This!*" Her head lolled to the side.

"Pleasing you makes me happy."

Persistently kissing her, finger-fucking her, he brought her to the edge.

Then he sucked a nipple into his mouth, licking and stretching it, then gently biting.

Sobbing, she shattered — every part of her relieved to finally be back with him.

Even though he kissed her, caressed her, whispered soothing words, he wasn't finished with her.

Instead, he resumed the flogging, this time with easy strokes. With a sigh of pleasure, she allowed herself to go limp, surrendering in total trust.

Though she'd spent years traveling, playing with numerous Doms, she'd never met anyone who could make her lose control so completely.

By measures, he increased the harshness of his strokes.

"Thank you, Sir." With each little lick from the strands, she began to float.

He moved around her in a complete circle, marking every part of her body.

After a few initial flinches, she closed her eyes.

Within moments, she resided somewhere else where reality blurred, and time no longer existed.

"Subspace?" he asked.

Though she tried to answer him, her mouth was dry, as if it had been stuffed with cotton, and she couldn't speak.

Her amazing Dom continued to light up her body, catching her everywhere, leaving nothing off-limits.

"Talk to me, darlin'."

"Mmm…" That, and a tiny sigh was the best she could manage.

Over time, she noticed he'd eased a little, but thankfully he continued, warming the backs of her legs again.

Eventually, bliss engulfed her.

Then later, as if it were happening to someone else, she was aware of her arms being released and she was swept from the floor.

She slept, dreamed, all snuggled in a protective embrace and a cozy blanket.

Sydney had no idea how much time had elapsed when he pressed a bottle of water to her lips.

Dutifully, she took a sip.

After she had, he brushed strands of her hair back behind her ear then once more cradled her close.

Secure, she drifted off again.

When she managed to blink her eyes open, darkness had fallen. "I think I was gone."

"Subspace?"

Gently, she pressed her palm to his massive chest and eased herself back so she could look at him. "Not long ago, I used to argue that it didn't exist."

"Until you submitted to me?"

"Arrogant, much?" she teased.

"Well, if you didn't believe in it and now you do…" His grin was ridiculously, endearingly triumphant.

"I concede your point."

"Let me know when you're ready to visit there again." He lifted her hand and raised it to his lips.

"I need you as much as I crave my next breath."

Possessiveness flared in the depth of his eyes. Beneath her, his cock hardened. "Will you fuck me?" she asked.

"Are you sure you're up for it? There's nothing I want more. But I have an obligation to care for you."

Reassuringly touching his face, she promised, "Then that's the best way to do it. *Please.*"

"Fuck, Sydney." His voice held a feral growl. "I can resist anything but the way you say that and that longing in your gaze."

If she had any idea what he was talking about, she'd ensure she always looked at him that way.

Keeping the blanket wrapped around her, he moved her to the side, then he stood.

The magnificent man removed his clothes then strode across the floor in all his masculine glory to open a drawer and pull a condom from a box.

As he walked back, he sheathed his pulsing, hard cock. The motion made his biceps ripple, flexing the wings on the eagle on his arm.

"Have I told you how sexy I find your tattoo?"

"We should get you a matching one."

"Really, Sir? I'd like that."

"Would you? It's my brand."

This moment mattered, the importance making the air heavy. "I'd wear it proudly."

"I honor the fact you said that you didn't want to be any man's submissive."

Except yours. "And you said we get to define our own version of D/s. We decide what it means to us."

"Oh, fuck, Sydney." He growled, a feral, hungry sound. "I want you on my lap, facing me," he told her. "Stay where you are. I don't want you to move."

Masterfully, he took hold of her and managed it so that he was sitting, and she was in the position he wanted.

"I get to be on top, Sir?"

"But not in charge."

"Of course not." Cheekily, she grinned as she raised herself up onto her knees while he guided himself to her entrance.

Then, trying to accommodate his impressive girth, she sank onto him, exhaling by small measures as she did so.

"Ride me, darlin'. Ride me like you mean it."

Leaning forward, she snaked her arms around his neck.

Her hair spilled erotically over him as she worked her body up and down his shaft, some of the strokes shallow, others longer.

Within moments, her insides constricted.

"Wait," he commanded.

Unsure that was possible, she sank her teeth into her lower lip, hoping to distract herself so she could obey his command.

He clamped his hands on her waist, helping her to complete several dozen more strokes before he relented. "Now, Sydney."

Screaming, she climaxed, her internal compressions squeezing him hard, driving his orgasm.

After they'd ridden out their pleasure together, she collapsed against him, staying there as he stroked her back and she caught her breath.

On some level she was aware of time passing, but she never wanted to leave this beautiful little cocoon he'd created where the outside world didn't exist.

"I don't want to scare you…"

Despite herself, a small tendril of fear nipped at her happiness. Since his voice was low, but serious, she tipped her head back.

"You don't have to respond, and I have no expectations of you."

"But...?" She waited for unwanted words to follow.

"I love you."

"You...?"

He captured her wrist, as if afraid she might flee, but that was the last thing she wanted to do.

Blinking back tears, she smiled. "Thank you for saying that. Being apart has been so hard. Soon after leaving, I discovered the truth. I missed you so much because I love you, too."

With that, her tears fell.

Right after, kisses and laughter flowed.

"Having you here makes me the happiest man in the world."

"One more thing we agree on, because you've made me the happiest woman in the world."

"Shall we celebrate our reunion? A glass of wine and dinner, followed by making love and a long soak in the bathtub."

"Sounds wonderful."

He narrowed his eyes. "You don't need to leave?"

That he asked made her blink back fresh tears. "I'd like to stay. If you'll have me."

"Forever, if you want."

Maybe, just maybe that would work for her.

"I need to be sure you're not too sore to play again soon."

The truth was, she was so greedy for him that she would endure any pain just to feed their connection.

Still, he tenderly rubbed arnica into her shoulders and on her red marks, and she appreciated his ministrations.

Then he helped her to dress.

Sydney tipped her head to the side, studying him as he pulled up his jeans. "You know you're a seriously sexy man, Sir. That flogging was amazing. Thank you."

"Did you learn anything from your punishment?"

That I'll intentionally misbehave every day. "Uhm…I'm afraid that may take some time, Sir."

"We've got plenty of that," he replied, sliding his gaze purposefully over her.

Inside, he poured the wine he'd promised and offered a toast.

"To our home. To us. And to many tomorrows."

She clinked her glass with his. "I love you, Sir."

"And I love you, Sydney."

"Uhm…" She slid her stemware back onto the counter. "About making love…"

In interest, he raised his eyebrows, and she arrowed her index finger down the row of buttons on his shirt, stopping when she reached his silver belt buckle.

Then she plucked his glass from his hand and placed it next to hers.

"You're playing with fire."

"Yes, Sir."

"Get upstairs, darlin, and be quick about it."

With a giggle, she dashed away, only to be swept from her feet at the landing and carried the rest of the way to his bed.

"I'm going to spend the rest of my life sexing you up as much as you want."

"Well, Sir…" She blinked seductively. "What are you waiting for?"

Epilogue

"I needed to meet the woman who stole my brother's heart."

Sydney glanced over at Melanie, Michael's sister.

She'd arrived about twenty minutes ago, along with her adorable girls, who were, in Melanie's words, "Holy terrors and a total handful."

After checking that Sydney would be okay if he took his nieces out to play with Chewie and down to the river, the three had headed out the door, leaving Sydney alone with Melanie, who promptly took a seat on a barstool and looked at Sydney.

"He told you I stole his heart?" Sydney asked.

"Absolutely not." With a laugh, Melanie shook her head. "Michael doesn't tell me anything, so I have to read between the lines. When I can't do that, I just make shit up."

As far as she was concerned, Melanie could visit anytime she wanted. The more often, the better.

She'd arrived in an enormous SUV packed with food, homemade yeasty rolls and, several salads — macaroni, potato, and fruit.

Sydney had lost track of how many items Melanie had placed in the fridge.

But she hadn't stopped there. She'd brought an angel food cake and strawberries, along with a decadent looking flourless chocolate torte. "Made with the most expensive chocolate in the world," she'd said when she slid the platter onto the counter.

Michael was planning to grill hamburgers and hot dogs in an hour or so. Even though he'd ordered plenty of sides and snacks from a catering company and told his sister she didn't need to bring anything, Melanie had shown up with enough provisions for a week.

"Can I offer you a lemonade? Michael made it this morning. Evidently from your grandmother's recipe."

"Hell no. That's for the kids." Wrinkling her nose, she left her perch to open the fridge. "I brought my favorite champs. Want some?"

"Absolutely."

With the familiarity that came with being raised in the house, Melanie pulled out the bottle while Sydney grabbed a couple of flutes from a cabinet.

As far as she was concerned, Melanie could visit anytime she wanted. The more often, the better.

And now she uncovered a charcuterie board.

"I can't believe you provided a whole feast."

"Cooking is a stress reliever for me." She blew out a breath. "Just wish exercise was."

Today was the first time Sydney and Michael had entertained since she'd all but moved in a month ago.

She still had her condo, and she'd stayed there once after the weather had delayed her flight home to

Denver. It had been well after midnight when she'd touched down at the airport, and she'd been exhausted.

After talking to Michael, she'd opted to spend the rest of the night in Evergreen, then finished the drive in the morning, after a few hours of sleep and a coffee stop at Misty Mountain.

Except for being able to indulge in a triple chocolate muffin and a large Americano with an extra shot of espresso, she'd made a bad choice.

Her sleep had been restless, and she'd missed being in his arms.

By the time she'd arrived home, she was every bit as tired as she'd been at midnight.

Home.

A concept she now truly embraced.

At some point, she'd started thinking of Eagle's Bend as her place, too. And that was a big change of heart for her.

Surprising herself, she enjoyed tending to the land, hanging out with Jeb around the firepit, taking care of the chickens, giving Chewie baths, and overseeing plans for the holiday sleigh rides, as well as future expansions.

Though he occasionally grumbled, Michael had approved a budget, hired a crew, and even swung a hammer himself.

Watching her man do physical labor—his muscles flexing and rippling—was the sexiest thing ever.

After Michael had shown her the space he'd converted for her in the existing barn, she'd agreed with him. The dungeon was their private spot, and there was no way she was giving up the place where they spent so much time.

The final building she envisioned wouldn't be completed until spring, but that meant they still might be able to book some late-summer weddings.

Suddenly aware of the silence, Sydney shook her head.

Without her being aware of it, she'd glanced out the window, searching for a glimpse of the man she adored. "Sorry. I was miles away."

"That happens here, doesn't it? It's easy to get lost in the view."

Sydney considered Michael's little sister. "Do you miss it?"

"Not at all. I like the idea of living out here, but I'm a city girl at heart. I prefer a coffee shop to be in walking distance."

Sydney laughed. "You could be besties with my friend Vanessa." Who was scheduled to come up next weekend.

They were planning a shopping day in Winter Park, and although Sydney would have preferred they skied, Vanessa had gasped in horror at the suggestion. The most she would agree to was spending a day at one of the town's renowned spas.

After uncorking the bottle, Melanie poured them each a glass of bubbles. "After the bullshit with Jane, his ex, I never thought Michael would actually trust again."

"Oh?"

"That bitch did a number on him." Over the rim of her glass, Melanie studied Sydney. "He wouldn't tell me how you met…"

Knowing the woman was fishing for information—not that she could blame her—Sydney pretended to place a lock on her sealed lips.

Melanie sighed. "So I'm not getting anything out of you, either?"

"Sorry."

"It was worth a try. Drink up. Maybe you'll let a secret or two slip later."

"Afraid not." Sydney shook her head. If Michael wanted to keep a secret, she'd honor that.

"Spoilsport. But no matter what, I'm glad he met you."

The two women toasted each other.

Since she hadn't been sure whether or not Melanie would be protective of her brother, the words helped Sydney to relax. "That means a lot, thank you. He's been good for me."

"So, he's pretty closed lipped. But I was able to find out that you run an outdoor adventure company. Does that mean you like to do extreme things?"

Moreso in the past than right now. "I do." She gave Melanie a brief overview of the way she'd been raised and outlined a couple of trips she'd put together for people.

"I'd never have the courage to do half that." Then she scoffed. "That's an outright lie. I wouldn't have the courage to do *anything* you said."

"You can start as small as you want." Not everyone summited their first fourteen-thousand-foot peak at age three like she had.

"I'll stick to baking."

They laughed together.

"Everyone has their place. I'm the least domesticated person on the planet."

"Don't let anyone tame you."

"I appreciate that."

"But I'd love to see pictures of your adventures."

"I'll send you a few. But if you ever decide you want to experience some outdoor fun, I'll be happy to take you. I can plan trips for your family. Ziplining, things like that."

Melanie shuddered. "No way you'd get me to step off firm ground." Frantically, she shook her head. "But occasionally I wonder if I should encourage the girls to try new experiences. Not sure it's good for them to grow up with a mom who's a scaredy-cat."

"Let's talk to them later, see what they might be interested in." She hadn't provided many activities for kids, and the idea appealed to her. "You can come along on anything as an observer. I promise not to make you participate."

"Does that include roller coasters? Lottie is desperate to ride one."

"I love them. Next summer, let's go to the amusement park."

"The youngest and I will be at the children's museum."

"Fair enough."

As they sipped the light and crisp champagne, they began to get plates and napkins ready for their upcoming meal.

"Michael tells me you have suggestions of things to do with the ranch."

"I hope I'm not stepping on toes."

"Oh not at all!" Melanie hastened to reassure her. "I'm glad you love this place as much as Michael does."

Sydney outlined a few ideas, all of which Melanie endorsed. "That's a great way to share the beauty of Eagle's Bend with others."

Shortly after that, Michael returned with the girls, and Chewie tried to follow them into the house.

"She needs a companion," Melanie said.

"We wouldn't have her at all if you hadn't bought her without asking permission." Michael leveled a severe look at his sibling. "I didn't even know she was showing up."

"The outrage!" Melanie gasped. "Your nieces wanted her. Not me." Batting her eyes, she said, "You can't deny them anything and you know it."

"Yeah." He glanced at the two who were pouring themselves lemonade. "They've got me wrapped around their little fingers."

Sydney considered him in a new light. His affection and easygoing manner with the kids proved he'd make an excellent father.

The shocking, unexpected thought didn't frighten her like it used to.

He made his way to her and dropped a gentle kiss on her forehead. "Everything okay here? Mel hasn't badgered you with a million questions about who you are and our relationship?"

"Me?" Melanie demanded, aghast once more. "No. Of course not. I'm a total angel."

"Yeah. Sure you are." But there was lightness in his tone.

"I behaved. Really." She winked at Sydney. "Tell him."

"We had a nice chat," Sydney replied.

"Which means she asked a thousand questions, but you artfully dodged them."

Their good-natured banter made Sydney regret being an only child. There was a shared history between brother and sister that she would never have. "I'm staying out of this."

"Smart woman." He gave her a second kiss before heading for the refrigerator to pull out the platter of meat that he'd seasoned earlier. "Who wants hot dogs?"

"Me!" Lottie called out.

"And who wants cheese on their burger?"

After everyone had placed their orders, he went back outside while she and Melanie arranged the side dishes and tucked spoons into the containers.

Since the sun was shining and it was a gorgeous fall day, they ate outside on the patio.

Then once the dishes were handled and leftovers stored, they moved on to coffee and dessert.

Since the girls were more interested in their horse than strawberry shortcake, Michael walked them over to the corral.

One of the hands said he'd be happy to watch the kids and give them each a turn on horseback.

Much later, after Sydney had devoured a second slice of chocolate torte, Melanie rounded up her family and headed for the car.

As Sydney and Michael waved goodbye, he draped an arm around her shoulders.

"Finally. I thought they'd never leave."

She could guess what he had on his mind. "I enjoyed the visit."

"Glad to hear that. It helps that you like her. Jane didn't."

Which was surprising. Melanie was delightful and easygoing.

"Enough about that." He looked at her. "I am relieved to finally have you all to myself."

"I'll make the wait worth your while."

"Will you?" He stroked her upper arm. "You always do."

After he gave her a spectacular kiss, she wiggled away from him.

"Keep in mind, brat, I don't like to be kept waiting."

Which certainly did not encourage her to hurry up.

Aware of his heated gaze on her rear, she walked up the path, swaying her hips provocatively.

"You're going to be in trouble for that."

At the doorway, she looked back and blew a kiss over her shoulder.

With a groan, he followed her inside.

Quickly, she headed upstairs to the room that she had claimed as her office, opened her desk drawer, and took out the present she'd ordered for herself.

She opened the box, wincing when her finger snagged on a pointed metal stud. Then, with his surprise in hand, she headed into their bedroom and changed into a short skirt.

Next, she removed her bra and pulled on a tight white sweater that left her midriff bare.

Finally, breaths unsteady, she fastened the collar around her neck before slipping into the wicked, studded heels he'd bought for her.

In front of the mirror, she scrunched her hair, styling it around her face.

"Holy fuck."

Startled, she glanced in the mirror again to see an image of her lover lazing against the doorjamb.

Lips parted, Sydney turned to face him.

Before she could react further, he was in front of her.

Right above the collar, he wrapped his hands around her neck. "We're not going to make it outside to the barn."

With the desire stoked in his eyes, she didn't doubt him.

"I need to be inside you. *Now.*"

Capturing her hand, he stripped off her sweater, then guided her to the bed, turned her to face it, then forced her body down, smashing her breasts into the mattress.

Carefully, he maneuvered the collar around so that the D-ring faced the back. Then he lifted her skirt and rubbed her ass, tenderly at first, then with more vigor before blazing her skin with his hand.

"Oh, God! *Oh, God!*"

"This evening, you may come as often as you like, my sweet. You earned it."

He left her long enough to grab a condom from the nightstand. Then, behind her, he dropped his jeans but didn't undress, obviously as impatient as she was.

In a single stroke, he claimed her, then he fucked her hard — the way she liked.

Her Dominant buried his hand beneath her pelvis in order to play with her clit, and when she was writhing, he moved up to plump and squeeze her breasts.

Within seconds, she was panting, consumed by orgasm after orgasm.

Offering approving words, he pulled away long enough to snatch his belt from its loops.

He placed the leather next to her face.

Then, voice gruff, he demanded, "Do you want to feel this? It was around my body, and it's mine. Just like you, Sydney. Got it?"

Yes. "Yes to everything, Sir."

Continually, he laid the leather to her curves, then he hooked a finger into the D-ring on her collar and very slightly pulled her neck up. "Why did you do this?" he demanded, voice hoarse.

"Sir," Sydney protested, in search of an orgasm, not capable of a conversation until she'd reached the pinnacle. "Just fuck me, please."

"Tell me, brat."

In his typical Dominant fashion, he demanded answers, even though she couldn't string two thoughts together.

"You knew I'd love this."

But she hadn't guessed just how much.

"Tell me."

Confounding her, he stopped belting her, and she cried out. "You told me I could come when I was ready."

"And I asked a question."

Her body vibrated with sexual hunger.

"It's a symbol." Forcing words was almost impossible. "That I'm no longer afraid." She turned her head to the side, wishing she could see him. "That I left the past behind."

"And your doubts?" Quiet desperation shrouded his voice.

"Gone." As if they had never existed.

"You're *my* sub, Sydney."

From the first moment they'd met, she had been, even if she hadn't wanted to admit it. With her words — her desperate confession — he once again used his belt on her, bringing her to the edge.

Then he sealed the deal, impaling his cock inside her until they were one, and she had no idea where he ended and she began.

Unraveled, grabbing the bedcovers, she climaxed.

He fucked her hard and long. Then with a possessive, primal roar, he orgasmed.

For the first time, she wished there was no barrier between them.

The realization shook her, leaving her breathless. What would it be like to have children with him? Something she'd never considered before she'd seen him with his nieces.

When they were both replete, he walked into the bathroom and returned with a warm cloth to bathe her swollen pussy.

She appreciated the way he nurtured her, ensuring that he never pushed her too far. It mattered to him that they could always enjoy another scene.

Afterward, he removed her collar.

As she slowly pushed herself upright, he stripped.

Pleasantly worn out, she kicked off her shoes and climbed onto the bed.

When he was naked, he joined her, snuggling her into his arms.

For a while they were quiet, and she lingered in a world that only she and Michael shared.

When she blinked her eyes open, he wasn't in the bed.

The bathroom light was on, but no sound reached her. Curious, she padded across the floor to see if he was in there.

A bubble bath awaited her, and the counter was ablaze with dozens of lit candles.

He was hanging a big, fluffy robe nearby when he noticed her.

"You must have liked your surprise, Sir."

"Yeah, brat." He drank her in. "I liked it."

Being his brat had its own rewards, but so did being his darling.

"My sister left an unopened bottle of champagne. Would you like some?"

The wonderful, effervescent bubbly had instantly become her new favorite. "Sounds divine."

She sank into the tub that was just the right temperature to soothe her muscles.

When he returned, he was dressed only in jeans, and he held two glasses.

"You're welcome to wear that collar anytime you want."

"Maybe you should get me one that you like, Sir."

He froze. "Go on."

"I was reading about options. Some submissives wear a bracelet. You know, something unobtrusive that wouldn't get in the way of ranch work or mountaineering."

"Have you seen anything that appeals to you?"

"I was looking at some with beads or charms that have some sort of symbolism."

"Send me links to some that you might enjoy."

Of course, he would have his own Dominant dictates. Had she really expected otherwise?

"And if you see one that you would like to wear when we scene or go to the Den, send me that as well."

"I haven't looked at those," she admitted.

"No hurry. Whenever you are ready."

She sat up long enough to accept his offering. Despite the heat and humidity in the room, her nipples hardened.

Maybe that was in response to the way his always-ready dick pushed against the front of his jeans.

"Take your time and enjoy your soak." His eyes telegraphed his desire. "Join me whenever you're ready."

A few minutes later, eager to spend more time together, she emerged from the tub and wrapped herself in the robe he'd provided.

In their bedroom, he was standing near the window, backlit by moonlight.

Glass in hand, she crossed to him and tipped her head back to meet his gaze. "Sir?"

"My timing isn't always good."

As her pulse turned thready, he lowered himself to one knee and lifted her left hand.

An impossible, loud buzzing filled her ears.

"Sydney Wallace, you complete my heart and my life. I want to spend the rest of my days making you happy."

Suddenly, she couldn't breathe.

"Will you do me the honor of being my wife and standing by my side as my partner?"

Her knees weakened, and in response, he tightened his grip, offering his strength to support her.

"Say something, Sydney. Anything."

Words failed her, and the champagne sloshed in its glass.

This was everything she'd once dreamed of.

After Lewis, she'd shoved aside her ideas of a happily ever after, telling herself her fantasies were childish and ridiculous, and she'd pretended they didn't matter.

But secretly, she'd yearned for a relationship as beautiful as the one her parents shared and like she had seen with others.

"As I said, I know my timing is not always perfect, but I want you to know that whenever you are ready — if you ever are — you have my total commitment."

Like her, he'd been through a lot. And entrusting her with his heart and his land was a massive step.

"We could have the first wedding ever on Eagle's Bend, try out that arbor that you insisted I build. After all, you'll need photos for the website you're building, right?"

"Oh my God, Michael..." Giddiness lodged in her throat.

He reached into his pocket and pulled out a two-tone pink-and-gray ring, with mountains and trees etched into it.

"Silicone," he explained. "I honor who you are, and this is something you can wear even when you're in the world's most dangerous places, and you'll be safe."

Is there a more perfect man for me?

"If it gets destroyed, it's easily replaced."

The sentimental value mattered to her. He'd considered her needs, not just what worked for him.

Shocking her, he didn't ask her to accept it.

Instead, he placed it on the nightstand, then he reached back into his pocket and pulled out the most spectacular engagement ring she'd ever seen. A massive square-cut diamond was flanked by three smaller ones on each side.

"I don't have to put this on you until you're ready." Still holding her hand, he sought her gaze.

The idea of a summer wedding near the arbor and a reception in a new barn sounded perfect. "Yes." Despite her best efforts, her voice cracked on the word. "I'm ready now." Happy tears stung her eyes. "Yes,

Michael... *Sir*. I'll marry you. There's nothing I want more than to be your wife and partner."

He slid the beautiful piece of jewelry onto her finger, and the moonlight danced across the radiant facets.

Once the symbol of their union and love was in place, he stood, removed the flute from her grip and set it on the nightstand, then took her by the shoulders, pulling her against him to capture her mouth in a dizzying kiss.

"Once more, you've made me the happiest man on the planet, Sydney."

His words, jagged with emotion, made her tears fall.

Against her belly, his cock was harder than she ever recalled.

After he released her, leaving her reeling and gasping, he picked up both glasses of champagne and gave hers back to her.

She tipped her head to one side. "The bubbly was intentional then."

"It was. I was hoping we could toast our upcoming marriage, but if not, every day with you is worth celebrating."

How did he always know the right things to say?

He lifted his glass. "To a long, beautiful future," he offered.

"Yes, Sir." *My love.*

After allowing her a single sip, he removed the glass from her hand and lifted her onto the mattress, where he joined her.

"I want to be balls deep in you."

Looking into his beautiful eyes, she traced the strong chiseled line of his jaw. "I want that too, Sir."

Taking his time, he brought her to full arousal before easing his sheathed cock inside her. "This is a heck of a way to begin our lives together, Sir."

"Get used to it." Steely intent flashed in his eyes. "There's a lot more of this to come."

"Let's get started on forever, Sir."

He kissed her. "Forever, darlin'."

Want to see more from this author?
Here's a taster for you to enjoy!

Mastered: In His Cuffs
Sierra Cartwright

Excerpt

Finally.

She'd made it.

Maggie smoothed the front of her short leather skirt and followed her friend Vanessa through the front door of the Den, Colorado's spectacular BDSM club nestled in the Rocky mountains.

Music blasted from the back patio and the bass seemed to shake the walls. Half-naked people — men, mostly — were everywhere, and cool air whispered in through open windows.

Gregorio, the Den's caretaker, met them in the foyer.

"Welcome to Ladies' Night." His dark eyes were sharp, taking in everything. At times she wondered if he saw into people's souls as well as their hearts.

As he moved, the wink of his silver earring made him resemble a pirate, sending a shiver through her.

"I'm here for the debauchery," Maggie said. After the week — *week? More like weeks* — she'd survived at work — she needed it.

"You've come to the right place," he assured her with a grin.

Maggie had been looking forward to this outing for over a month. Not only had she spent her lunch hours shopping online for a new outfit and killer shoes, but she'd also purchased a sparkly collar.

Every day at five o'clock, she'd happily slashed through the date on her calendar.

The fat, red mark served as a reward for surviving another workday with the insufferable David Tomlinson, and it was a visual reminder that she was closer to a night at the Den, where she would hopefully get a sizzling spanking that would satisfy her deepest cravings.

"Are you planning to scene tonight, Maggie?" Gregorio asked.

She nodded. *Definitely.*

"Sex?"

With the right man – Dominant – possibly. "I'm not planning to, but I won't rule it out."

"Condoms are provided in all the private rooms. House Monitors also have them. I take it you want to participate as a sub, not a Domme?"

"That's correct." She wondered how he managed to keep up with the particulars of each guest. But then, that was why he ran the place.

"Are you looking to play with a man or a woman? Both? Multiples?"

Oh. It definitely is Ladies Night. "Strictly het," she replied.

Several different colored wristbands lay on a nearby table. Gregorio selected a white one and affixed it to her wrist.

"Switches are in yellow," he continued.

"That's the one I want," Vanessa chimed in.

"Seriously?" An eyebrow raised, she looked at her friend.

Vanessa shrugged. "You never know what opportunities might present themselves."

"As always, Tops have red bands," Gregorio informed them. "So that's what you'll be looking for, Maggie."

"Got it," she replied, anxious to start the festivities.

Over the years, she'd visited the Den often enough that she could take Gregorio's place at the door. But she also knew he wouldn't hurry through the ritual, despite her impatience.

"House Monitors have black bands around their upper arm. House subs have purple ones. The Den's safe word is 'halt'. Use it at any time. Enjoy yourselves."

"I will, for sure," Vanessa said.

Brandy, a woman Maggie knew as a house sub, took their jackets and purses. Her motions were easy, elegant, something Maggie would never be able to replicate.

Any night at this glorious property owned by Master Damien was fabulous, but four times a year, the owner went all out for the house's single ladies, providing entertainment, demonstrations, Doms and Dommes, exotic non-alcoholic beverages, and the most mouthwatering desserts imaginable.

For over a week, she'd saved up her calories with the intention of indulging in all her favorite things. Not that it mattered, really. If she had her way, she'd burn plenty of energy during a BDSM scene or two.

Playing would also help with her stress level. Orgasms had a magical way of soothing most of her emotional upsets. Tonight, though, she'd need at least a dozen of them to forget the crappy hell her life had become.

With luck, it would take less than half an hour to find someone to take her to the downstairs dungeon.

She and Vanessa made their way toward the kitchen and looked out the patio doors.

A fire danced and popped in a pit. People in all sorts of outfits, from street clothes to club wear, milled about. A stage had been set up near the back of the paved area where singer and guitarist Zephyr 'Zeph' Rockwell all but made love to a microphone.

"I'll have a double shot of that deliciousness," Vanessa said against Maggie's ear.

"Zeph?" Oozing sex appeal, he wore an unbuttoned black shirt, and unbelievably tight leather pants that left nothing to the imagination. A recent video of him had gone viral, thanks to a publicity stunt by Chelsea Barton, one of the Den's members. The sensational musician was now giving women all over the world heart palpitations.

"I'd let him put his guitar under my bed," Vanessa replied enthusiastically. "And he can strum any part of me that he wants to."

At her friend's outrageousness, Maggie laughed.

"But no. I'm talking about the Top standing to the right of the stage. I think he has on a black band. I love a man who has authority and knows how to wield it."

Since the party attracted so many newbies, Master Damien brought in extra House Monitors—male and female—to ensure everyone's safety and answer questions.

"I don't know who you're talking about." Her platform shoes added much-needed inches, but even they couldn't help Maggie see through the crowd.

"Over there." Vanessa pointed. "Near the speaker. Short dark hair. Jeans. No shirt. Can you see him yet?"

"No."

"Wait. I think that's a pair of handcuffs on his belt loop." She made a show of exaggeratedly fanning herself. "Damn."

Maggie craned her head.

"Do you need me to lift you up?"

She glared at Vanessa. Vanessa was five inches taller than Maggie and never missed an opportunity to point that out.

"Would you care for a chocolate-covered strawberry?" a server asked, distracting them.

"Oh, God, yes," Maggie said.

Vanessa and Maggie both turned away from the huge glass windows and toward the hot man standing near them. He was over six feet tall, with long hair she itched to run her fingers through.

She took her time selecting a treat from the silver serving platter. If nothing else, she enjoyed keeping him next to her for an extra few seconds. Not only did he smell of expensive, spicy cologne, but he had on a bow tie and remarkable, shimmery gold pants. His chest was devoid of hair, and his skin glistened as if oiled. Master Damien *definitely* knew how to please his guests.

She chose a strawberry with the most chocolate coating, and since she'd done that, Vanessa selected two. "You got more chocolate than I did," she explained.

Where Maggie was deliberate, Vanessa seized every opportunity that came along. The fact they were so different had made the friendship all sorts of interesting over the last eight years. Maggie nibbled at her dessert while Vanessa bit hers in half.

"Another, ladies?" the man tempted.

"Could you leave the tray?" Vanessa asked.

"No! Don't you dare," Maggie countered.

Vanessa picked up another treat while Maggie shook her head. The man winked at Maggie before moving off.

"The sexy man I was looking at earlier is gone. You never saw him, did you?"

"Not like it's a loss. There's plenty of them here."

"True enough. But I like handcuffs. So do you, right?"

Enthusiastically, Maggie nodded. She loved any kind of restraint.

"So, have you seen anyone you're interested in?" Vanessa asked.

After she'd eaten her strawberry, Maggie surveyed the crowd in the kitchen and great room. "I wouldn't mind sceneing with the Top I played with last time, if he's here. He knew his way around my body without a map." The man had flogged her hard and had gotten her off. "How about you?"

"I'm greedy. I want two men."

"Two?" Even though Gregorio had mentioned it, Maggie hadn't considered trying a ménage, but now that Vanessa said she was interested...

"It *is* Ladies' Night," Vanessa pointed out.

"So it is."

The music trailed off and raucous applause followed. After wiping her hands on a cocktail napkin, Maggie joined in. Zeph was so much better than the wannabe who used to perform up here.

A few seconds later, he introduced his next song — the single that was accelerating up the charts — then nodded to his band who cranked up the sound.

"Ready to get your kink on?" Vanessa asked.

"Almost." Nerves assailed her, a heady combination of adrenaline and expectation.

"If we don't leave at the same time, we'll meet up at the Chalet?"

Maggie nodded. Because it was a special evening, they'd splurged on a hotel room in Winter Park. Master Damien had thoughtfully provided a shuttle between the Den and several stops in the nearby tourist town. "If you go home with anyone, send me a text. Let me know where you are and who you're with." Even though the Den's members were vetted, it didn't hurt to be safe.

"Same for you."

"Yeah." Maggie rolled her eyes. "As if."

"Hey, you could shock the world and do something totally out of character."

Ever since her breakup with Samuel, she'd been in a sexual drought. Then again, it had been all but barren while they were together. He'd tried, at least at first. But after several months, he'd lost his temper.

During one of their arguments, he'd shouted that she was insatiable and that no man could keep her happy. That wasn't true. She would have been fine if he'd ever tied her to the bed and used her vibrator on her. A spanking once a week would have satisfied her needs. Well…at least she thought it would have. If it was hard enough, the after-effects would remind her of the pain, then the anticipation would have carried her through the remaining days.

Then again, perhaps the more she got, the more she'd want.

After all, how would she know?

She'd never had a relationship that had made it past six months. If she found a man who was demanding in the bedroom, he tended to be an arrogant son of a bitch outside it. If he was considerate about sharing chores, he tended to bore her once the lights were turned down.

Two men she'd dated insisted it wasn't right to ever spank a woman. More than once she'd tried to explain the difference between consensual play and striking out in anger, but neither of them had been persuaded to give it a try.

Since then, Maggie had learned to embrace her single status.

She didn't have to answer to anyone if she worked late. If she didn't feel like getting out of her pajamas on a Saturday morning, she didn't have to. In fact, she could eat ice cream for dinner or skip vacuuming for so long that dust bunnies threatened to strangle her.

All in all, that suited her, especially with her awful boss's ridiculous demands.

Instead of struggling to juggle her professional and personal lives, she'd recently canceled all her dating site memberships. Forget Mr. Right. All she had time for was Mr. Right Now.

At the Den, she wasn't shamed for her desires, and she could play with a different Top every time she visited. The exhilaration of not knowing what to expect added to her delirium.

"Targets acquired." With a little wave, Vanessa confidently headed toward a group of men in the great room.

Maggie snagged a virgin piña colada from the granite island in the kitchen then walked into the backyard.

She stood to one side and watched a few couples dance in front of the stage. Off to the left, a tall, broad male knelt in front of a woman who wore a red wristband. Though the image was erotic, it didn't do much for her.

When she was here, she preferred giving up control. At work, she engaged in constant battles with her self-appointed boss and had to be on guard all the time. Letting go and surrendering to her submissive tendencies was critical to her mental health.

"Would you like to dance?"

She turned and smiled at a man who'd approached her. He was tall and lanky, wearing a plaid shirt. At least he'd skipped the pocket protector.

Part of her knew she was being unfair. He had an earnest smile, and she was sure he was a nice man. He had on a red band, but somehow, she didn't see him as a Top. There was something lacking in his tone, a certain confidence. And his expression was more hopeful than assertive.

She smiled back and waited a few seconds. Though he continued to look at her, she had no compulsion to cast her gaze at the ground, and not a single spark of attraction raced through her.

If she was going to bare her body — or at least parts of it — to a stranger, she wanted a man with a razor-edge of danger about him.

Maybe because of the way he dressed or held his shoulders, he reminded her of Samuel, and there was no greater turn-off. "Thank you," she said, tightening her grip on her glass. "Perhaps another time."

"It was worth a try," he said easily before moving onto the next possibility, a woman who was swaying as she listened to Zeph.

Maggie sipped her cool drink, loving the blend of pineapple, coconut, and whipped cream on her tongue. Since the mocktail had juice in it, she told herself the beverage was somewhat healthy.

She was ready to take a second drink when she caught sight of a shirtless man. Her knees weakened and the glass almost slipped from her fingers.

David Tomlinson.

Her bosshole.

The one man on the planet she couldn't stand.

Her nemesis.

The man who tormented her days and haunted her nights.

What the hell are you doing here?

How could this be possible?

She'd come here tonight to escape him.

Trembling, she lowered her hand.

He was kinky? And no doubt he was all six-foot-three of raw Dominance.

Tomlinson stood near a speaker, arms folded. His dark hair was spiked, and he could have been poured into his jeans.

Then he turned slightly, enough for her to glimpse the black band on his rippled biceps.

No. He couldn't be a House Monitor. *Crap.* It wasn't enough that he was here, but he had to hold a position of authority?

Then silver flashed in the dim lighting, making her gawk.

Handcuffs.

Was the jackass the man Vanessa had noticed?

If Maggie didn't know him so well, she might agree that he was sexy. But his good looks were a shell that hid the fact no heart beat in his chest. If he had a soul, she'd be surprised.

With her own eyes, she'd watched him manipulate people to his own ends. Sure, he was one of the smartest people she'd ever met, but so what? He never did anything good with it. Instead, he used his intelligence for shitty purposes.

Still staring at him in shock, she took a few steps back, as if that ridiculous act could somehow make her invisible.

How the heck was she supposed to proceed now?

Should she offer a nonchalant hello? Ignore him and hope he didn't see her? Or... Sighing, she considered catching the shuttle back to Winter Park.

Immediately she dismissed that idea.

She was here to have a good time, and under no circumstance was the relentless jerk's presence going to stop that.

Pretending she hadn't seen him wasn't her normal style, and she didn't intend to spend the entire night skulking around and looking over her shoulder.

That left dealing with him straight-up. And really, that was the only option that suited her personality.

As if sensing her gaze, he looked at her.

He scowled—a ferocious, all-too-familiar expression.

Obviously he was as surprised and as unhappy to see her as she was to see him. *Good.* She shouldn't be the only one suffering.

A tall, willowy sub walked up to him, claiming his attention.

Relieved at the reprieve, Maggie pushed out a hot breath, then took a sip of her drink, desperately trying to regroup.

We're both adults. And they'd each sought out the Den for a reason. There was absolutely no reason their existing relationship should have any bearing on what happened here.

Determinedly, she pivoted and strode back inside to wander into the living room. A trio near the fireplace were placing bets on the outcome of tomorrow's Denver Broncos game.

Near the window, a Dom rested his shoulders on the wall.

Though he wasn't overly tall, he was broad, and his T-shirt revealed beefy biceps. He could probably wield a flogger for a good long time.

After pointedly glancing at her wrist, he returned his gaze to her face.

Her heart rate increased, and she tightened her grip on her drink as she cast her gaze at the ground, silently signaling both her submissiveness and willingness.

Long seconds later, she raised her head, stunned to see him striding away from her, out of the room.

"I told him if he touches you, he won't survive the night."

The rich, deep voice—as controlled as it was reviled—came from behind her, freezing her in place.

When she caught her breath, she swung to face her adversary. She looked a long way up into his dark blue, penetrating eyes.

His jaw was set, and his arms were once more folded across his chest.

"Damn you, David. Isn't it enough that you ruin every one of my days?"

"It's *Master* David, or I'm open to Mr. Tomlinson. I've always wanted to have you over my lap for the good spanking you deserve." He captured her hand, raised it slightly, then traced the wristband that informed him she was a sub. "You're here to suffer, Maggie? I'll ensure you do."

Her frantic pulse lodged in her throat, strangling her.

"And while you're at it? You'll sure as hell call me Sir."

About the Author

Born in northern England and raised in the Wild West, Sierra Cartwright pens books that are as untamed as the Rockies she calls home.

She's an award-winning, multi-published writer who wrote her first book at age nine and hasn't stopped since.

Sierra invites you to share the complex journey of love and desire, of surrender and commitment. Her own journey has taught her that trusting takes guts and courage, and her work is a celebration for everyone who is willing to take that risk.

Sierra loves to hear from readers. You can find her contact information, website details and author profile page at https://www.totallybound.com

Home of Erotic Romance

Sign up for our newsletter and find out about all our romance book releases, eBook sales and promotions, sneak peeks and FREE romance books!